THE WAPSHOT SCANDAL

THE
WAPSHOT
SCANDAL
JOHN CHEEVER

PERENNIAL LIBRARY
Harper & Row, Publishers
New York, Evanston, San Francisco, London

This book was originally published by Harper & Row, Publishers, Inc. in 1963. It is here reprinted by arrangement. Six parts of this book appeared in *The New Yorker* and one part in *Esquire*, and the author is grateful to the editors for their permission to reprint.

First PERENNIAL LIBRARY edition published 1973.

STANDARD BOOK NUMBER: 06–080296–0

79·03

To W.M.

All the characters in this work are fictional, as is much of the science.

PART ONE

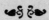

CHAPTER I

❦ ❧

The snow began to fall into St. Botolphs at four-fifteen on Christmas Eve. Old Mr. Jowett, the stationmaster, carried his lantern out onto the platform and held it up into the air. The snowflakes shone like iron filings in the beam of his light, although there was really nothing there to touch. The fall of snow exhilarated and refreshed him and drew him—full-souled, it seemed—out of his carapace of worry and indigestion. The afternoon train was already an hour late, and the snow (whose whiteness seems to be a part of our dreams, since we take it with us everywhere) came down with such open-handed velocity, such swiftness, that it looked as if the village had severed itself from its context on the planet and were pressing its roof and steeples up into the air. The remains of a box kite hung from the telephone wires overhead—a reminder of the year's versatility. "Oh, who put the overalls in Mrs. Murphy's chowder?" Mr. Jowett sang loudly, although he knew that it was all wrong for the season, the day and dignity of a station agent, the steward of the town's true and ancient boundary, its Gate of Hercules.

Going around the edge of the station he could see the lights of the Viaduct House, where at the very moment a lonely traveling salesman was bending down to kiss a picture of a pretty girl in a mail-order catalogue. The kiss tasted faintly of ink. Beyond the Viaduct House were the rectilinear lights of the village green, but the village itself was circular and did not conform in any way to the main road that wound seaward to Travertine, or to the railroad track, or even to the curve of the river, but to the pedestrian needs of its inhabitants, putting them within walking

3

distance of the green. Thus it was the shape, really, of an ancient place, and seen from the air on a fairer day might have been in Etruria. Mr. Jowett could see into the windows, across from the Viaduct House and above the ship chandler's, of the Hastings apartment, where Mr. Hastings was decorating the Christmas tree. Mr. Hastings stood on a ladder, and his wife and children passed him ornaments and told him where to hang them. Then suddenly he bent and kissed his wife. It was the sum of his feeling for the holiday and for the storm, Mr. Jowett thought, and it made him very happy. He seemed to feel happiness in the stores and houses, happiness everywhere. Old Dog Tray trotted happily up the street, on his way home, and Mr. Jowett thought affectionately of the dogs of St. Botolphs. There were wise dogs, foolish dogs, bloodthirsty and thieving dogs, and as they raided clotheslines, upset garbage pails, bit the mailman and disturbed the sleep of the just, they seemed like diplomats and emissaries. They seemed, in their chaffing way, to keep the place together.

The last of the shoppers were going home, carrying a pair of mittens for the ash man, a brooch for Grandmother and a Teddy bear stuffed with sawdust for baby Abigail. Like Old Dog Tray, everybody was going home, and everybody had a home to go to. It was one place in a million, Mr. Jowett thought. Even with his pass, he had never wanted much to travel. The village, he knew, had, like any other, its brutes and its shrews, its thieves and its perverts, but like any other it meant to conceal these facts under a shine of decorum that was not hypocrisy but a guise or mode of hope. At that hour most of the inhabitants were decorating their Christmas trees. The druidical significance of bringing a green tree into the house at the solstice had certainly never crossed the minds of any of the natives, but they treated their chosen trees (at the time of which I'm writing) with more instinctive respect than is the case today. The trees were not, at the end of their usefulness, stuck into ashcans or fired into the ditch by the railroad tracks wearing a few strands of angel's hair. The men and boys burned them ceremoniously in the back yard, admiring the surge of flame and the smell of balsam smoke. People did not, as they presently would, say that the Tremaines' tree was skinny, that the Wapshots' tree had a bare place in the middle, that the Hastings' tree was stumpy and that the Guilfoyles must have suffered economic reverses, since they had only paid fifty cents for their tree. Fancy illuminations, competitiveness and disregard for the symbols involved would all come, but they would come later. The lights, at the time of which I am writing, were spare and rudimentary and the ornaments were commemorative like the table silver, and were handled respectfully, as if one were counting over the bones of the family. They were, naturally, in disrepair—the birds without tails, the bells without clappers and the angels sometimes without wings. It was a conservatively dressed population that performed this tree-trimming ceremony. All the men wore trousers and all the women wore skirts, excepting Mrs. Wilston, who was a widow, and Alby Hooper, who was an itinerant carpenter. They had been drinking bourbon for two days and wore nothing at all.

On the ice pond—Parson's Pond at the north end of town—two boys were struggling to keep clear enough ice for a hockey game in the morning. They skated back and forth, pushing coal shovels ahead of them. It was an impossible task. This was clear to both of them, and yet they continued to go back and forth, toward and away from the roar of the falls at the dam, with an unaccountable feeling of eagerness. When the snow got too deep for skating, they propped their shovels against a pine tree and sat down in its shelter to unlace their skates.

"You know, Terry, I miss you when you're away at school."

"They throw so much work at me in school that I don't have a chance to miss anyone."

"Smoke?"

"No, thanks."

The first boy took from his pocket a pouch full of sassafras root that had been ground in a clean pencil sharpener, poured some of this onto a square of coarse, yellow toilet paper, and rolled a loose cigarette that flared up like a torch, lighting his thin face, with its momentary look of suavity, and dropping embers all over his trousers. Drawing on his cigarette, he could taste its components—the raw

village know each other

gassy flavor of burning toilet paper and the sweetness of sassafras. He shuddered as it touched his lungs, and yet he was rewarded by his smoke with a sense of wisdom and power. When their skates were unlaced and the fire in the cigarette had died, they started back toward the village. The first house they passed was the Ryders', distinguished in St. Botolphs because, for as long as anyone could remember, the parlor window shades had been drawn and the parlor door locked. What did the Ryders have hidden in their parlor? There was no one in the village who hadn't wondered. Was there a dead body there, a perpetual-motion machine, a collection of eighteenth-century furniture, a heathen altar, a laboratory for hellish experiments on dogs and cats? People had made friends of the Ryders in the hope of getting into their parlor, but no one had ever succeeded. The Ryders themselves, a peculiar but not really unfriendly family, were decorating their tree in the dining room, which was where they lived. Next to the Ryders' was the Tremaines' and, passing here, the boys could see a gleam of something yellow—copper or brass— a clue to the richness of color in that house. Traveling through Persia as a young man, Dr. Tremaine had cured the shah of boils and had been rewarded with rugs. The Tremaines had rugs on their tables, their piano, their walls and their floors, and the brilliant dyes could be seen through the lighted windows. Suddenly, for one of the boys —the smoker—the bitterness of the storm and the warmth of color in the Tremaines' house seemed to converge. It was like a discovery, and so exciting that he began to run. His friend jogged along beside him to the corner, where they could hear the bells of Christ Church.

The rector was about to bless the carolers who stood in his living room. A rancid and exciting smell of the storm came from their clothes. The room was neat and clean and warm, and had been—before they entered in their snowy clothes—fragrant. Mr. Applegate had cleaned the room himself, they knew, because he was unmarried and did not employ a housekeeper. He did not enjoy having women in his sanctuary. He was a tall man with an astonishing and somehow elegant curvature of the spine, formed by an enlarged lower abdomen, which he carried in a stately and contented way, as if it contained money and securities. Now and then he patted his paunch—his pride, his friend, his solace, his margin for error. With his spectacles on he gave the impression of a portly and benign ecclesiastic, but when he removed his eyeglasses to clean them his gaze was penetrating and haggard and his breath smelled of gin.

His life was a lonely one, and the older he grew the more harried he was by doubts about the Holy Ghost and the Virgin Mary, and it was true that he drank. When he first took over the parish, the spinsters had embroidered his stoles and illuminated his prayer books, but when it appeared that he was not interested in their attentions, they urged the vestry and bishop to discharge him as a drunk. Drunkenness was not what infuriated them. His claim to be celibate, his unmarriedness, had offended their womanhood and they longed to see him disgraced, defrocked, scourged and harried down the Wilton Trace past the old pill factory to the village boundaries. On top of this, Mr. Applegate had recently begun to suffer from an hallucination. It seemed to him that as he passed the bread and wine he could hear the substance of his parishioners' prayers and petitions. Their lips did not move, so he knew this was an hallucination, a kind of madness, but as he moved from one kneeling form to another he seemed to hear them asking, "Lord God of Hosts, shall I sell the laying hens?" "Shall I take up my green dress?" "Shall I cut down the apple trees?" "Shall I buy a new icebox?" "Shall I send Emmett to Harvard?" " 'Drink this in remembrance that Christ's Blood was shed for thee, and be thankful,' " he said, hoping to scour his mind of this galling illusion, but he still seemed to hear them asking, "Shall I fry sausage for breakfast?" "Shall I take a liver pill?" "Shall I buy a Buick?" "Shall I give Helen the gold bracelet or wait until she's older?" "Shall I paint the stairs?" It was the feeling that all exalted human experience was an imposture, and that the chain of being was a chain of humble worries. If he had confessed to the vice of drinking and to his serious doubts about blessedness, he would end up licking postage stamps in some diocesan office, and he felt too old for this. "Almighty God," he said loudly, "bless these Thy servants in the task of celebrating the birth of Thine only Son, by

Whom and with Whom in the unity of the Holy Ghost all honor and glory be to Thee, O Father Almighty world without end. Amen!" The blessing smelled distinctly of juniper. They sang an Amen and a verse of "Christus Natus Hodie."

Absorbed and disarmed by the business of singing, their faces seemed unusually open, like so many windows, and Mr. Applegate was pleased to look into them, they seemed at that moment so various. First was Harriet Brown, who had worked for the circus, singing romantic music for the living statues. She was married to a wastrel, and it was she who kept the family together these days, baking cakes and pies. Her life had been stern, and her pale face was sternly marked. Next to Harriet stood Gloria Pendleton, whose father ran the bicycle-repair shop. They were the only colored family in the village. The ten-cent necklace that Gloria wore seemed to be of inestimable value, and she dignified everything she touched. This was not a primitive or a barbaric beauty, it was the extraordinary beauty of race, and it seemed to accentuate the plumpness and the paleness of Lucille Skinner, who stood on her right. Lucille had studied music in New York for five years. Her education was estimated to have cost in the neighborhood of ten thousand dollars. She had been promised an operatic career, and wouldn't your head swim at the thought of San Carlo and La Scala, that uproarious applause that seems to be the essence of the world's best and warmest smile! Sapphires and chinchilla! But the field is crowded, as everyone knows, and dominated by unscrupulous people, and she had come home to make an honest living teaching the piano in her mother's front parlor. Her love of music— it was true of most of them, Mr. Applegate thought—had been a consuming and disenchanting passion. Next to Lucille stood Mrs. Coulter, the wife of the village plumber. She was Viennese, and she had been a seamstress before her marriage. She was a frail, dark-skinned woman with shadows like lampblack under her eyes. Beside her stood old Mr. Sturgis, who wore a celluloid collar and a brocade ascot, and who had sung in public whenever possible ever since he had been admitted to his college glee club, fifty years ago.

Behind Mr. Sturgis stood Miles Howland and Mary Perkins, who would be married in the spring but who had been lovers since last summer, although no one knew. He had first undone her clothes in the pine copse behind Parson's Pond during a thunderstorm, and after this they had thought mostly of how, where, when next—moving, on the other hand, through a world lit by the intelligent and trusting faces of their parents, whom they loved. They took a picnic lunch to Bascom's Island and didn't put their clothing on the whole day long. Lovely, it was lovely. Was this sinful? Would they burn in Hell, suffer agues and strokes? Would he be killed by a bolt of lightning during a baseball game? Later that same Christmas Eve, he would serve on the altar at Holy Communion, wearing fresh white and scarlet and raking the dark church, as he appeared to pray, for the shape of her face. In the light of all the vows he had taken, that was heinous, but how could it be, since if his flesh had not informed his spirit he would never have known this sense of strength and lightness in his bones, this fullness of heart, this absolute belief in the glad tidings of Christmas, the star and the kings? If he walked her home from church in the storm her kind parents might ask him to spend the night and she might come to him. In his mind he heard the creaking of the stairs, saw the color of her instep, and he thought, in his innocence, how wonderful was his nature that he could at the same moment praise his Saviour and see the shape of his lady's foot. Beside Mary stood Charlie Anderson, who had the gift of an unusually sweet tenor voice, and beside him were the Basset twins.

In the dark, mixed clothing they had put on for the storm, the carolers looked uncommonly forlorn, but the moment they began to sing they were transformed. The Negress looked like an angel, and dumpy Lucille lifted her head gracefully and seemed to cast off her misspent youth in the rainy streets around Carnegie Hall. This instantaneous transformation of the company was thrilling, and Mr. Applegate felt his faith renewed, felt that an infinity of unrealized possibilities lay ahead of them, a tremendous richness of peace, a renaissance without brigands, an ecstasy of light and color, a kingdom! Or was this gin! The carolers seemed absolved and purified as long as the music lasted, but when the final note was broken off they were just as suddenly themselves. Mr. Applegate thanked them, and they started for his front door. He drew old Mr. Sturgis aside and said tactfully, "I know you enjoy very good health, but don't you think this snowstorm might be a little too severe for you to go out in? It said on the radio that there hasn't been such a snowstorm in a hundred years."

"Oh, no, thank you," said Mr. Sturgis, who was deaf. "I had a bowl of crackers and milk before I came out."

The carol singers left the rectory for the village green. The music could be heard in the feed store, where Barry Freeman was closing up. Barry had graduated from Andover Academy, and during Christmas vacation of his senior year he had worn his new tuxedo to the Eastern Star Dance. There was general laughter as soon as he appeared. He approached one girl and then another, and when they all refused to dance with him he tried to cut in, but he was laughed off the floor. He stood against the wall for nearly half an hour before he put on his coat and walked home through the snow. His appearance in a tuxedo had not been forgotten. "My oldest daughter," a woman might say, "was born two years after Barry Freeman wore his monkey suit to the Eastern Star Dance." It was a turning point in his life. It may have accounted for the fact that he had never married and would go home on Christmas Eve to an empty house.

The music could be heard in Bryant's General Store ("Rock Bottom Prices"), where old Lucy Markham was talking on the telephone. "Do you have Prince Albert in the can, Miss Markham?" a child's voice asked.

"Yes, dear," Miss Markham said.

"Now, you stop hectoring Miss Markham," said Althea Sweeney, the telephone operator. "You're not supposed to use the telephone for hectoring people on Christmas Eve."

"It's against the law," said the child, "to interfere in private telephone conversations. I'm just asking Miss Markham if she has Prince Albert in the can."

"Yes, dear," said Miss Markham.

"Then let him out," said the child, her voice breaking with laughter. Althea turned her attention to a more interesting conversation—an eighty-five-cent call to New Jersey, made from Prescott's drugstore.

"It's Dolores, Mama," a strange voice said. "It's Dolores. I'm in a place called St. Botolphs. . . . No, I'm not drunk, Mama. I'm not drunk. I just wanted to wish you a Merry Christmas, Mama. . . . I just wanted to wish you a Merry Christmas. And a Merry Christmas to Uncle Pete and Aunt Mildred. A Merry Christmas to all of them . . ." She was crying.

" '. . . on the Feast of Stephen,' " sang the carolers, " 'when the snow lay round about . . .' " But the voice of Dolores, with its prophecy of gas stations and motels, freeways and all-night supermarkets, had more to do with the world to come than the singing on the green.

The singers turned down Boat Street to the Williamses' house. They would not be offered any hospitality here, they knew—not because Mr. Williams was mean but because he felt that hospitality might reflect on the probity of the bank of which he was president. A conservative man, he kept in his study a portrait photograph of Woodrow Wilson framed in an old mahogany toilet seat. His daughter, home from Miss Winsor's, and his son, home from St. Mark's, stood with their father and mother in the doorway and called "Merry Christmas! Merry Christmas!" Next to the Williamses' was the Brattles', where they were asked in for a cup of cocoa. Jack Brattle had married the Davenport girl from Travertine. It had not been a happy marriage, and, having heard somewhere that parsley was an aphrodisiac, Jack had planted eight or ten rows of parsley in his garden. As soon as the parsley matured, rabbits began to raid it, and, going into his garden one night with a shotgun, Jack blew an irreparable hole in the stomach of a Portuguese fisherman named Manuel Fada, who had been his wife's lover for years. He stood trial on a manslaughter charge in the county court and was acquitted, but his wife ran off with a yard-goods salesman, and now Jack lived with his mother.

Next to the Brattles were the Dummers, where the carol singers were passed dandelion wine and sweet cookies. Mr. Dummer was a frail man who sometimes did needlework and who was the father of eight. His enormous children ranged behind him in the living room, like some excessive authentication of his vigor. Mrs. Dummer seemed pregnant again, although it wasn't easy to tell. In the hallway was a photograph of her as a pretty young woman, posed beside a cast-iron deer. Mr. Dummer had labeled the picture "Two Dears." The singers pointed this out to one another as they left the house for the storm.

Next to the Dummers were the Bretaignes, who ten years ago had been to Europe, where they had bought a crèche, which everyone admired. Their only daughter, Hazel, was there with her husband and children. During Hazel's marriage ceremony, when Mr. Applegate asked who gave the girl away, Mrs. Bretaigne got up from her pew and said, "I do. She's mine, she's not his. I took care of her when she was sick. I made her clothes. I helped her with her homework. He never did anything. She's mine, and I'm the one to give her away." This unconventional behavior did not seem to have affected Hazel's married happiness. Her husband looked prosperous and her children were pretty and well behaved.

At the foot of the street was old Honora Wapshot's house, where they knew they would get buttered rum, and in the storm the old house, with all its fires burning, all its chimneys smoking, seemed like a fine work of man, the kind of homestead some greeting-card artist or desperately lonely sailor sweating out a hangover in a furnished room might have drawn, brick by brick, room by room, on Christmas Eve. Maggie, the maid, let them in and passed the rum. Honora stood at the end of her parlor, an old lady in a black dress that was sprinkled liberally with either flour or talcum powder. Mr. Sturgis did the honors. "Say us the poem, Honora," he asked.

She backed up toward the piano, straightened her dress, and began:

> Announced by all the trumpets of the sky,
> Arrives the snow, and, driving o'er the fields,
> Seems nowhere to alight; the whited air
> Hides hills and woods, the river and the heaven,
> And veils the farmhouse at the garden's end. . . .

She got through to the end without making a mistake, and then they sang "Joy to the World." It was Mrs. Coulter's favorite, and it made her weep. The events in Bethlehem seemed to be not a revelation but an affirmation of what she had always known in her bones to be the surprising abundance of life. It was for this house, this company, this stormy night that He had lived and died. And how wonderful it was, she thought, that the world had been blessed with a savior! How wonderful it was that she should have such a capacity for joy! When the carol ended she dried her tears and said to Gloria Pendleton: "Isn't it wonderful?" Maggie filled their glasses again. Everyone protested, everyone drank a cup, and going back into the snow again they felt, like Mr. Jowett, that there was happiness everywhere, happiness all around them.

But there was at least one lonely figure on the scene, lonely and furtive. It was old Mr. Spofford, moving with the particular agility of a thief, down the path to the river. He carried a mysterious sack. He lived alone at the edge of town, supporting himself by repairing watches. His family was formerly well-to-do, and he had traveled and been to college. What could he be carrying to the river on Christmas Eve in an epochal snowstorm? It must be some secret, something he meant to destroy, but what documents might a lonely old man possess, and why should he choose this of all nights to hide his secret in the river?

The sack he carried was a pillowcase, and in it were nine live kittens. They made a lumpy burden, mewing loudly for milk, and their mistaken vitality distressed him. He had tried to give them away to the butcher, the fish man, the ash man and the druggist, but who wants a stray cat on Christmas Eve, and he couldn't take care of nine himself. It was not his fault that his old cat conceived—it was no one's fault, really—and yet the closer he got to the river, the heavier was his burden of guilt. It was the destruction of their vitality, their life, that pained him. Animals are not supposed to apprehend death, and yet the struggle in the pillowcase was vigorous and apprehensive; and he was cold.

He was an old man, and he hated the snow. Pushing on toward the river, he seemed to see in the storm the mortality of the planet. Spring would never come again. The valley of the West River would never again be a bowl of grass and violets. The lilacs would never bloom again. Watching the snow blow over the fields, he knew in his bones the death of civilizations—Paris buried in snow, the Grand Canal and the Thames frozen over, London abandoned, and in the caves of the escarpment at Innsbruck a few survivors huddled over a fire of chair and table legs. This cruel, this dolorous, this Russian winter, he thought; this death of hope. Cheer, valor, all good feelings had been extinguished in him by the cold. He tried to cast the hour into the future, to invent some gentle thaw, some clement southwest wind—blue and moving water in the river, tulips and hyacinths in bloom, the plump stars of a spring night hung about the tree of heaven—but he felt instead the chill of the glacier, the ice age, in his bones and in the painful beating of his heart.

The river was frozen, but there was some open water along the banks where the current turned. It would be easiest to drop a stone into the pillowcase, but this might hurt the kittens that he meant to murder. He knotted the top of the sack, and as he approached the water the noise in the pillowcase got louder and more plaintive. The banks were icy. The river was deep. The snow was blinding. When he put his sack into the water, it floated, and in trying to submerge it he lost his balance and fell into the water himself. "Help! Help! Help!" he cried. "Help! Help! Help! I'm drowning!" But no one heard him, and it would be weeks before he was missed.

Then the train whistle sounded—the afternoon train that had pushed its cowcatcher through the massive drifts, bringing home the last to come, bringing them back to the old houses on Boat Street, where nothing was changed and nothing was strange and nobody worried and nobody grieved, and where in an hour or two the souls of men would be sifted out, the good getting toboggans and sleds, skates and snowshoes, ponies and gold pieces, and the wicked receiving nothing but a lump of coal.

CHAPTER II

The Wapshot family settled in St. Botolphs in the seventeenth century. I knew them well, I made it my business to examine their affairs, indeed I spent the best years of my life, its very summit, on their chronicle. They were friendly enough. When you met them on the streets of St. Botolphs they behaved as if this chance meeting were something they had anticipated but if you told them anything—told them that the West River had flooded or that Pinkham's Folly had burned to the ground—they would convey, in a fleeting smile, the fact that you had made a mistake. One did not tell the Wapshots anything. Their resistance to receiving information seemed to be a family trait. They thought well of themselves; they esteemed themselves so healthy that it seemed impossible to them that they would not have known about the flood or the fire, even though they might have been in Europe. I went to school with the boys, raced with Moses at the Travertine Boat Club and played football with them both. They used to cheer one another loudly as if shouting the family name across a playing field would give it some immortality. I spent a lot of pleasant time at their house on River Street and yet what I remember is that it was always in their power to make me feel alone, to make it painfully clear that I was an outsider.

Moses, when I knew him best, had the kind of good looks and presence that sweeps a young man triumphantly through secondary school and disappointingly enough not much farther. He had dark yellow hair and a sallow complexion. Everybody loved Moses, including the village dogs, and he comported himself with the purest, the most impulsive humility. Everybody did not love Coverly. He had a long neck and a disagreeable habit of cracking his knuckles. Sarah Wapshot, their mother, was a fair and slender woman who wore a pince-nez, mispronounced the word "interesting" and claimed to have read *Middlemarch* sixteen times. She used to leave her books in the garden and their set of George Eliot was foxed and buckled by the rain. Their father, Leander, was one of those Massachusetts Yankees who look forever like a boy although toward the end he looked like a boy who had seen the Gorgon. He had a high color, fine blue eyes and thick white hair. He said "marst" for "mast" and "had" for "hard" and spent the last years of his life running a launch between Travertine and the amusement park in Nangasakit. Leander drowned while swimming. Mrs. Wapshot died two years later and ascended into heaven, where she must have been kept very busy since she was a member of that first generation of American women to enjoy sexual equality. She had exhausted herself in good works. She had founded the Woman's Club, the Current Events Club, and was a director of the Animal Rescue League and the Lambert Home for Unwed Mothers. As a result of all these activities the house on River Street was always filled with dust, its cut flowers long dead, the clocks stopped. Sarah Wapshot was one of those women whose grasp of vital matters had forced them to consider the simple tasks of a house to be in some way perverted. Coverly married a girl named Betsey Marcus from the Georgia badlands; a counter girl in a Forty-second Street milk bar. At the time of which I'm writing he worked at the Talifer Missile Site. Moses had thrown up his job as a banking apprentice to work for Leopold and Company, a shady brokerage house. He married Melissa Scaddon. Both Moses and Coverly had sons.

Spread them out on some ungiven summer evening on the lawn between their house and the banks of the West River, in the fine hour before dinner. Mrs. Wapshot is giving Lulu, the cook, a lesson in landscape painting. They have set up their easel a little to the right of the group. Mrs. Wapshot is holding a paper frame up to the river view and saying: *"Cherchez la motif, Lulu. Cherchez la motif."* Leander is drinking bourbon and admiring the light. For a man who is, in all his ways, plainly provincial, Leander's

life has possessed more latitude than one would have
guessed. He once traveled as far west as Cleveland with a
Shakespearean company and, a few years later, ascended
one hundred and twenty-seven feet in a hot-air balloon at
the county fair. He is proud of himself, proud of his sons;
pride is some part of the calm and inquisitive gaze he gives
to the river banks, thinking that all the rivers of the world
are old but that the rivers of his own country seem oldest.

Coverly is burning tent moths out of the apple trees.
Moses folds a sail. From the open windows of their house
they can hear the Waldstein Sonata being played by their
cousin Devereaux, who is practicing for his concert debut
in the fall. Devereaux has a harried, dark face and is not
quite twelve years old. "Light and shadow, light and
shadow," says old Cousin Honora of the music. She would
say the same for Chopin, Stravinsky or Thelonious Monk.
She is a redoubtable old woman in her seventies, dressed
all in white. (She will switch to black on Labor Day.) Her
money has saved the family repeatedly from disgrace or
worse and while her own home is on the other side of town
she gives this landscape and its cast a proprietary look. The
parrot, in his cage by the kitchen door, exclaims: "Julius
Caesar, I am thoroughly *disgusted.*" It is all he ever says.

How orderly, clean and sensible the world seems; above
all how light, as if these were the beginnings of a world,
a chain of mornings. It is late in the day, late in this history
of this part of the world, but this lateness does nothing to
eclipse their ardor. Presently there is a cloud of black
smoke from the kitchen—the rolls are burning—but it
doesn't really matter. They eat their supper in a cavernous
dining room, play a little whist, kiss one another good night
and go to sleep to dream.

CHAPTER III

ঙ§ ৡ৹

The trouble began one afternoon when Coverly Wapshot
swung down off the slow train, the only south-bound train
that still stopped at the village of St. Botolphs. It was in the
late winter, just before dark. The snow was gone but the
grass was dead and the place seemed not to have rallied
from the February storms. He shook hands with Mr. Jowett
and asked about his family. He waved to the bartender
in the Viaduct House, waved to Barry Freeman in the feed
store and called hello to Miles Howland, who was coming
out of the bank. The late sky was brilliant and turbulent
but it shed none of its operatic lights and fires onto the
darkness of the green. This awesome performance was
contained within the air. Between the buildings he could
see the West River with its, for him, enormous cargo of
pleasant memory and he took away from this brightness
the unlikely impression that the river's long history had
been a purifying force, leaving the water fit to drink. He
turned right at Boat Street. Mrs. Williams was sitting in
her parlor, reading the paper. The only light at the Brattles'
was in the kitchen. The Dummers' house was dark. Mrs.
Bretaigne, who was saying good-bye to a caller, welcomed
him home. Then he turned up the walk to Cousin Honora's.

Maggie answered the door and he gave her a kiss. "They
ain't nothing but dried beef," Maggie said. "You'll have to
kill a chicken." He went down the long hall past the seven
views of Rome into the library, where he found his old
cousin with an open book on her lap. Here was home-
sweet-home, the polished brass, the applewood fire. "Coverly dear," Honora said in an impulse of love and kissed
him on the lips. "Honora," Coverly said, taking her in his
arms. Then they separated and scrutinized one another
cannily to see what changes had been made.

Her white hair was still full, her face leonine, but her new false teeth were not well fitted and they made her look like a cannibal. This hinted savagery reminded Coverly of the fact that his cousin had never been photographed. In all the family albums she appeared either with her back to the camera as she ran away or with her face concealed by her hands, her handbag, her hat or a newspaper. Any stranger looking at the albums would have thought she was wanted for murder. Honora thought Coverly looked under-fed and she said so. "You're skinny," she said.

"Yes."

"I'll have Maggie bring you some port."

"I'd rather have a whisky."

"You don't drink whisky," Honora said.

"I didn't used to," Coverly said, "but I do now."

"Will wonders never cease?" Honora asked.

"If you're going to kill a chicken," Maggie said from the doorway, "you'd better kill it now or you won't get supper much before midnight."

"I'll kill the chicken now," Coverly said.

"You'll have to speak louder," Honora said. "She can't hear."

Coverly followed Maggie back through the house to the kitchen. "She's crazier than ever," Maggie said. "Now she claims she can't sleep. She claims she ain't slept for years. Well, so I come into the parlor one afternoon with her tea and there she is. Sound asleep. Snoring. So I say, 'Wake up, Miss Wapshot. Here's your tea.' She says, 'What do you mean, wake up? I wasn't asleep,' she says. 'I was just lost in deep meditation.' And now she's thinking of buying an automobile. Dear Jesus, it would be like setting a hungry lion loose in the streets. She'll be running over and killing innocent little children if she don't kill herself first."

The relationship between the old women stood four-square on a brand of larcenous backbiting that appeared to contain so little in the way of truth that it could be passed off as comical. Maggie's hearing was perfect but for some years Honora had told everyone she was deaf. Honora was eccentric but Maggie told everyone in the village that she was mad. The physical and mental infirmities they invented for one another had a pristine quality that made it nearly

K. W. Chickens

impossible to believe there was any grimness in the contest.

Coverly found a hatchet in the back pantry and went down the wooden steps to the garden. Somewhere in the distance he could hear children's voices, distinctly accented with the catarrhal pronunciations of that part of the world. There was a gaggle of sound from the hen house beyond the hedge. He felt uncommonly happy in this sparsely populated place; felt some marked loosening of his discontents. It was the hour, he knew, when the pinochle players would be drifting across the green to the firehouse and when the yearnings of adolescence, exacerbated by the smallness of the village, would be approaching a climax. He could remember sitting himself on the back steps of the house on River Street, racked with a yearning for love, for friendship and renown, that had made him howl.

He went on through the hedge to the hen house. The laying hens had retired but four or five cockerels were feeding in their yard. He chased them into their house and after an undignified scuffle caught one by its yellow legs. The bird squawked for mercy and Coverly spoke to it soothingly, he hoped, as he lay its neck on the block and chopped off its head. He held the struggling body down and away from him to let the blood drain into the ground. Maggie brought him a bucket of scalding water and an old copy of the St. Botolphs *Enterprise* and he plucked and eviscerated the bird, losing his taste for chicken, step by step. He brought the carcass back to the kitchen and joined his old cousin in the library, where Maggie had set out whisky and water.

"Can we talk now?" Coverly asked.

"I guess so," Honora said. She put her elbows on her knees and leaned forward. "You want to talk about the house on River Street?"

"Yes."

"Well, nobody'll rent it and nobody'll buy it and it would break my heart to see it torn down."

"What is the matter?"

"The Whitehalls rented it in October. They moved in and moved right out again. Then the Haverstraws took it. They lasted a week. Mrs. Haverstraw told everybody in the stores that the house was haunted. But who," she asked, raising her face, "would there be to haunt the place? Our family has always been a very happy family. None of us have ever paid any attention to ghosts. But just the same it's all over town."

"What did Mrs. Haverstraw say?"

"Mrs. Haverstraw spread it around that it's the ghost of your father."

"Leander," Coverly said.

"But what would Leander want to come back and trouble people for?" Honora asked. "It wasn't that he didn't believe in ghosts. He just never had any use for them. I've heard him say many times that he thought ghosts kept low company. And you know how kind he was. He used to escort flies and moth millers out the door as if they were guests. What would he come back for except to eat a bowl of crackers and milk? Of course he had his faults."

"Were you with us," Coverly asked, "the time he smoked a cigarette in church?"

"You must have made that up," Honora said, fending for the past.

"No," Coverly said. "It was Christmas Eve and we went to Holy Communion. I remember that he seemed very devout. He was up and down, crossing himself and roaring out the responses. Then before the Benediction he took a cigarette out of his pocket and lighted it. I saw then that he was terribly drunk. I told him, 'You can't smoke in church, Daddy,' but we were in one of the front pews and a lot of people had seen him. What I wanted then was to be the son of Mr. Pluzinski the farmer. I don't know why, except that the Pluzinskis were all very serious. It seemed to me that if I could only be the son of Mr. Pluzinski I would be happy."

"You ought to be ashamed of yourself," Honora said. Then she sighed, changed her tone and added uneasily: "There was something else."

"What?"

"You remember how he used to give away nickels on the Fourth of July."

"Oh, yes." Coverly then saw the front of their house in many colors. A large flag hung from the second floor, its crimson stripes faded to the color of old blood. His father stood on the porch, after the parade and before the ball game, passing out new nickels to a line of children that reached up River Street. The trees were all leafed out and in his reverie the light was quite green.

"Well, as you may remember he kept the nickels in a cigar box. He had painted it black. When I was going through the house I found the box. There were still some nickels in it. Many of them were not real. I believe he made them himself."

"You mean . . ."

"Shhhh," said Honora.

"Supper's ready," said Maggie.

Honora seemed tired after supper so he kissed her good night in the hallway and walked to his own home on the other side of town. The place had been empty since fall. There was a key on the windowsill and the door swung open onto a strong smell of must. This was the place where he had been conceived and born, where he had awakened to the excellence of life, and there was some keen chagrin at finding the scene of so many dazzling memories smelling of decay; but this, he knew, was the instinctual foolishness that leads us to love permanence when there is none. He turned on the lights in the hall and the parlor and got some logs from the shed. He was absorbed in laying and lighting a fire but when the fire was set he began to feel, surrounded by so many uninhabited rooms, an unreasonable burden of apprehension, as if his presence there were an intrusion.

It was his and his brother's house, by contract, inheritance and memory. Its leaks and other infirmities were his responsibility. It was he who had broken the vase on the mantelpiece and burned a hole in the sofa. He did not believe in ghosts, shades, spirits or any other forms of unquietness on the part of the dead. He was a man of twenty-eight, happily married, the father of a son. He weighed one hundred and thirty-eight pounds, enjoyed perfect health and had eaten some chicken for dinner. These were the facts. He took a copy of *Tristram Shandy* down from the shelf and began to read. There was a loud noise in the kitchen that so startled him the sweat stood out on his hands. He raised his head long enough to em-

brace this noise in the realm of hard fact. It could be a
shutter, a loose piece of firewood, an animal or one of those
legendary tramps who were a part of local demonology and
who were supposed to inhabit the empty farms, leaving
traces of fire, empty snuff cans, a dry cow and a frightened
spinster. But he was strong and young and even if he
should encounter a tramp in the dark hallway he could
take care of himself. Why should he feel so intensely uncomfortable? He went to the telephone intending to ask
the operator the time of night but the telephone was dead.

He went on reading. There was noise from the dining
room. He said something loud and vigorous to express his
impatience with his apprehensions but the effect of this was
to convince him overwhelmingly that he had been heard.
Someone was listening. There was a cure for this foolishness. He went directly to the empty room and turned on
the light. There was nothing there and yet the beating of
his heart was accelerated and painful and sweat ran off his
palms. Then the dining room door slowly closed of itself.
This was only natural since the old house sagged badly and
while half the doors closed themselves the other half
wouldn't close at all. He went through the swinging door
on into the pantry and the kitchen. Here again he saw
nothing but felt again that there had been someone in the
room when he turned on the light. There were two sets
of facts—the empty room and the alarmed condition of his
skin. He was determined to scotch this and he went out
of the kitchen into the hallway and climbed the stairs.

All the bedroom doors stood open, and here, in the dark,
he seemed to yield to the denseness of the lives that had
been lived here for nearly two centuries. The burden of
the past was palpable; the utterances and groans of con-
ception, childbirth and death, the singing at the family
reunion in 1893, the dust raised by a Fourth of July
parade, the shock of lovers meeting by chance in the hallway, the roar of flames in the fire that gutted the west wing
in 1900, the politeness at christenings, the joy of a young
husband bringing his wife back after their marriage, the
hardships of a cruel winter all took on some palpableness
in the dark air. But why was the atmosphere in this darkness distinctly one of trouble and failure? Ebenezer had

made a fortune. Lorenzo had introduced child-welfare legislation into the state laws. Alice had converted hundreds of Polynesians to Christianity. Why should none of these ghosts and shades seem contented with their work? Was it because they had been mortal, was it because for every last one of them the pain of death had been bitter?

He returned to the fire. Here was the physical world, fire-lit, stubborn and beloved, and yet his physical response was not to the parlor but to the darkness in the rooms around him. Why, sitting so close to the fire, did he feel a chill slide down his left shoulder and a moment later coarsen with cold the skin of his chest, as if a hand had been placed there? If there were ghosts, he believed with his father that they kept low company. They consorted with the poorhearted and the faint. He knew that we sometimes leave after us, in a room, a stir of love or rancor when we are gone. He believed that whatever we pay for our loves in money, venereal disease, scandal or ecstasy, we leave behind us, in the hotels, motels, guest rooms, meadows and fields where we discharge this much of ourselves, either the scent of goodness or the odor of evil, to influence those who come after us. Thus it was possible that this passionate and eccentric cast had left behind them some ambiance that made his presence seem like an intrusion. It was time to go to bed and he got some blankets out of a closet and made up a bed in the spare room, nearest the stairs.

He woke at three. There was enough radiance from the moon or the night sky itself to light the room. What had waked him, he knew immediately, was not a dream, a reverie or an apprehension; it was something that moved, something that he could see, something strange and unnatural. The terror began with his optic nerves and reverberated through his whole person but it was in the beam of his eye that the terror had begun. He was able to trace the disturbance back through his nervous system to his pupil. The eye counted on reality and what he had seen or thought he had seen was the ghost of his father. The chaos set into motion by this hallucination was horrendous and he shook with psychic and physical cold, he shook with terror, and sitting up in bed he roared: "Oh, Father, Father, Father, why have you come back?"

The loudness of his voice was some consolation. The ghost seemed to leave the room. He thought he could hear stair lifts give. Had he come back to look for a bowl of crackers and milk, to read some Shakespeare, come back because he felt like all the others that the pain of death was bitter? Had he come back to relive that moment when he had relinquished the supreme privileges of youth—when he had waked feeling less peckery than usual and realized that the doctor had no cure for autumn, no medicine for the north wind? The smell of his green years would still be in his nose—the reek of clover, the fragrance of women's breasts, so like the land-wind, smelling of grass and trees—but it was time for him to leave the field for someone younger. Spavined, gray, he had wanted no less than any youth to chase the nymphs. Over hill and dale. Now you see them; now you don't. The world a paradise, a paradise! Father, Father, why have you come back?

There was the noise of something falling in the next room. The knowledge that this was a squirrel, as it was, would not have brought Coverly to his senses. He was too far gone. He grabbed his clothing, flew down the stairs and left the front door standing open. He stopped on the sidewalk long enough to draw on his underpants. Then he ran to the corner. Here he put on his trousers and shirt but he ran the rest of the way to Honora's barefoot. He scribbled a farewell note, left it on her hall table and caught the milk train north, a little after dawn, past the Markhams', past the Wilton Trace, past the Lowells', who had changed the sign on their barn from BE KIND TO ANIMALS to GOD ANSWERS PRAYERS, past the house where old Mr. Sturgis used to live and repair watches.

new world of guissdles etc

class sttucte

CHAPTER IV

◆§ ₿◆

Going back to Talifer where he lived with Betsey, Coverly had the choice of concluding that he was demented or that he had seen his father's ghost. He chose the latter, of course, and yet he could not say so to his wife; he could not explain to his brother Moses why the house on River Street was empty. The specter of his father seemed to sit beside him in the plane that took him west. Oh, Father, Father, why have you come back! What, he wondered, would Leander have made of Talifer?

The site for Missile Research and Development had a population of twenty thousand, divided, like any society, whatever its aspirations, into first class, second class, third class and steerage. The large aristocracy was composed of physicists and engineers. Tradesmen made up the middle class, and there was a vast proletariat of mechanics, ground crewmen and gantry hands. Most of the aristocracy had been given underground shelters and while this fact had never been publicized it was well known that in the case of a cataclysm the proletariat would be left to scald. This made for some hard feeling. The vitals of the place were the twenty-nine gantries at the edge of the desert, the mosque-shaped atomic reactor, the underground laboratories and hangars and the two-square-mile computation and administration center. The concerns of the site were entirely extraterrestrial, and while common sense would scotch any sentimental and transparent ironies about the vastness of scientific research undertaken at Talifer and the capacity for irrational forlornness, loneliness and ecstasy among the scientists, it was a way of life that presented some strenuous intellectual contrasts.

Security was always a problem. Talifer was never men-a place w/o a past + present

tioned in the newspapers. It had no public existence. This
concern with security seemed to inhibit life at every level.
One Saturday afternoon Betsey was watching television.
Coverly had taken Binxey for a trip to the shopping center.
Out of her window she saw that Mr. Hansen, who lived
across the street, was taking down his storm windows and
putting up his screens. He had a stepladder, which he
planted carefully in his flowerbeds, then he raised and un-
hooked his windows and carried them into the garage. His
wife and children seemed to be off. There were no other
signs of life around the place. When he had removed the
windows from the first floor he started on the upstairs
bedrooms. His ladder didn't reach these and he had to
work by leaning out of the open windows, unhooking the
frames and drawing them on their rectilinear bias into the
house. The hardware for one of the windows seemed
warped or rusted. It would not come loose. He straddled
the windowsill and yanked at the frame. He fell out of the
window and landed with a thud onto a little terrace that
he had paved with cement block a few weeks earlier.
Betsey looked out of the window long enough to see that
his body was inert. Then she returned to her television set.
Twenty minutes later she heard a siren and an ambulance
came down the street and took the still inert form away
on a stretcher. She learned that evening that he had been
instantly killed. Some children had given the alarm. But
why hadn't she? How could she account for her unnatural
behavior? The general concern for security seemed to be at
the bottom of her negligence. She had not wanted to do
anything that would call attention to herself, that would
involve giving testimony or answering questions. Presumably her concern for security had led her to overlook the
death of a neighbor.

Coverly would have had some difficulty explaining to
Leander that while he had been trained as a taper and subprogrammer, he had been switched to public relations
when he was transferred from the Remsen to the Talifer
Site. This was a mistake, made by one of the computations
machines in personnel, but there was no appeal. They lived
in a mixed neighborhood. Betsey wanted a shelter and
Coverly had applied for a transfer to another neighborhood

bureaucracy

but the government-operated real-estate office was
swamped with such applications and anyhow Coverly was
not unhappy where he was. Ginkgo trees had been planted
along the sidewalks where children roller-skated, and song
birds had nested in the trees. Sitting in his back yard before
dinner he could watch the sere and moving mountain twilight—that sour and powerful glow—beyond the distant
gantries. They had a little garden and a grill for cooking
meat. The house on their right was owned by a man named
Armstrong, who was in the World Relations Department.
Armstrong had developed a dry, manly and monosylla-
bic prose style for ghosting the chronicles of astronauts.
The house on their left was owned by a gantry-crew man
named Murphy, who got drunk and beat up his wife on
Saturday nights. The Wapshots did not get along with the
Murphys. One morning when Coverly was at work the
signal board indicated that there was a telephone call for
him. He left the security area to take the call. It was
Betsey. "She stole my garbage pail," Betsey said.

"I don't understand, sugar," Coverly said.

"Mrs. Murphy," Betsey said. "The garbage man came
this morning, he always comes on Tuesdays, and when he
took away the garbage she took that nice, new, tin, gal-
vanized garbage pail of mine and carried it right up to the
back of her house, leaving me with that cracked, plastic old
thing they brought from Canaveral."

"Well, I can't do anything about it now," Coverly said.
"I'll be home at half-past five."

Betsey was still excited when he returned. "You go right
over there now and get it back," she said. "They'll fill it
up with garbage and claim that it's theirs. You should
have painted our name on it. You go right over there now
and get it away from them. There he is, he's cutting the
grass."

Coverly left the house and walked to the boundary of his
lot. Pete Murphy had just started up his lawn mower. The
distant mountains were blue. The time of day, the sameness
of the houses, the popping noise of the one-cylinder engine
and the two men in their white shirt sleeves gave to the
scene some unwonted otherness, as if Coverly were not
about to accuse his neighbor, or his neighbor's wife, of

theft, but was about to remark that merchandising indices showed in their uptrend the inarguable power of direct-mail advertising. In short, their reality and their passions seemed challenged. The distant mountains had been formed by fire and water but the houses in the valley looked so insubstantial that they seemed, in the dusk, to smell of shirt cardboards. Coverly cracked his knuckles nervously and signaled to Pete with a jerk of his head. Pete pushed the lawn mower directly past him and muffled Coverly's words with noise of the motor. Coverly waited. Pete made a second circle of the lawn and then throttled down the motor and stopped in front of Coverly.

"My wife tells me you stole our garbage pail," Coverly said.

"So what?"

"Are you in the habit of helping yourself to other people's property?" Coverly was more perplexed than angry.

"Listen, chicken," Murphy said. "Where I grew up you either helped yourself or you ate dirt."

"But this doesn't happen to be where you grew up," said Coverly. It was the wrong tack. He seemed to be foot-noting the dispute. Then, confident of his rightness he spoke sternly and in a full voice, marred by some old-fashioned or provincial haughtiness.

"Would you be good enough to return our garbage pail?" he asked.

"Listen," Murphy said. "You're trespassing. You're on my land. Get off my land or you'll go home a cripple for life. I'll gouge out your eyes. I'll break your nose. I'll tear off your ears."

Coverly swung a right from the hip, and Murphy, a big man and a coward, it seemed, went down. Coverly stood there, a little bewildered. Then Murphy came forward on his hands and knees and sank his teeth into Coverly's shin. Coverly roared. Betsey and Mrs. Murphy came running out of their kitchens. Just then a missile left its pad and, in the dusk, shed a light as bright as the light of a mid-summer's day over the valley and the site, throwing the shadows of the combatants, their houses and their ginkgo trees blackly onto the grass, while air waves demarked the earth-shaking roar so that it sounded like the humble click of track joints. The missile ascended, the light faded with it, and the two women took their husbands home.

Oh, Father, Father, why have you come back?

The computation and administration center where Coverly worked appeared from a distance to be a large, one-story building but this single story merely contained the elevator terminals and the security offices. The other offices and the hardware were underground. The one visible story was made of glass, tinted darkly to the color of oily water. The darkened glass did not diminish but it did alter the light of day. Beyond these dim glass walls one could see some flat pasture land and the buildings of an abandoned farm. There was a house, a barn, a clump of trees and a split-rail fence, and the abandoned buildings with the gantries beyond them had a nostalgic charm. They were signs of the past, and whatever the truth may have been, they appeared to be signs of a rich and a natural way of life. The abandoned farm evoked a spate of vulgar and bucolic imagery—open fires, pails of fresh milk and pretty girls swinging in apple trees—but it was nonetheless persuasive. One turned away from this then to the dark, oil-colored glass and moved into another world, buried six stories beneath the cow pasture. It was a new world in every way. Its newness was most apparent in an atmosphere of enthusiasm and usefulness that seems lost to most of us today. To observe that the elevators sometimes broke down, that one of the glass walls had cracked, and that the pretty receptionists in the security office had a primitive and an immemorial appeal was like burdening oneself with the observations of some old man, pushed by time past the boundaries of all usefulness. The crowds that went to and from the computation center had a look of contentment and purpose that you won't find in the New York or Paris subways, where we seem to regard one another with the horror and dismay of a civilization of caricaturists. Leaving his office late one night Coverly had heard Dr. Cameron, the site director, ending a dispute with one of his lieutenants. The doctor was shouting, "You'll never get a Goddamned man onto the Goddamned moon, and if you do, it won't do you any Goddamned good."

Oh, Father, Father, why have you come back?

Betsey had hoped to be transferred to Canaveral and was disappointed in Talifer. They had been there two months then but no one had come to call. She had made no friends. In the evening she could hear the sounds of talk and laughter but she and Coverly were never included in these gatherings. From her window Betsey could see Mrs. Armstrong working in her flower garden and she interpreted this interest in flowers as the sign of a kindly nature. One day, when Binxey was taking his nap, Betsey went next door and rang the bell. Mrs. Armstrong answered the door. "I'm Betsey Wapshot," Betsey said, "and I'm your next-door neighbor. My husband Coverly was trained as a subprogrammer but they've got him on public relations right now. I've seen you in your garden and I thought I'd pay you a call." The woman kindly invited her in. She seemed not inhospitable but subdued. "What I wanted to ask you about," Betsey said, "was my neighbors. We've been here two months now but we just seem to have been too busy to make friends. We don't know anybody and so I thought I'd like to give a little cocktail party and see who's who. I want to know who to ask."

"Well, my dear, I'd wait a little while, if I were you," Mrs. Armstrong said. "For some reason this seems to be quite a conservative community. I think you'd better meet your neighbors before you invite them."

"Well, I come from a small town," Betsey said, "where everybody's neighbors, and I often say to myself that if I can't trust in the friendliness of strangers, well, then what in the world is there that I can trust in?"

"I see what you mean," said Mrs. Armstrong.

"I've lived in all kinds of places," Betsey said. "High society. Low society. My husband's family came over on the *Arbella*. That's the ship that came after the *Mayflower* but it had a higher class of people. It seems to me that people are all the same, under their skins. What I want you to do is to give me a list of twenty-five or thirty of the most interesting people in the neighborhood."

"But, my dear, I'm afraid I couldn't do that."

"Why not?"

"There isn't time."

small town v. suburb

"Well, it wouldn't take very long, would it?" Betsey asked. "I've got a pencil and paper right here. Now just tell me who lives in the house on the corner."

"The Seldons."

"Are they interesting?"

"Yes, they're quite interesting but they're not terribly friendly."

"What's his first name?"

"Herbert."

"Who lives in the house next to them?"

"The Trampsons."

"Are they interesting?"

"Yes, they're terribly interesting. He and Reginald Tappan discovered the Tappan Constant. He's been nominated for a Nobel Prize but he's not terribly friendly."

"And then on the other side of them?" Betsey asked.

"The Harnecks," Mrs. Armstrong said. "But I must warn you, my dear, that you'll be making a mistake if you ask them before you've been introduced."

"And that's where I think you're wrong," Betsey said. "You just wait and see. Who lives on the other side of them?"

In the end she went away with a list of twenty-five names. Mrs. Armstrong explained that she would be unable to come to the party herself because she was going to Denver. With the thought of a party to occupy her Betsey was happy and at peace with the world. She explained her plans to the proprietor of a liquor store in the shopping center. He told her what she would need and gave her the telephone number of a couple—a maid and barman—who would mix the drinks and prepare the food. At the stationery store she bought a box of invitations and happily spent an afternoon and an evening addressing these. On the day of the party the couple arrived at three. Betsey dressed herself and her little son, Coverly came home at five, when the first guests were expected, and the scene was set.

When no one had come by half-past five Coverly opened a beer and the barman made a whisky and ginger ale for Betsey. Cars went to and fro on the street but none of them stopped at the Wapshots'. She could hear the sounds of a tennis game from a court in the next block; laughter and talk. The bartender said kindly that the neighborhood was a strange one. He worked in Denver and he longed to get back to a place where people were more courteous and predictable. He halved limes, squeezed lemons, arranged a row of cocktail glasses on the table and filled these with ice. At six o'clock the maid took a paper-back novel out of her bag and sat down to read. At a little after six the back doorbell rang and Betsey hastened to answer it. It was the delivery man from the dry-cleaners. Coverly heard Betsey ask him in for a drink. "Oh, I'd love to, Mrs. Wapshot," the man said, "but I have to go home now and cook my supper. I'm living alone now, I guess I told you. My wife ran off with one of the butchers in the food express. The lawyer told me to put the kids in an orphanage, he said I'd get custody quicker that way, so I'm all alone. I'm so alone that I talk with the flies. There's a lot of flies where I live but I don't kill them. I just talk with them. They're like friends. 'Hello, flies,' I say. 'We're all alone, you and me. You're looking good, flies.' I suppose you might think I was crazy for talking with the flies but that's the way it is. I don't have anybody else to talk to."

Coverly heard the door close. Betsey drew some water in the sink. When she came back into the room her face was pale. "Well, let's have a party," Coverly said. "Let's you and I have a party." He got her another drink and passed her a tray of sandwiches but she seemed so stiff with pain that she could not turn her head and when she drank her whisky she spilled some on her chin. "The things you read about in these paper books," the maid said. "I don't know. I been married three times but right here in this book they're doing something and I don't know what it is. I mean I don't know what they're doing. . . ." She glanced at the little boy and went on reading. Coverly asked the couple if they wouldn't like a drink but they both politely refused and said that they didn't drink on duty. Their presence seemed to amplify a pain of embarrassment that was swiftly turning into shame; their eyes seemed to be the eyes of the world, civil as they were, and Coverly finally asked them to go. They were enormously relieved. They had the good taste not to say that they were sorry; not to

say anything but good-bye. "We'll leave everything out for
the latecomers," Betsey called gallantly after them as they
went out the door.

It was her last gallantry. The pain in her breast threatened to overwhelm her. Her spirit seemed about to break
under the organized cruelty of the world. She had offered
her innocence, her vision of friendly strangers, to the community and she had been wickedly spurned. She had not
asked them for money, for help of any kind, she had not
asked them for friendship, she had only asked that they
come to her house, drink her whisky and fill the empty
rooms with the noise of talk for a little time and not one
of them had the kindness to come. It was a world that
seemed to her as hostile, incomprehensible and threatening
as the gantry lines on the horizon, and when Coverly put
an arm around her and said, "I'm sorry, sugar," she pushed
him away from her and said harshly, "Leave me be, leave
me be, you just leave me be."

In the end Coverly, by way of consolation, took Betsey
to a coffee house in the commercial center. They bought
their tickets and sat in canvas chairs with mugs of coffee to
drink. A young woman with yellow hair drawn back over
her ears was plucking a small harp and singing:

> "Oh Mother, dear Mother, oh Mother,
> Why is the sky so dark?
> Why does the air smell of roach powder?
> Why is there no one in the park?"

> "It's nothing, my darling daughter,
> This isn't the way the world ends,
> The washing machine is on spinner,
> And I'm waiting to entertain friends."

> "But Mother, dear Mother, please tell me,
> Why does your Geiger counter tick?
> And why are all those nice people
> Jumping into the creek?"

> "It's nothing, it's nothing, my darling,
> It's really nothing at all,
> My Geiger counter simply records
> An increase in radioactive fall."

"But Mother, dear Mother, please tell me,
Before I go up to bed,
Why are my yellow curls falling,
Falling off of my head?
And why is the sky so red?
Why is the sky so red . . ."

There was something in Coverly's nature—something
provincial no doubt—that made this sort of lamentation
intolerable and he seized Betsey's hand and marched out
of the coffee house, snorting like someone much older.
It wasn't much of a night.

Oh, Father, Father, why have you come back?

CHAPTER V

Moses and Melissa Wapshot lived in Proxmire Manor, a
place that was known up and down the suburban railroad
line as the place where the lady got arrested. The incident
had taken place five or six years before, but it had the
endurance of a legend, and the lady had seemed briefly to
be the genius of the pretty place. The facts are simple. With
the exception of one unsolved robbery, the eight-man
police force of Proxmire Manor had never found anything
to do. Their only usefulness was to direct traffic at wed-
dings and large cocktail parties. They listened day and
night on the interstate police radio to the crimes and
alarms in other communities—car thefts, mayhem, drunkenness and murder—but the blotter in Proxmire Manor
was clean. The burden of this idleness on their self-esteem
was heavy as, armed with pistols and bandoleers of ammu-
nition, they spent their days writing parking tickets for
the cars left at the railroad station. It was like a child's
game, ticketing commuters for the most trifling infractions

of the rules the police themselves invented, and they played it enthusiastically.

The lady—Mrs. Lemuel Jameson—had similar problems. Her children were away at school, her housework was done by a maid, and while she played cards and lunched with friends, she was often made ill-tempered by abrasive boredom. Coming home from an unsuccessful shopping trip in New York one afternoon, she found her car ticketed for being a little over a white line. She tore the ticket to pieces. Later that afternoon, a policeman found the pieces in the dirt and took them to the police station, where they were pasted together.

The police were excited, of course, at this open challenge to their authority. Mrs. Jameson was served with a summons. She called her friend Judge Flint—he was a member of the Club—and asked him to fix it. He said that he would, but later that afternoon he had an attack of acute appendicitis and was taken to the hospital. When Mrs. Jameson's name was called in traffic court and there was no response, the police were alert. A warrant for her arrest was issued, the first such warrant in years. In the morning two patrolmen, heavily armed and in fresh uniforms and in the company of an old police matron, drove to Mrs. Jameson's house with the warrant. A maid opened the door and said that Mrs. Jameson was sleeping. With at least a hint of force, they entered the beautiful drawing room and told the maid to wake Mrs. Jameson. When Mrs. Jameson heard that the police were downstairs she was indignant. She refused to move. The maid went downstairs, and in a minute or two Mrs. Jameson heard the heavy steps of the policemen. She was horrified. Would they dare enter her bedroom? The ranking officer spoke to her from the hall. "You get out of bed, lady, and come with us or we'll get you up." Mrs. Jameson began to scream. The police matron, reaching for her shoulder holster, entered the bedroom. Mrs. Jameson went on screaming. The matron told her to get up and dress or they would take her to the station house in her nightclothes. When Mrs. Jameson started for the bathroom, the matron followed her and she began to scream again. She was hysterical. She screamed at the policemen when she encountered them in the upstairs hallway, but she let herself be led out to the car and driven to the station house. Here she began to scream again. She finally paid the one-dollar fine and was sent home in a taxi.

Mrs. Jameson was determined to have the policemen fired, and the moment she walked into her house she began to organize her campaign. Counting over her neighbors for someone who would be eloquent and sympathetic, she thought of Peter Dolmetch, a free-lance television writer, who rented the Fulsoms' gatehouse. No one liked him, but Mrs. Jameson sometimes invited him to her cocktail parties, and he was indebted to her. She called and told him her story. "I can't believe it, darling," he said. She said that she was asking him, because of his natural eloquence, to defend her. "I'm against Fascism, darling," he said, "wherever it raises its ugly head." She then called the mayor and demanded a hearing. It was set for eight-thirty that night. Mr. Jameson happened to be away on business. She called a few friends, and by noon everyone in Proxmire Manor knew that she had been humiliated by a policewoman, who followed her into the bathroom and sat on the edge of the tub while she dressed, and that Mrs. Jameson had been taken to the station house at the point of a gun. Fifteen or twenty neighbors showed up for the hearing. The mayor and his councilmen numbered seven, and the two patrolmen and the matron were also there. When the meeting was called to order, Peter stood and asked, "Has Fascism come to Proxmire Manor? Is the ghost of Hitler stalking our tree-shaded streets? Must we, in the privacy of our homes, dread the tread of the Storm Troopers' boots on our sidewalks and the pounding of the mailed fist on the door?" On and on he went. He must have spent all day writing it. It was all aimed at Hitler, with only a few passing references to Mrs. Jameson. The audience began to cough, to yawn, and then to excuse themselves. When the protest was dismissed and the meeting adjourned, there was no one left but the principals, and Mrs. Jameson's case was lost, but it was not forgotten. The conductor on the train, passing the green hills, would say, "They arrested a lady there yesterday"; then, "They arrested a lady there last month"; and presently, "That's

the place where the lady got arrested." That was Proxmire
Manor.

The village stood on three leafy hills north of the city,
and was handsome and comfortable, and seemed to have
eliminated, through adroit social pressures, the thorny
side of human nature. This knowledge was forced on
Melissa one afternoon when a neighbor, Laura Hilliston,
came in for a glass of sherry. "What I wanted to tell you,"
Laura said, "is that Gertrude Lockhart is a slut." Melissa
heard the words down the length of the room as she was
pouring sherry, and wondered if she had heard correctly,
the remark seemed so callous. What kind of tidings were
these to carry from house to house? She was never sure—
how could one be, it was all so experimental?—of the exact
nature and intent of the society in which she lived, but did
it really embrace this kind of thing?

Laura Hilliston laughed. Her laughter was healthy and
her teeth were white. She sat on the sofa, a heavy woman
with her feet planted squarely on the rug. Her hair was
brown. So were her large, soft eyes. Her face was fleshy,
but with a fine ruddiness. She was long married and had
three grown sons, but she had recently stepped out of the
country of love—briskly and without a backward glance,
as if she had spent too much time in its steaming jungles.
She was through with all *that,* she had told her wretched
husband. She had put on some perfume for the visit, and
she wore a thick necklace of false gold that threw a brassy
light up onto her features. Her shoes had high heels, and
her dress was tight, but these lures were meant to establish
her social position and not to catch the eyes of a man.

"I just thought you ought to know," Laura said. "It isn't
mere gossip. She has been intimate with just about everybody. I mean the milkman, and that old man who reads
the gas meter. That nice fresh-faced boy who used to de-
liver the laundry lost his job because of her. The truck
used to be parked there for hours at a time. Then she began
to buy her groceries from Narobi's, and one of the delivery
boys had quite a lot of trouble. Her husband's a nice-looking man, and they say he puts up with it for the sake of
the children. He adores the children. But what I really
wanted to say is that we're getting her out. They have a

twenty-eight-thousand-dollar mortgage with a repair clause, and Charlie Peterson at the bank has just told them that they'll have to put a new roof on the house. Of course, they can't afford this, and so Bumps Trigger is going to give them what they paid for the place, and they'll have to go somewhere else. I just thought you might like to know."

"Thank you," Melissa said. "Will you have some more sherry?"

"Oh, no, thank you. I must get along. We're going to the Wishings'. Aren't you?"

"Yes, we are," Melissa said.

Laura put on a short mink jacket and stepped out of the house with that grace, that circumspection, that gentle and unmistakable poise of a lady who has said farewell to love.

Then the back doorbell rang. The cook was out with the baby, and so Melissa went to the back door and let in one of Mr. Narobi's grocery boys. She wondered if he was the one Mrs. Lockhart had tried to seduce. He was a slender young man with brown hair and blue eyes that shed their light evenly, as the eyes of the young will, and were so unlike the eyes of the old—those haggard lanterns that shed no light at all. She would have liked to ask him about Mrs. Lockhart, but this, of course, was not possible. She gave him a quarter tip, and he thanked her politely, and she went upstairs to bathe and dress for the Wishings' dance.

The Wishings' dance was an annual affair. As Mrs. Wishing kept explaining, they gave it each year before the rugs were put down. There was a three-piece orchestra, a fine dinner, with glazed salmon, *boeuf en daube,* a dark flowery claret and a bar for drinks. By quarter after ten, Melissa felt bored and would have asked Moses to take her home, but he was in another room. Lovely and high-spirited, she was seldom bored. Watching the dancers, she thought of poor Mrs. Lockhart, who was being forced out of this society. On the other hand, she knew how easy, how mistaken it was to assume that the exceptions—the drunkard and the lewd—penetrate, through their excesses, the carapace of immortal society. Did Mrs. Lockhart know more about mankind than she, Melissa? Who did have the power of penetration? Was it the priest who saw how their hands trembled when they reached for the chalice, the doctor who had seen them stripped of their clothing, or the psychiatrist who had seen them stripped of their obdurate pride, and who was now dancing with a fat woman in a red dress? And what was penetration worth? What did it matter that the drunken and unhappy woman in the corner dreamed frequently that she was being chased through a grove of trees by a score of naked lyric poets? Melissa was bored, and she thought her dancing neighbors were bored, too. Loneliness was one thing, and she knew herself how sweet it could make lights and company seem, but boredom was something else, and why, in this most prosperous and equitable world, should everyone seem so bored and disappointed?

Melissa went to the bathroom. The Wishings' house was large and she lost her way. She stepped by mistake into a dark bedroom. The moment she entered the room another woman, who must have been waiting, embraced her, groaning with ardor. Then realizing her mistake she said: "I'm terribly sorry," and went out the door. Melissa saw only that she had dark hair and full skirts. She stood in the dark room for a moment, trying, with no success at all, to fit this encounter somewhere into the distant noise of dance music. It could only mean that two of her neighbors, two housewives, had fallen in love and had planned a rendezvous in the middle of the Wishings' dance. But who could it have been? None of her neighbors seemed possible. It must have been someone from out of town; someone from the wicked world beyond Proxmire Manor. She stepped into the lighted hallway and found her way to where she had been going in the first place and all she seemed able to do was to forget the encounter. It had not happened.

She asked Bumps Trigger to get her a drink, and he brought her back a glass of dark bourbon. She felt a profound nostalgia, a longing for some emotional island or peninsula that she had not even discerned in her dreams. She seemed to know something about its character—it was not a paradise—but its elevating possibilities of emotional richness and freedom stirred her. It was the stupendous feeling that one could do much better than this; that the

reality was not Mrs. Wishing's dance; that the world was
not divided into rigid parliaments of good and evil but was
ruled by the absolute authority and range of her desire.

She began to dance then, and danced until three, when
the band stopped playing. Her feelings had changed from
boredom to a ruthless greed for pleasure. She did not ever
want the party to stop, and stayed until dawn, when she
then yielded to Moses' attentions. Moses was a very attentive husband. He was attentive in boathouses and leaky
canoes, on beaches and mossy banks, in motels, hotels,
guest rooms, sofas, and day beds. The house rang nightly
with his happy cries of abandon but within this lather of
love there were rigid canons of decency and some forms
of sexual commerce seemed to him shocking and distaste-
ful. In the light of day (excepting Saturdays, Sundays and
holidays) his standards of decency were exacting. He
would smash any man in the nose who told a dirty story
in mixed company and once spanked his little son for
saying damn. He was the sort of paterfamilias who inspires
sympathy for the libertine. Nightly he romanced Melissa,
nightly he climbed confidently into bed, while the poor
libertine enjoys no such security. He—love's wanderer—
must write letters, spend his income on flowers and jewelry,
squire women to restaurants and theaters and listen to interminable reminiscences—How Mean My Sister Was To
Me and The Night the Cat Died. He must apply his intelligence and his manual dexterity to the nearly labyrinthine complications of women's clothing. He must anticipate problems of geography, caprices of taste, jealous
husbands, suspicious cooks, all for a few hours', sometimes
a few moments', stolen sweetness. He is denied the
pleasures of friendship, he is a suspicious character to the
police, and it is sometimes difficult for him to find employment, while the world smiles gently on that hairy brute,
his married neighbor. This volcanic area that Moses shared
with Melissa was immense, but it was the only one. They
agreed on almost nothing else. They drank different
brands of whisky, read different books and papers. Outside
the dark circle of love they seemed almost like strangers,
and glimpsing Melissa down a long dinner table he had
once wondered who was that pretty woman with light hair.

That this boisterousness, this attentiveness, was not entirely spontaneous was revealed to Melissa one morning when she opened a drawer in the hall table and found a series of clipped memos dated for a month or six weeks and titled: "Drink Score." The entries ran: "12 noon 3 martinis. 3:20 1 pickmeup. 5:36 to 6:40 3 bourbons on train. 4 bourbons before dinner. 1 pint moselle. 2 whiskies after." The entries didn't vary much from day to day. She put them back into the drawer. It was something else to be forgotten.

CHAPTER VI

§ ?

Incredible as it may seem, Honora Wapshot had never paid an income tax. Judge Beasely, who was nominally in charge of her affairs, assumed that she was cognizant of the tax laws and had never questioned her on the subject. Her oversight, her criminal negligence, might have been explained by her age. She may have felt herself too old to begin something new such as paying taxes or she may have felt that she would die before she was apprehended. Now and then the thought of her dereliction would waveringly cross her mind and she would suffer a fleeting pang of guilt, but, as she saw it, one of the privileges of age was a high degree of irresponsibility. In any case, she had never paid a tax and thus, one evening, a man named Norman Johnson got off the same train that had brought Coverly to St. Botolphs the night he saw his father's ghost.

Mr. Jowett guessed from his clothing that he was a salesman and directed him to the Viaduct House. Mabel Moulton, who had been running the hotel since her father's stroke, led him up the stairs to a room on the second floor back. "It isn't much," she explained, "but it's all we have." She left him alone to amplify her observation. The single window looked out across the river to the table-silver factory. In the corner there was a pitcher and a basin for washing. He saw a chamber pot under the bed. These primitive arrangements disturbed him. Imagine using a chamber pot at a time when men freely explored space! But did astronauts use chamber pots? Motormen's helpers? What *did* they use? He dropped this subject to sniff the air of the room but the Viaduct House was a very old hotel and forgiveness was all you could bring to its odors. He hung both the suit he wore and the one in his bag in the closet. The collection of tin coat-racks there chimed the half-hour when he touched them. This ghostly music startled him and then the stillness of the place rushed in. There were footsteps in the room overhead. A man's? A woman's? The heels were hard but the step was heavy and he guessed they belonged to a man. But what was he doing? First the stranger walked from the window to the closet. Then he walked from the closet to the bed. Then he walked from the bed to the washstand and then from the washstand back to the window. His step was brisk, quick and urgent, but his comings and goings were senseless. Was he packing, was he dressing, was he shaving or was he, as Johnson knew from his own experience, simply moving aimlessly around an empty place, wondering what it was that he had forgotten?

Johnson, wearing a shirt and underpants, sat on the edge of the bed. (His underpants were printed with poker hands and dice.) He opened a bottle of sherry and drank a glass. In the heterogeneous and resurgent stream of faces that surrounds us there are those that seem to be the coins of a particular realm, that seem to have a sameness of feature and value. One would have seen Johnson before; one would see him again. He had the kind of long face to which the word "maturity" could not in any sense be applied. Time had been a series of unsuspected losses and rude blows, but in half-lights and cross-lights this emotional scar tissue was unseen and the face seemed earnest, simple and inscrutable. Some of us go around the world three times, divorce, remarry, divorce again, part with our children, make and waste a fortune, and coming back to our beginnings we find the same faces at the same windows, buy our cigarettes and newspapers from the same old man, say good morning to the same elevator operator, good night to the same desk clerk, to all those who seem, as Johnson did, driven into life by misfortune like the nails into a floor.

He was a traveler, familiar with the miseries of loneliness, with the violence of its sexuality, with its half-conscious imagery of highways and thruways like the projections of a bewildered spirit; with that forlorn and venereal limbo that must have flowed over the world before the invention of Venus, unknown to good and evil, ruled by pain. His father had died when he was a boy and he had been raised by his mother and her sister, a schoolteacher and a seamstress. He had been a good boy, industrious and hard-working, and while the rest of the kids were running up and down the street after a football he had sold arch supporters, magazine subscriptions, hot-water heaters, Christmas cards and newspapers. He stored his dimes and nickels in empty prune-juice jars and deposited them in his savings account once a week. He paid his own tuition for two years at the university and then he was drafted into the infantry. He could have gotten a deferred job at the ore-loading docks in Superior and made a fortune during the war but he didn't learn this until it was too late.

He landed in Normandy on the fourth day of the invasion. His burly first sergeant shot himself in the foot as soon as they landed and his bloodthirsty company commander cracked up after three hours of combat. The modest and decent men like himself were the truly brave. He was wounded on his third day in combat and flown back to a hospital in England. When he returned to his company he was transferred to headquarters and he stayed there until his discharge. That was four years out of his life, four years cut out of the career of a young man. When he got back to Superior his aunt was dead and his mother was dying. When he buried her he was left with three thousand dollars in medical bills, a fourteen-hundred dollar bill from the undertaker and a seven-thousand-dollar mortgage on a house nobody wanted to buy. He was twenty-seven years old. He poured himself another glass of sherry. "I never had an electric train," he said aloud. "I never had a dog."

He got a job in the Veterans Administration in Duluth and learned another lesson. Most men were born in debt, lived in debt and died in debt. Conscientiousness and industry were no match for the burdens of indebtedness. What he needed was an inspiration, a gamble, and standing on a little hill outside Superior one night he had an inspiration. In the distance he could see the lights of Duluth. Below him were the flat roofs of a cannery. The evening wind from Duluth blew in his direction and on this wind he heard the barking of dogs. His thinking took these lines. Two thousand people lived on the hill. Everyone on the hill had a dog. Every dog ate at least a can of food a day. People loved their dogs and were ready to pay good money to feed them but who knew what went into a can of dog food? What did dogs like? Table scraps, garbage and horse buns. Stray dogs always had the finest coats and enjoyed the best health. All he needed was a selling point. Ye Olde English Dog Food! England meant roast beef to most people. Put a label like that on a can and dog owners would pay as high as twenty-five cents. The noise from the cannery fitted in with all of this and he went happily to bed.

He experimented with dogs in the neighborhood and settled on a formula that was ninety per cent floor sweepings from the breakfast-food factory, ten per cent horse buns from the riding stable and enough water to make the mixture moist. He had a label designed and printed with a heraldic shield and "Ye Olde English Dog Food" in a florid script. The cannery agreed to process a lot of a thousand and he rented a truck and took a load to the cannery in ashcans. When the cans were labeled and crated and stored in his garage he felt that he possessed something valuable and beautiful. He bought a new suit and began going around to the markets of Duluth with a sample can of Olde English.

The story was the same everywhere. The grocers bought from the jobbers and when he approached the jobbers they explained that they couldn't handle his food. The dog food they sold was pushed by the Chicago meat-packers on a price tie-in basis with the rest of their products and he couldn't compete with Chicago. He tried peddling his dog food on the hill but you can't sell dog food door to door and he learned a bitter lesson. The independent doesn't have a chance. Duluth was full of hungry dogs and he had a thousand cans of feed stored in his garage but as an independent he was helpless to bring them profitably together. Remembering this, he had another glass of sherry.

It was dark by then. The light had gone from the window and he dressed to go down for supper. He was the only customer in the dining room, where Mabel Moulton brought him a bowl of greasy soup in which a burnt match was swimming. The burnt match, like the chamber pot, made his hatred of St. Botolphs implacable. "Oh, I'm awful sorry," Mabel said, when he showed her the match. "I'm awful sorry. You see, my father had a stroke last month and we're awful shorthanded. Things aren't the way we'd like to have them. The pilot light on the gas range isn't working and the cook has to keep lighting the range with matches and I expect that's how a match got into your soup. Well, I'll take away your soup and bring you the pot roast and I'll make sure there's no matches in that. Notice that I'm taking off your plate with my *left* hand. I sprained my left hand last winter and it's never been right since but I keep doing things with it to see if I can't get it back into condition that way. The doctor tells me that if I keep using it, it'll get better. Of course it's easier for me to use my right hand all the time but every now and then . . ." She saw that he was unfriendly and moved on. She had waited on a thousand lonely men and most of them liked to hear about her aches, pains and sprains while she admired the pictures of their wives, children, houses and dogs. It was a light bridge of communication but it was better than nothing and it passed the time.

Johnson ate his pot roast and his pie and went into the bar. It was crudely lighted by illuminated beer signs and smelled like a soil excavation. The only customers were two farmers. He went to the end of the bar farthest from them and drank another glass of sherry. Then he bowled

a game on the miniature bowling machine and went out
the side door onto the street. The town was dark; turned
back on itself, totally unfamiliar with the needs of
travelers, wanderers, the great flowing world. Every store
was shut. He glanced at the Unitarian church across the
green. It was a white frame building with columns, a bell
tower and a spire that vanished into the starlight. It
seemed incredible to him that his people, his inventive kind,
the first to exploit glass store fronts, bright lights and continuous music, should ever have been so backward as to
construct a kind of temple that belonged to the ancient
world. He went around the edges of the green and turned
up Boat Street as far as Honora's. Lights burned here and
there in the old house but he saw no one. He went back
to the bar and watched a fight on television.

The favorite was an aging club fighter named Mercer.
The challenger was a man named Santiago who could have
been Italian or Puerto Rican. He was fleshy, muscular and
stupid. Mercer had it all his way for the first two rounds.
He was a fair, slight man, his face lined, so Johnson
thought, with common domestic worries. He would have
kissed his wife good-bye in some kitchen an hour ago and
he was fighting to keep up the payments on the washing
machine. Agile, intelligent and tough, he seemed unbeat-
able until early in the third round when Santiago opened a
cut over his right eye. Blood streamed down Mercer's face
and chest and he slipped on the bloody canvas. Santiago
reopened the cut in the fifth and Mercer was blinded again
and staggered helplessly around the ring. The fight was
stopped in the sixth. Mercer's spirit would be crushed, his
wife and children would be heartbroken and his washing
machine would be taken away. Johnson went upstairs, got
into a suit of pajamas printed with scenes of a steeplechase
and read a paper-back novel.

His novel was about a young woman with millions of
dollars and houses in Rome, Paris, New York and Hono-
lulu. In the first chapter she made it with her husband in a
ski hut. In the second chapter she made it with a butler in
the pantry. In the third chapter her husband and the butler
made it in the swimming pool. The heroine then made it
with a chambermaid. Her husband discovered them and

joined the fun. The cook then made it with the postman
and the cook's twelve-year-old daughter made it with the
groom. On it would go for six hundred pages. It would
end, he knew, in religious institutions. The heroine, having
practiced every known indecency, would end up in a clois-
tered order with a shaven head and a lead ring. The last
you saw of her depraved husband would be his feet in the
rude sandals of a monk as he pressed through a snowstorm carrying a vial of antibiotics to a sick whore in the
mountains. It seemed like a poor fare for a lonely man
and he felt from the hard mattress where he lay an accrual
of loneliness from the thousands like himself who had lain
there, hankering not to be alone. He turned off the light,
slept and dreamed of swans, a lost suitcase, a snow-covered
mountain. He saw his mother lifting the ornaments off the
Christmas tree with trembling hands. He woke in the
morning feeling natural, boisterous and even loving, but
the stranger with a hidden face is always waiting by the
lake, there is always a viper in the garden, a dark cloud in
the west. The eggs that Mabel brought him for breakfast
were swimming in grease. As soon as he stepped out of the
Viaduct House a dog began to bark at him. The dog followed him across the green, snapping at his ankles. He ran
up Boat Street and some children on their way to school
laughed uproariously at his panic. When he got to Honora's his high spirits were spent.

Maggie answered the doorbell and led him into the library, where Honora was sitting by the window, picking
over a large assortment of fireworks heaped in a wash-
basket. At the sound of a man's footsteps she took off her
spectacles. She hoped to look younger. She could not see
much without her glasses and when Johnson entered the
library the indistinctness with which she saw his face made
her think that he was a young man with keen appetites,
enthusiasms, an open heart. She felt for his very blurred
image an impulse of friendship or pity. "Good morning,"
she said. "Please sit down. I was just looking over my fireworks. I bought these last year, you know, and I thought
I'd have a little party, you know, but it was very dry last
July, it didn't rain for six weeks and the fire chief asked
me not to shoot them off. I put them in the coat closet and

I completely forgot about them until this morning. I love fireworks," she said. "I love to read the labels on the packages and imagine what they'll look like. I *love* the smell of gunpowder."

"I'd like to know something about your Uncle Lorenzo," Johnson said.

"Oh, yes," Honora said. "Is this about the commemorative plaque?"

"No," Johnson said. He opened his briefcase.

"Well, a man came last year," Honora said, "and urged me to have a commemorative plaque made for Lorenzo. At first I thought he represented some committee but then I discovered that he was just a salesman. You're not a salesman?"

"No," Johnson said. "I'm from the government."

"Well, Lorenzo served in the state legislature, you know," Honora said. "He introduced the child-labor laws. You see, my parents were missionaries. You wouldn't know it to look at me, would you, but I was born in Polynesia. My parents sent me back here to school but they died before I could return. Lorenzo raised me. He was never an awfully friendly man." She seemed deeply reflective. "But you might have described him as both my father and mother," she said with a sigh of obvious discontent.

"This was his house?"

"Oh, yes."

"Your uncle left you his estate?"

"Yes, he had no other family."

"I have some correspondence here from the Appleton Bank and Trust Company. They estimate the value of your uncle's estate at the time of his death to have been about a million dollars. They claim to have paid you an annual income ranging from seventy thousand to a hundred thousand dollars."

"I don't know," Honora said. "I give most of my money away."

"Have you any proof of this?"

"I don't keep records," Honora said.

"Have you ever paid an income tax, Miss Wapshot?"

"Oh, no," Honora said. "Lorenzo made me promise that I wouldn't give any of his money to the government."

"You are in grave trouble, Miss Wapshot." Then he felt
tall and strong, felt the supreme importance of those who
bring black tidings. "This will lead to a criminal indictment."

"Oh, dear," Honora said.

She had been caught and she knew it; caught like any
clumsy thief waving a water pistol at a bank teller. If her
knowledge of the tax laws was not much more than a
dream, she knew them to be the laws of her country and
her time. What she did then was to go to the fireplace and
light the pile of shavings, paper and wood that the gardener
had laid on the irons. The reason she did this was that fire
was for her a sovereign pain-killer. When she was discon-
tented with herself, troubled, bewildered or bored, to light
a fire seemed to incinerate her discontents and transform
her burdens into smoke. She approached the light and heat
of a fire like an aboriginal. The shavings and paper exploded into flame, filling the library with a dry, gaseous
heat. Honora stoked the blaze with dry apple wood; felt
that once the fire was hot enough she would have burned
away her fears of the poor farm and the jail. A log exploded and an ember landed in the basket of fireworks. A
Roman candle was the first to go. "Mercy," Honora said.
Purblind without her spectacles, she reached for a vase of
flowers to extinguish the Roman candle but her aim was
off and she got Johnson square in the face with a pint or so
of bitter flower water and a dozen hyacinths. By this time
the Roman candle had begun to ejaculate its lumps of
colored fire and these ignited something called The Golden
Vesuvius. A rocket took off in the direction of the piano
and then the lot went up.

CHAPTER VII

The two stories about Honora Wapshot that were most frequently told in the family concerned her alarm clock and her penmanship. These were not told so much as they were performed, each member of the family taking a part, singing an aria so to speak, while everyone joined in on the Grand Finale like some primitive anticipation of the conventions of nineteenth-century Italian opera. The alarm clock incident belonged to the remote past when Lorenzo had been alive. Lorenzo was determined to appear pious and liked to arrive at Christ Church for morning worship at precisely quarter to eleven. Honora, who may have been genuinely pious but who detested appearances, could never find her gloves or her hat and was always tardy. One Sunday morning Lorenzo, in a rage, led his niece by the hand into the drugstore and bought her an alarm clock. So they went to church. Mr. Briam, Mr. Applegate's predecessor, had started on an interminable sermon about the chains of St. Paul when the alarm clock went off. Since most of the congregation was asleep they were startled and confused. Honora shook the clock and then proceeded to unwrap it but by the time she got through to the box in which it sat the ringing had stopped. Mr. Briam then picked up the chains of St. Paul and the alarm clock, on repeat, began to ring again. This time Honora pretended that it wasn't her clock. Sweating freely, she sat beside this impious engine while Mr. Briam went on about the significance of chains until the mechanism had unwound. It was an historic Sunday. The tales about her penmanship centered on a morning when she had written to the local coal dealer protesting his prices and then had written to Mr. Potter to share with him his sorrow over the sudden loss of his sainted wife. She got the letters in the wrong envelopes but since Mr. Potter could read nothing of her letter but the signature he was touched by her thoughtfulness and since Mr. Sumner, the coal dealer, was unable to read the letter of condolence he received he mailed it back to Honora. She had been taught Spencerian penmanship but something redoubtable or coarse in her nature was left unexpressed by this style and the conflict between her passions and the tools given to her left her penmanship illegible.

At about this time Coverly received a letter from his old cousin.

Someone more persevering might have broken the letter down word by word and diagnosed its content but Coverly was not this gifted or patient. He was able to decipher a few facts. A holly tree that grew behind her house had been attacked by rust. She wanted Coverly to return to St. Botolphs and have it sprayed. This was followed by an indecipherable paragraph on the Appleton Bank and Trust Company in Boston. Honora had set up trusts for Coverly and his brother and he supposed she was writing of these. The income enabled Coverly to live much more comfortably than he would have been able to on his government salary and he hoped nothing was wrong here. This was followed by a clear sentence stating that Dr. Lemuel Cameron, director of the Talifer site, had once received a scholarship endowed by Lorenzo Wapshot. She closed with her customary observations on the rainfall, the prevailing winds and the tides.

Coverly guessed that her reference to the holly tree meant something very different but he didn't have the emotional leisure to discover what was at the back of the old woman's mind. If there was trouble with the Appleton Bank and Trust Company—and his quarterly check was late—there was nothing much he could do. The remark about Dr. Cameron might or might not have been true since Honora often exaggerated Lorenzo's bounty and had, like any other old woman, a struggle to remember names. The letter arrived at a bad time in his affairs and he forwarded it on to his brother.

Betsey had not rallied from the failure of her cocktail

party. She hated Talifer and squarely blamed Coverly for
making her live there. She avenged herself by sleeping
alone and by not speaking to her husband. She complained
loudly to herself about the noise, the neighborhood, the
kitchen, the weather and the news in the papers. She swore
at the mashed potatoes, cursed the pot roast, she damned
the pots and pans to hell and spoke obscenely to the frozen
apple tarts, but she did not speak to Coverly. Every surface
of life—tables, dishes and the body of her husband—
seemed to be abrasive facets of a stone that lay in her path.
Nothing was right. The sofa hurt her back. She could not
sleep in her bed. The lamps were too dim to read by, the
knives were too dull to cut butter, the television programs
bored her although she watched them faithfully. The great-
est of Coverly's hardships was the breakdown in their sexual relationship. It was the crux, the readiest source of
vitality in their marriage, and without this her companion-
ship became painful.

Coverly tried to throw a ring of light around her figure
and saw or thought he saw that she might be heartlessly
overburdened by a past of which he knew nothing. We are
all, he thought, ransomed to our beginnings, and the sum
in her case might have been exorbitant. This might account
for that dark side of her nature that seemed more mysterious to him than the dark face of the moon. Were there
instruments of love and patience that could explore this
darkness, discover the wellsprings of her misery and by
charting it all draw it all into the area of reasonableness;
or was this the nature of her kind of woman to stand forever half in a darkness that was unknown to herself? She
looked nothing like a moon goddess, sitting in front of the
television set, but of all the things in the world her spirit
with its irreconcilable faces seemed most like the moon to
him.

One Saturday morning when he was shaving he heard
Betsey's voice—strident and raised in anger—and he went
downstairs in his pajamas to see what was the matter. Betsey was upbraiding a new cleaning woman. "I just don't
know what the world's coming to," Betsey said. "I just
don't *know*. I suppose you expect me to pay you good
money for just sitting around, for just sitting around smok-

ing my cigarettes and watching my television." Betsey turned to Coverly. "She can hardly speak English," Betsey said, "and she doesn't even know how to work a vacuum cleaner. She doesn't even know how to do that. And you. Look at you. Here it is nine o'clock and you're still in your pajamas and I suppose you're going to spend the day just sitting around the house. It just makes me sick *and* tired. Well, you take her upstairs and you show her how to work the vacuum cleaner. Now you march, both of you. You get upstairs and do something useful for a change."

The cleaning woman had dark hair and olive skin. Her eyes were wet with tears. Coverly got the vacuum cleaner and carried it up the stairs, admiring the stranger's ample rump. There was between them the instantaneous rapport of unhappy children. Coverly plugged in the cord and turned on the motor but when he smiled at the stranger things took a different turn. "Now we put it in here," Betsey heard him say. "That's right. That's the way. We have to get it into the corners, way into the corners. Slowly, slowly, slowly. Back and forth, back and forth. Not too fast . . ." Downstairs Betsey thought angrily that Coverly had at last found something useful to do on Saturday mornings and that at least one room would be clean. She went into the bathroom where she had a vision—not so much of the emancipation of her sex as the enslavement of the male.

Routine progress—a feminine President and a distaff Senate—did not appear in Betsey's reverie. Indeed, in her vision the work of the world was still largely done by men, although this had been enlarged to include housework and shopping. She smiled at the thought of a man bent over an ironing board; a man dusting a table; a man basting a roast. In her vision all the public statuary commemorating great men would be overthrown and dragged off to the dump. Generals on horseback, priests in robes, solons in tailcoats, aviators, explorers, inventors, poets and philosophers would be replaced by attractive representations of the female. Women would be granted complete sexual independence and would make love to strangers as casually as they bought a pocketbook, and coming home in the evening they would brazenly describe to their depressed husbands (sprinkling Adolph's meat tenderizer on the London broil) the high points of their erotic adventures. She would not go so far as to imagine any legislation that would actually restrict the rights of men; but she saw them as so browbeaten, colorless and depressed that they would have lost the chance to be taken seriously.

Now the love song of Coverly Wapshot was slapstick and vainglorious and at the time of which I'm writing he had developed an unfortunate habit of talking like a Chinese fortune cookie. "Time cures all things," he would say or, "The poor man goes before the thief." In addition to his habit of cracking his knuckles he had acquired an even more irritating habit of nervously clearing his throat. At regular intervals he would emit from his larynx a reflective, apologetic, complaining and irresolute noise. "Grrgrum," he would say to himself as he washed the dishes. "Arhum, arrhum, grrumph," he would say as if these noises subtly expressed his discontents. He was the sort of man who at the PR conventions he sometimes attended always dropped his name tag (Hello! I'm Coverly Wapshot!) into the wastebasket along with the white carnation that was usually given to delegates. He seemed to feel that he lived in a small town where everyone would know who he was. Nothing, of course, could be further from the truth. Betsey was one of those women who, like the heroines in old legends, could turn herself from a hag into a beauty and back into a hag again so swiftly that Coverly was kept jumping.

Coverly, like some despot, was given to the capricious rearrangement of the facts in his history. He would decide cheerfully and hopefully that what had happened had not happened although he never went so far as to claim that what had not happened had happened. That what had happened had not happened was a refrain in his love song as common as those lyrical stanzas celebrating erotic bliss. Now Betsey was a complaining woman or, as Coverly would put it, Betsey was not a complaining woman. She had been unhappy at Remsen and had wanted to be transferred to Canaveral, where she saw herself sitting on a white beach, counting the wild waves and making eyes at a lifeguard. If Betsey had been painted she would have been painted against the landscapes of northern Georgia where she had spent her mysterious childhood. There would be razorback hogs, a dying chinaberry tree, a frame house that needed paint and as far as the eye could see acres of swept red dirt that would turn slick and wash off in the lightest rains. There was not enough topsoil in that part of the state to fill a bait can. Coverly had seen this landscape fleetingly from the train window and of her past he only knew that she had a sister named Caroline. "I was so disappointed in that girl Caroline," Betsey said. "She was my only, only sister and I just wanted to enjoy a real sisterhood with her but I was disappointed. When I was working in the five-and-dime I gave her all my salary for her trousseau but when she got married she just went away from Bambridge and she never once wrote me or told me her whereabouts in any way, shape or form." Then Caroline began to write Betsey and there was a *bouleversement* in Betsey's feeling for her sister. Coverly was pleased with this since, with the exception of the television set, Betsey's loneliness in Talifer was unrelieved and it did not seem to be in his power to make the place more sociable. In the end Caroline, who was divorced, was invited to visit.

What had not happened or what might possibly have happened and been overlooked by Coverly's way of thinking began with Caroline's visit. She arrived on a Thursday. All the windows were lighted when Coverly came home from work and when he stepped into the house he could hear their voices from the living room. Betsey seemed happy for the first time in months and met him with a kiss. Caroline looked up at him and smiled, the color and cast of her eyes concealed by a large pair of spectacles that reflected the room. She was not a heavy woman but she sat like a heavy woman, her legs wide apart and her arms hung gracelessly between them. She was wearing a traveling costume—blue pumps that pinched her feet and a tight blue skirt that was rucked and seamed like a skin. Her smile was sweet and slow and she got to her feet and gave Coverly a wet kiss. "Why, he looks just like Harvey," she said. "Harvey was this boy in Bambridge and you look just like him. He was a nice-looking boy. His family had a nice house on Spartacus Street."

"They didn't live on Spartacus Street," Betsey said. "They used to live on Thompson Avenue."

"They lived on Spartacus Street until his father got the Buick agency," Caroline said. "Then they moved to Thompson Avenue."

"I thought they always lived on Thompson Avenue," Betsey said.

"It was that other boy that used to live on Thompson Avenue," Caroline said. "The one that had curly hair and crooked teeth.

There was a bottle of bourbon on the coffee table and they each had a drink. When Betsey went into the kitchen to heat up the supper Caroline remained with Coverly. It was at this point that Coverly would decide that what had happened had not happened. Caroline spoke to him in a whisper. "I just been dying to meet the man Betsey married," Caroline said. "Nobody in Bambridge ever thought Betsey'd get married, she's so *queer*."

There was a moment before Coverly decided, as he would, that what had been said had not been said when he was confronted with the venom in this remark. He could only conclude that "queer" in Georgia meant charming, original and fair.

"I don't understand," he said.

"Why, she's just queer, that's all," Caroline whispered. "Everybody in Bambridge knew Betsey was queer. I don't think it was her fault. I just think it was because Steppappy was so mean to her. He used to whip her, he used to take off his belt and whip her with no provocation whatever. I just think he whipped the common sense right out of her."

"I didn't know any of this," Coverly said; or didn't say.

"Well, Betsey was never one to tell anybody anything," Caroline whispered. "That was one of the queer things about her."

"Dinner's served," Betsey said in her sweetest and most trusting manner. This much, in retrospect, would appear to be true.

The talk about Bambridge went on through dinner and it was a conversation that, led by Caroline, seemed strangely morbid. "Bessie Pluckette has another mongoloid idiot," Caroline exclaimed, not cheerfully but with definite enthusiasm. "Unfortunately it's just as healthy as it can be and poor Bessie can just expect to spend the rest of her life taking care of it. Poor thing. Of course she could put it into the state institution but she just doesn't have the heart to have her little son starved to death and that's what they do in the state institution, they starve them to death. Alma Pierson had a mongoloid too but mercifully that one died. And remember that Brasie girl, Betsey, the one with the shriveled right arm?" She turned to Coverly and explained. "She has this shriveled right arm, no longer than your elbow and right at the end of it there's this teeny-weeny hand. Well, she learned how to play the piano. Isn't that wonderful? I mean she could only play chords of course with this teeny-weeny hand but she could play the rest of the music with her left hand. Her left hand was normal. She took piano lessons and everything; that is, she took piano lessons until her father fell down the elevator shaft at the cotton mill and broke both legs." Was this morbidity, Coverly wondered, or were these the facts of life in Georgia?

Caroline stayed three days and was (if one forgot her remarks before dinner) a tolerable guest excepting that her knowledge of tragic, human experience was inexhaustible and that she left lipstick stains on everything. She had a broad mouth and she painted it heavily and there were purple lipstick stains on the cups and glasses, the towels and napkins; the ashtrays were full of stained cigarette ends and in the toilet there was always a piece of Kleenex stained purple. This seemed to Coverly not carelessness but much more—some atavistic way of impressing herself upon this household in which she would spend so short a time. The purple stains seemed to mark her as a lonely woman. When Coverly went to the site on the day she left Caroline was asleep and she had gone by the time he got home. She had left a smear of purple lipstick on his son's forehead; there seemed to be purple lipstick everywhere he looked, as if she had marked her departure this way. Betsey was watching television and eating from a box of candy that Caroline had given her as a present. She did not look up when he came in and brushed away the place on her cheek where he kissed her. "Leave me be," she said, "leave me be. . . ."

After Caroline's departure Betsey's discontents only seemed to increase. Then there was a night that, according to Coverly's habit of eliminating facts, especially did not happen. He was kept late at the site and didn't get home until half-past seven. Betsey sat in the kitchen, weeping. "What's the matter, sugarluve," he asked, or didn't ask.

"Well, I made myself a nice cup of tea," Betsey sobbed, "and a piece of hot Danish and I was just sitting down to enjoy myself when the telephone rang and there was this woman selling magazine subscriptions and she talked and by the time she was done talking my tea and my Danish were all cold."

"That's all right, sugar," Coverly said. "You can heat it up again."

"It isn't all right," Betsey said. "It just isn't all right. Nothing's all right. I hate Talifer. I hate it here. I hate you. I hate wet toilet seats. The only reason I live here is because there's no place else in the world for me to go. I'm too lazy to get a job and I'm too plain to find another man."

"Would you like to take a trip, sugar, would you like a change?"

"I been all over this country, it's the same everywheres."

"Oh, come back, sugar, come back," he said, speaking in great love and tiredness. "I feel as if I were walking up a street calling after you, asking you to come back and you never turn your head. I know what the street looks like, I've seen it so often. It's nighttime. There's a place on the corner where you can buy cigarettes and papers. Stationery. I can see you walking up this street and I'm behind you, calling you to come back, to come back, but you never turn your head." Betsey went on sobbing, and thinking that his words had moved her Coverly put an arm around her shoulders but she wrenched herself convulsively out of his embrace and screamed: "Leave me be." The scream, like the piercing and hideous noise of brakes, seemed to be apart from the fitness of things.

"But, sugar."

"You beat me," she screamed. "You took off your belt and you beat me and you beat me and you beat me."

"I never beat you, sugar. I never hit anybody but Mr. Murphy the night he stole our garbage pail."

"You beat me and beat me and beat me," she screamed.

"When was this, sugar, when did I do this?"

"Tuesday, Wednesday, Thursday, Friday, I can't remember every time." She fled to her room and shut the door. He was stunned (or would have been stunned if any of this had happened) and it was a minute or two before he realized (or would have realized) that Binxey was crying in terror. He seized the little boy as an object of reason, love, animal warmth. He crushed him in his arms and took him into the kitchen. This was no time, it seemed, for reflection or decision. He cooked some hamburgers and after supper told the boy an asinine story of space travel as he did each night. These stories were no worse than the stories of talking rabbits he had been told as a boy but the talking rabbits had the charm of innocence. He turned off the light, kissed the boy good night and stopped at the bedroom door to ask Betsey if she wanted some dinner. "Let me alone," she said. He drank a beer, read an old copy of *Life,* went to the window and looked at the lights on the street.

Here was (or would have been had he admitted the facts) the forlornness, the pain of an unexampled dilemma. The thief and the murderer all have their brotherhood and their prophets but he had none. Psychiatry, psychiatry, the word came to his mind as we put one foot in front of the other, but if he went to a doctor he would jeopardize his security clearance and his job. Any association with mental instability made a man unemployable in Talifer. The only way he could cling to his conviction that the devastating blows of life fell in some usable sequence was to claim that these especial blows had not fallen; and so making this claim he made a bed on the sofa and went to sleep.

This curious process of claiming that what had happened had not happened and what was happening was not happening went on in the morning when Coverly went to get a shirt and found that Betsey had cut the buttons off all of his shirts. This was inadmissible. He fastened a shirt with his tie, tucked it into his trousers and went to work but in the middle of the morning he went to the men's room and wrote Betsey a note:

"Darling Betsey," he wrote, "I am going away. I am desperate and I am not interested in desperation, especially quiet desperation. I have no address but I don't suppose that makes much difference because in all the years we've been together you've never sent me a postcard and I don't suppose you're going to start writing me piles of letters now. I have thought of taking Binxey with me but of course this would be against the law. I love him more than I have ever loved anyone in the world and please be kind to him. You might want to know why I am going away and why I am desperate although I somehow cannot imagine you asking yourself any questions about my disappearance. I don't know any of your family excepting Caroline and I sometimes wish I knew them better because I sometimes think you've got me mixed up with someone who caused you pain long ago. I know that I have a very difficult personality my family always said that Coverly was very odd and perhaps I am much more to be blamed than I will ever know. I do not like to cherish resentments, I do not like to be bitter or resentful and yet I often am. In the mornings of our life together when the alarm wakes me the first thing I want to do is to take you in my arms but if I do I know you will fling yourself away from me and so that is the way the days begin and usually the way they end. I won't bother about saying anything else. As I said in the beginning I am not interested in desperation, particularly quiet desperation and so I am going away."

Coverly mailed the letter, bought some shirts, cleared some annual leave and left for Denver that night, where he checked into a fourth-string hotel. There were cigarette butts on the bathroom floor and a pier glass arranged at the foot of the bed for questionable reasons. He had some drinks and went to a movie. When he came in at about midnight the elevator man asked if he wanted a girl, a boy, some dirty pictures or filthy comics. He said no thanks and went to bed. He went to a museum in the morning, to another movie and was having a drink at dusk in a bar when he felt his spirit genuflect, bend, stoop and kneel before what happened to be the image of those worn Indian moccasins, ornamented with beads, that Betsey wore around the house. He had another drink and went to another movie. When he came in the elevator operator asked again if he wanted, a girl, a boy, a dirty massage, filthy pictures or obscene comics. He wanted Betsey.

The secrets of a marriage are most scrupulously guarded. Coverly might speak freely of his infidelities; it was his passion for fidelity that he would hide. It didn't matter that she had accused him wrongly and cut the buttons off his shirt. It wouldn't matter if she burned holes in his underpants and served him arsenate of lead. If she locked the door against him he would climb in at the window. If she locked the bedroom door he would break the lock. If she met him with a tirade, a shower of bitter tears, an ax or a meat cleaver it didn't matter. She was his millstone, his ball and chain, his angel, his fate, and she held in her hands the raw material of his most illustrious dreams. He called her then and said he was coming home. "That's all right," Betsey said. "That's all right."

He had some trouble making connections for the return trip and it was not until ten that he got back the next night. Betsey was in bed, filing her nails. "Hi, sugar," he said and sat on the bed, making a groaning sound. "Well, all right," Betsey said, but she flung her nail file onto the table, preserving this much of her sovereignty. She went into the bathroom, closing the door, and Coverly heard the various sounds of running water, diverse and cheerful as the fountains in Tivoli. But she did not return. What had happened? Had she hurt herself? Had she climbed out the window? He threw open the bathroom door and found her sitting naked on the edge of the tub, reading an old copy of *Newsweek*. "What's the matter, sugar?" he asked.

"Nothing," Betsey said. "I was just reading."

"But that's an old copy," Coverly said. "That's about a year old."

"Well, it's very interesting," Betsey said. "I find it very interesting."

"But you're not interested in current events," Coverly said. "I mean you don't even know the name of the vice president, do you?"

"That's none of your business," said Betsey.

"But do you know the name of the vice president?"

"That's just none of your business," Betsey said.

"Oh, sugar," groaned Coverly, his feeling swamped with love, and he raised her up in his arms. Then the verdure of venery, that thickest of foliage, filled the room. Sounds of running water. Flights of wild canaries. Lightly, lightly, assisting one another at every turn they began their effortless ascent up the rockwall, the chimney, the flume, the long traverse, up and up and up until over the last ridge one had a view of the whole, wide world and Coverly was the happiest man in it. But according to him none of this had happened. How could it have?

CHAPTER VIII

Judge Beasely's offices were on the second floor of the Trowbridge Block. Enid Moulton, Mabel's sister, let Honora into the farther room where the judge sat examining or pretending to examine papers. Honora guessed that he had been asleep and she looked at him gloomily. Time, that she had seen turn so many things and men into their opposites, had forced him into the image of a hawk. She did not mean that he seemed predatory—only that the thinness of his face made what had always been a sharp nose hooked like a beak and that his thin gray hair lay on his scalp like moulting feathers. He humped his shoulders like a roosted bird. His voice was cracked but then it always had been. The skin of his nose had peeled here and there, showing a violet-colored underskin. He had been a lady-killer—she remembered that—and at eighty he still seemed proud of his prowess. Above his desk was a large, varnished painting of some antlered deer, leaving a gloomy wood to drink at a pond. The frame of the picture was festooned with Christmas tinsel. Honora gave this a glance. "I see you're all ready for Christmas," she said meanly.

"Hmmm," he said, uncomprehending.

Honora told him her problem, trying to estimate its magnitude by the degrees of consternation on his thin face. His memory, his reason, seemed not impaired but retarded. When she was done he made a temple of his fingers. "County court won't convene for another five weeks," he said, "so they can't indict you until then. Have they put a lien on your accounts?"

"I don't believe so," Honora said.

"Well, my advice, Honora, is that you go directly to the bank, withdraw a substantial sum of money and leave the country. Extradition proceedings are complicated and prolonged and the tax authorities are not altogether pitiless. They will invite you to return, of course, but I don't think a lady as venerable as you will be subjected to any unpleasantness."

"I am too old to travel," Honora said.

"You are too old to go to the poor farm," he said. The light in his eye seemed as uncomprehending as a bird and he seemed, like a drake, to have to turn his head from side to side to bring her into his vision. She said nothing more, neither thank you nor good-bye, and left the office. She stopped at the hardware store and bought a length of clothesline. When she got back to her own house she climbed directly to the attic.

Honora admired all sorts of freshness: rain and the cold morning light, all winds, all sounds of running water in which she thought she heard the chain of being, high seas but especially the rain. Liking all of this she felt, stepping into the airless attic holding a length of clothesline with which she meant to hang herself, an alien. The air was so close it would make your head swim; spicy as an oven. Flies and hornets at the single window made the only sounds of life. Calcutta trunks, hatboxes, a helm inlaid with mother-of-pearl (hers), a torn mainsail and a pair of oars stood by the window. She looped the clothesline she carried over a rafter on which was printed: PEREZ WAPSHOT'S GRAND MENAGERIE AND ANIMAL CIRCUS. Red curtains hung from the rafter marking the stage where they had performed on wet days, rain gentling that small, small world. Rodney Townsend had waked her as the sleeping beauty with a kiss. It was her favorite part. She went to the window to see the twilight, wondering why the last light of day demanded from her similes and resolutions. Why, all the days of her life, had she compared its colors to apples, to the sere pages of old books, to lighted tents, to sapphires and ashes? Why had she always stood up to the evening light as if it could instruct her in decency and courage?

The day was gray, it had been gray since morning. It would be gray at sea, gray at the ferry slip where the crowds waited, gray in the cities, gray at the isthmus, gray at the prison and the poor farm. It was a harsh and an ugly light, stretched like some upholstery webbing beneath the damask of the year. Responsive to all lights, the dark left her feeling vague and sad. The rewards of virtue, she knew, are puerile, odorless and mean, but they are none the less rewards and she could not seem to find enough virtue in her conduct to reflect upon. She had meant to bring Mrs. Potter chicken broth when Mrs. Potter was dying. She had meant to attend her funeral when she died. She had meant to spread the fireplace ashes on the lawn. She had meant to return Mrs. Bretaigne's copy of *The Bitter Tea of General Yen*. She had counted every stud, nail, pew, light and organ pipe in Christ Church while Mr. Applegate, year after year, had unfolded the word of God. Patroness, Benefactor, Virgin and Saint!

She had been proud of her ankles, proud of her hair, proud of her hands, proud of her power over men and women although she knew enough about love to know that this impulse has no reflection. Pridefully she had given toys to the poor on Christmas. Pridefully she had smiled at this image of her magnanimity. Pridefully she had invented a whispering chorus of admiration. Glorious Honora, Generous Honora, Peerless Honora Wapshot. One brought energy to life, there was nothing to equal its velocity, its discernment, but could the spirit of an old woman take wing on the rain wind? She had no boisterousness left. Her usefulness was over. She tied a noose in the clothesline and dragged a trunk to beneath the rafter.

This would be a trap for her gallows. The trunk lid was ajar and she saw that the papers inside had been rifled. They were family papers, private things. Who would have done this? Maggie. She was into everything: Honora's desk, Honora's pockets. She pieced together the torn letters in the fireplace. Why? Was it like the magic that an empty house works on a child? The King and Queen are dead. She roots through Daddy's stud box, puts on Mummy's beads, stirs up the humble contents of every drawer. Honora put on her glasses and looked at the disordered papers. "The President and the Board of Trustees of the Hutchins Institute for the Blind request . . ." Beneath this was a letter in faded ink: "Dear Honora, I shall be in Boston for perching cloathing for summer and fawl but will return thursday. I thinch its plaine enof now that Lorenzo wold like to have bought my land when he was theare. I am ankshus to sell. I know thears no prospect of getting a faire prise from him, jidging from the past. Dishonesty is his polesy but if you spoke with him it might affect a saile. . . ." Below this she read: "He who reads me when I am ashes is my son in wishes."

It was in Leander's hand, some pages of that execrable journal or autobiography that had occupied the last months of his life.

Cousin Honora Wapshot is a skin-flint [he had written]. Head-cheese of every local charity. Dispenser of skinny chickens and pullet's eggs to the poor. Prays loudly in church for those who travail and are heavy-laden but will not loan one hundred bucks to only, only cousin for safe investment and guaranteed income in local water-powered tack factory. No work in St. Botolphs. No coin. Village dying or dead. Writer at age nineteen forced by Honora's parsimony to take job as night desk clerk in Travertine Mansion House ten miles down river.

Travertine Mansion House ranked with wonders of the ages. Compared in free literature to monuments in Karnak, Acropolis in Greece, Pantheon in Rome. Large, frame, brine-soaked fire-trap with two-story piazzas, palatial public rooms, 80 bedrooms, 8 baths. Wash-basins and chamber-pots still widely in use. Accounted for poignant smell

in hallways. Public rooms and some suites lighted by gas
but many chambers still dependent on kerosene lamps for
illumination. Palm trees in lobby. Music played for all
meals, excepting breakfast. American plan. Twelve dollars
a day and upwards. Writer worked at desk from 6 P.M.
until last gun was fired, usually around midnight. Salary
was seventeen dollars including board wages. Wore swallow-tail coat and flower in buttonhole. Speaking tubes
but no telephones. Limited bell system connected to dry-
cell batteries. Fine view of beach from piazza. Tennis
courts and croquet lawn at side of hotel. Some saddle
horses brought up from livery stable. Some boating. Prin-
ciple evening recreation was attendance at lectures. Glories
of Rome. Glories of Venice. Glories of Athens. Also some
philosophical and religious subjects.

Among guests was Shakespearean actress. Lottie Beauchamp. Pronounced Beecham. Played supporting roles
with Farquarson Grant Stratford and Avon Shakespearean
Co. Traveled with own bed-linen, silver, jams and jellies.
Mlle. Beauchamp as she was then known to writer appeared at desk late in evening with sad tale. Had lost pearl
necklace on beach. Remembered where she had left it but
was reluctant to venture on dark shore alone. Writer ac-
companied star-boarder on search. Mild night. Moon,
stars, etc. Gentle swell. Found necklace on stone in sheltered cove. Admired scenery, warmth of night air, moon
riding in west. Mlle. Beauchamp breathing heavily. Pleasant hour ensued. Writer dozed off. Woke to find famous
Thespian jumping up and down in moonlight, holding
breasts to keep from jouncing. Moon madness? What are
you doing? Well, you don't want me to have a child do
you? says she. Jumped up and down. Never experienced
such behavior before or since. Seemed to work.

Lottie Beauchamp was 5′6″. 117 lbs. Age unknown.
Paine's Celery Compound Complexion. Light brown hair.
Would be called blonde nowadays. Excellent shape but
excessive topside structure by modern standards. Golden
voice. Could raise your hackles, also bring tears to every
eye. Noticeable English accent but not foreign sounding or
in any other way unpleasant. Fastidious nature. Traveled
with own bed-linen as noted above. Hot house flowers in

bedroom. Spoke however of humble beginnings. Daughter
of a Leeds mill worker. Mother was drunkard. Familiar
with cold, hunger, poverty, destitution, etc., in childhood.
A dungheap rose. Enjoyed ample stock of artistic tempera-
ment. Very volatile. Complained liberally to management
about lack of hot water and lumpiness of bed but was
always gracious to servants. Sometimes repented of life as
actress. All mummery and sham. Needed tenderness.
Writer happy to accommodate. No question of wrongdoing or so it seemed.

End of September business at Mansion House slow as
cold molasses. Some northerly winds. Also fine weather.
Bright sun. Warm air. Breeze up and down the mast.
Wouldn't blow a butterfly off your mainsail. Walked often
on beach with Thespian before commencing tour of duty.
Delightful company. Lingered in various coves, nooks,
also aboard catboat. Property of hotel. Tern. Fifteen foot.
Marconi rig. Wide waisted. Sailed like a butter-tub. Small
cabin with no amenities. So the days passed.

Maiden ladies composed majority of clientele at season's end. Some dear old ladies; some lemons. Front-porch
committee commanded by Dr. Helen Archibald. Famous
dietician. Also hygienist. Led daily course in calisthenics
in music saloon For Women Only. Never privileged to see
same but expect consisted of knee bends performed to old
music box tunes. Big music box. Called Regina. Music
produced by flat metal disks, two feet in diameter. Wide
selection. Opera. Marches. Songs of love.

Front-porch committee bored with counting whitecaps.
Got wind of romance. Famous dietician evinced sudden
interest in sea-shells. Shells of no particular interest on
Travertine beach. Sand dollars. Starfish. Usual produce of
cold northern waters. Few colored stones gleaming like
jewels when wet. Colorless when dry. Purpose of famous
dietician's seaside excursions was to spy. Shadowed Lottie
and me like moral gumshoe. Pretending to look for shells.
Upsoaring of self. Tramped the beach for hours. Got sand
in shoes. Ruined several costumes. Vigilance was rewarded. Writer, rising from recumbent position in sheltered cove, saw famous dietician scurrying back to Mansion House in full possession of damaging facts. All interest

in sea-shells forgotten. Was unable to pursue same, being
clad only in birthday suit. Lottie very calm. Planned campaign. She would return to Mansion House alone. Gallant.
Unafraid to beard front-porch committee. Writer would
travel cross-country and approach hostelry from opposite
direction. Did so. Walked through scrub pine woods to
village of Travertine and then down dirt road to shore via
so-called Great Western. Changed clothes and took up
position behind desk at 6 P.M. with fresh flower in buttonhole. String trio tuning instruments in Grand Dining Salon.
Handyman lighting gas chandeliers. (No daylight saving
time. September dusk fell swiftly.) All h——l broke loose.

Front-porch committee led by self-designated Grand
Marshal and Chief Bottle Washer Dr. Helen Archibald approached hotel manager and issued ultimatum. Unable to
hear terms from desk but surmised they dealt with Lottie.
Committee then entered dining salon in full panoply, sat
down and put on pince-nezs and other assorted storm windows, pretending to study menus. (Menus printed for
every meal.) Other guests entered and were seated. Music
of string trio did nothing to relieve tension. Soup is being
served when Lottie comes downstairs in salmon or coral-
colored dress. Beautiful! She is waylaid by hotel proprietor
who urges her sotto voce to dine in her suite at the ex-
pense of the management. No soap. On sweeps Lottie into
the lion's den. Considerable noise of dropped soup spoons.
Also storm windows. Then silence. Grand Marshal for the
opposition deals the first and only blow. "I will not eat off
the same dishes as that whore," says she. Then up spake
the desk clerk in the swallow-tail coat. "Apologize to Miss
Beauchamp, Dr. Archibald." "You're fired," says the manager. "When was this?" says I. "The day before yesterday," says he and the forces of Venus retired in confusion.
Lottie took a trip to Travertine and went up to Boston on
freight train with load of cranberries. I walked to St.
Botolphs, carrying my straw suitcase and, finding Cousin
Honora's dark, spent the night at the Viaduct House. Only
concern was indignation at having been fired. Was never
fired before or since during fifty-five years in business.

Went up to Boston on noon cars. Joined Lottie as per
arrangement in Brown's Hotel. Very tough joint. Lottie

preparing to open two weeks season with Farquarson and
Freedom. Urged writer to take job with company as bit-
player, walk-on, crowd recruiter and bouncer. Theater
more free and easy than today. Great attraction of times
was Count Johannes. Audience came armed with over-ripe
produce. Missiles began to fly before first act ended. Actors
served as moving targets for remainder of performance.
Sometimes produced bushel baskets and nets to catch
vegetables. No reflection on theatrical greats intended.
Julia Marlowe as Parthenia in Ingomar. Glorious! E. H.
Sothern in Romeo and Juliet. Basset D'Arcy's Lear. Howard Athenaeum then open. Also Boston Museum, Old
Boston Theatre and Hollis Street Theatre.

Accepted position with Farquarson and Freedom.
Played Marcellus in opening production of Hamlet with
Farquarson as Hamlet and Lottie as Ophelia. Played nu-
merous soldiers, sailors, gentlemen, guards and sundry
watch-men during two-week season. Opened National
Tour in Congress Opera House, Providence, R.I.

Tour included Worcester, Springfield, Albany, Rochester, Buffalo, Syracuse, Jamestown, Ashtabula, Cleveland,
Columbus and Zanesville. Suspected Lottie of concupis-
cence in Jamestown. Found naked stranger in clothes
closet in Ashtabula. Caught redhanded in Cleveland. Sold
gold cuff-links and returned to Boston via steam-cars on
March 18th. No hard feelings. Laugh and the world laughs
with you. Weep and you weep alone.

CHAPTER IX

❧ ❧❧

When Moses had Honora's letter he was much more
alarmed than his brother. He had mortgaged his trust on
the strength of Honora's age and he wrote directly to Boston. The Appleton Bank and Trust Company did not reply

and when he telephoned Boston they told him that the trust officer was skiing in Peru. On Sunday night Moses took a plane to Detroit, starting on a wild-goose chase across the country to see if he could raise fifty thousand dollars on the strength, largely, of his charm. Fifty thousand dollars would barely cover his obligations.

On Monday night, alone in the house with the cook and her son, Melissa had a sentimental dream. The landscape was romantic. It was evening, and since there was no trace anywhere of mechanical things—automobile tracks and the noise of planes—it seemed to her to be evening in another century. The sun had set, but a polished afterglow lighted up the sky. There was a winding stream with alders, and on the farther banks the ruins of a castle. She spread a white cloth on the grass and set this with long-necked wine bottles and a loaf of new bread, whose fragrance and warmth were a part of the dream. Upstream a man was swimming naked in a pool. He spoke to her in French, and it was part of the dream's lightness that it all transpired in another country, another time. She saw the man pull himself up onto the banks and dry himself with a cloth while she went on setting out the things for supper.

She was waked from this dream by the barking of a dog. It was 3 A.M. She heard the wind. It was changing its quarter and beginning to blow from the northwest. She was about to fall asleep when she heard the front door come open. Sweat started at her armpits and her young heart strained its muscles, although she knew it was only the wind that had opened the door. Not long ago, a thief had broken into a house in the neighborhood. In the garden, behind a lilac bush, a pile of cigarette ends had been found, where he must have waited patiently for hours for the lights of the house to be turned out. He had made an opening in a window with a glass cutter, rifled a wall safe of cash and jewelry, and left by the front door. In reporting the theft, the police had described his movements in detail: He had waited in the garden. He had entered by a back window. He had gone through the kitchen and pantry into the dining room. But who was he? Had he been tall or short, heavy or slender? Had his heart throbbed with terror in the dark rooms, or had he experienced the thief's supreme sense of triumph over a pretentious and gullible society? He had left traces of himself—cigarette ends, footprints, broken glass and a rifled safe—but he had never been found, and so he remained disembodied and faceless.

It was the wind, she told herself; no thief would have left the door standing open. Now she could feel the cold air spreading through the house, rising up the stairs and moving the curtains in the hall. She got out of bed and put on a wrapper. She turned on the hall light and started down the stairs, asking herself what it was she was afraid of in the dark rooms below. She was afraid of the dark, like a primitive or a child, but why? What was there about darkness that threatened her? She was afraid of the dark as she was afraid of the unknown, and what was the unknown but the force of evil, and why should she be afraid of this? She turned on the lights one after another. The rooms were empty, and the wind was enjoying the liberty of the place, scattering the mail on the hall table and peering under the edge of the rug. The wind was cold, and she shivered as she closed and locked the front door, but now she was unafraid and very much herself. In the morning she had a cold.

The doctor came several times during that week, and when she got no better he ordered her to go to the hospital. In the middle of the morning, she went upstairs to pack. She had been to the hospital in recent years only once, to have her son, and then the drives of pregnancy had carried her unthinkably through her preparations. This time she carried no life within her; she carried, instead, an infection. And, alone in her bedroom, choosing a nightgown and a hairbrush, she felt as if she had been singled out to make some mysterious voyage. She was not a sentimental woman, and she had no sad thoughts about parting from the pleasant room she shared with her husband. She felt weary but not sick, although there was a cutting pain in her chest. A stranger watching her would have thought she was insane. Why did she empty the carnations into the wastebasket and rinse out the vase? Why did she count her stockings, lock her jewelry box and hide the key, glance at her bank balance, dust off the mantelpiece and stand in the middle of the room, looking as if she were

listening to distant music? The foolish impulse to dust the
mantelpiece was irresistible, but she had no idea why she
did it, and anyhow it was time to go.

The hospital was new, and conscientious efforts had
been made to make it a cheerful place, but her loveliness
—you might say her elegance—was put at a disadvantage
by the undisguisable atmosphere of regimentation, and she
looked terribly out of place. A wheelchair was brought for
her, but she refused to use it. She would have looked crest-
fallen and ridiculous, she knew, with her coat bunched up
around her middle and her purse in her lap. A nurse took
her upstairs and led her into a pleasant room, where she
was told to undress and get into bed. While she was un-
dressing, someone brough her lunch on a tray. It was a
small matter, but she found it disconcerting to be given a
chop and some canned fruit while she was half-naked and
before the clocks had struck noon. She ate her lunch duti-
fully and the doctor came at two and told her she could
count on being in the hospital ten days or two weeks. He
would call Moses. She fell asleep, and woke at five with a
fever.

The imagery of her fever was similar to the imagery of
love. Her reveries were spacious, and she seemed to be
promised the revelation of some truth that lay at the center
of the labyrinthine and palatial structures where she
wandered. The fever, as it got higher, eased the pain in
her breast and made her indifferent to the heavy beating
of her heart. The fever dreams seemed like a healthy employment of her imagination to distract her from the struggle that went on in her breast. She was standing at the head
of a broad staircase with red walls. Many people were
climbing the stairs. They had the attitudes of pilgrims. The
climb was grueling and lengthy, and when she reached the
summit she found herself in a grove of lemon trees and lay
down on the grass to rest. When she woke from this dream,
her nightgown and the bed linen were soaked with sweat.
She rang for a nurse, who changed them.

She felt much better when this was done, and felt that
the fever had been a crisis and that, passing safely through
it, she had triumphed over her illness. At nine the nurse
gave her some medicine and said good night. Some time

later she felt the lassitude of fever returning. She rang, but no one came, and she could not resist the confusion in her mind as her temperature rose. The labored beating of her heart sounded like a drum. She confused it with a drum in her mind, and saw a circle of barbaric dancers. The dance was long, rising to a climax, and at the moment of the climax, when she thought her heart would burst, she woke, shaking with a fresh chill and wet with sweat. A nurse finally came and changed her clothing and her linen again. She was relieved to be dry and warm. The two attacks of fever had weakened her but left her with a feeling of childish contentment. She felt wakeful, got out of bed and by supporting herself on the furniture made her way to the window to see the night.

While she watched, clouds covered the moon. It must have been late because most of the windows were dark. Then a window in the wall at her left was lighted, and she saw a nurse introduce a young woman and her husband into a room identical to the one where she sat in the dark. The young woman was pregnant but not having labor pains. She undressed in the bathroom and got into bed, while her husband was unpacking her bag. The window, like all the others, was hung with a Venetian blind, but no one had bothered to close it. When the unpacking was done, he unfastened the front of her nightgown, knelt beside the bed and lay his head on her breasts. He remained this way for several minutes without moving. Then he got up—he must have heard the nurse approach—and covered his wife. The nurse came in and snapped the blinds shut.

Melissa heard a night bird calling, and wondered what bird it was, what it looked like, what it was up to, what its prey was. There was a deep octave of thunder, magnificent and homely, as if someone in heaven had moved a chest of drawers. Then there was some lightning, distant and discolored, and a moment later a shower of rain dressed the earth. The sound of the rain seemed to Melissa, with the cutting pain in her breast, like the repeated attentions of a lover. It fell on the flat roofs of the hospital, the lawns and the leaves in the wood. The pain in her chest seemed to spread and sharpen in proportion to her stubborn love of the night, and she felt for the first time in her life an unwillingness to leave any of this; a fear as senseless and powerful as her fear of the dark when she went down to shut the door; a horror of death.

CHAPTER X

Now that was the year when the squirrels were such a pest and everybody worried about cancer and homosexuality. The squirrels upset garbage pails, bit delivery men and entered houses. Cancer was a commonplace but men and women, at its mercy, were told that their pain was some trifling complication while behind their backs their brothers and their sisters, their husbands and wives, would whisper: "All we can hope is that they will go quickly." This cruel and absolute hypocrisy was bound to backfire and in the end no one could tell or count upon being told if that pain in the middle was the knock of death or some trifling case of gas. Most maladies have their mythologies, their populations, their scenery and their grim jokes. The Black Plague had masques, street songs and dances. Tuberculosis in its heyday was like a civilization where a caste of comely, brilliant and doomed men and women fell in love, waltzed and invented privileges for their disease; but here was the grappling hand of death disinfected by a social conspiracy of all its reality. "Why, you'll be up and around in no time at all," says the nurse to the dying man. "You want to dance at your daughter's wedding, don't you? Don't you want to see your daughter married? Well, then, we can't expect to get better if we're not more cheerful, can we?" She cleans his arm with alcohol and prepares the syringe. "Your wife tells me you're a great mountain-climber but if you want to get better and climb the mountains again you'll have to be more cheerful. You do want to climb the mountains again, don't you?" The contents of the syringe flow into his veins. "I've never climbed a mountain myself," the nurse says, "but I expect it must be very exciting when you get to the top. I don't think I'd like the climbing part of it very much but the view from the summit must be lovely. They tell me that in the Alps roses grow in the snow banks and if you want to see all these things again you'll have to be more careful." Now he is drowsy and she raises her voice. "Oh, you'll be up and around in no time at all," she exclaims and softly, softly she closes the door to his room and says to his family, gathered in the corridor: "I've put him to sleep again and all we can do is hope and pray that he will never wake up." Melissa was one of those unfortunate people who was to suffer from this attitude.

Moses returned from his wild-goose chase as soon as he learned of Melissa's illness, having borrowed enough money to at least give an impression of solvency. The fact that Melissa was convalescent when he returned might have seemed to account for the fact that he did not describe to her his financial embarrassments but this was not so. He would not have been able to describe them to her under any circumstances; no more could Coverly state that he had seen the ghost of his father. Had Moses lived in Parthenia he would have felt free to put a FOR SALE sign in his living room window and another in the windshield of his convertible but to do this in Proxmire Manor would have been subversive. He expressed his worries not in irritability but in a manner that was very broad and jocular. Melissa then had this forced jocularity to cope with as well as the absurd conviction that she had cancer. She could not convince herself that she was cured nor could she trust what the doctor told her. She telephoned the hospital and asked to speak with her nurse. She asked the nurse if they could meet for a drink. "Why not?" the nurse asked. "Sure. Why not?" She went off duty at four and Melissa planned to meet her at the traffic light by the hospital at four-fifteen.

They went to a bar near there, a roadside place. The nurse ordered a double martini. "I'm tired," she said. "I'm worn out. My sister, she's married, she called me last night and said would I take care of the baby while she and her husband go to a cocktail party. So I'd said sure, I'd take care of the baby if it was just for cocktails, an hour or two. So I went there at six and you know when they came home? Midnight! The baby didn't shut her eyes once. She bawled all the time. Kind sister, that's me."

"I wanted to ask you about my x-rays," Melissa said. "You saw them."

"What are you afraid of," the nurse asked, "cancer?"

"Yes."

"That's what they're all afraid of."

"I don't have cancer?"

"Not to my knowledge." She raised her face and watched the wind carry some leaves past the window. "Leaves," she said, "leaves, leaves, look at them. I've got a little apartment with a back yard and it's me that rakes the leaves. I spend all my spare time raking leaves. Just as soon as I get one bunch cleaned up down comes another. As soon as you get rid of the leaves it begins to snow."

"Would you like another drink?" Melissa asked.

"No, thanks. You know, I wondered what you wanted to see me about but I didn't think it was cancer. You know what I thought you wanted?"

"What?"

"Heroin."

"I don't understand."

"I thought maybe you wanted me to smuggle some heroin out to you. You'd be surprised at the number of people who think I can get them drugs. Top-ranking people, some of them. Oh, I could name names. Shall we go?"

She stood, late one afternoon, at her window watching the ring of golden light that crowned the eastern hills at that season and time of day. It rested on the Babcocks' lawn, the Filmores' ranch house, the stone walls of the church, the Thompsons' chimney—lambent, and as yellow and clear as strained honey and a ring, because, as she watched, she saw at the base of the hills a clear demarcation between the yellow light and the rising dark, and watched the band of light lift past the Babcocks' lawn, the Filmores' ranch house, the stone walls of the church and the Thompsons' chimney, up into thin air. The street was empty, or nearly so. Everyone in Proxmire Manor had two cars and no one walked with the exception of old Mr. Cosden, who belonged to the generation that took constitutionals. Up the street he came, his blue eyes fixed on the last piece of yellow light that touched the church steeple, as if exclaiming to himself, "How wonderful, how wonderful it is!" He passed, and then a much stranger figure took her attention—a tall man with unusually long arms. He was a stray, she decided; he must live in the slums of Parthenia. In his right hand he carried an umbrella and a pair of rubbers. He was terribly stooped and to see where he was going had to crane his neck forward and upward like an adder. He had not bent his back over a whetstone or a workbench or under the weight of a brick hod or at any other honest task. It was the stoop of weakmindedness, abnegation and bewilderment. He had never had any occasion to straighten his back in self-esteem. Stooped with shyness as a child, stooped with loneliness as a youth, stooped now under an invisible burden of social disregard, he walked now with his long arms reaching nearly to his knees. His wide, thin mouth was set in a silly half-grin, meaningless and sad, but the best face he had been able to hit on. As he approached the house, the beating of her heart seemed to correspond to his footsteps, the cutting pain returned to her breast, and she felt the return of her fear of darkness, evil and death. Carrying his umbrella and rubbers, although there was not a cloud in the sky, he duck-footed out of sight.

A few minutes later, Melissa was driving back from the village of Parthenia. The street was lighted erratically by the few stores that hung on at the edge of town—general stores smelling of stale bread and bitter oranges, where those in the neighborhood who were too lazy, too tired and too infirm to go to the palatial shopping centers bought their coffee rings, beer and hamburgers. The darkness of the street was sparsely, irregularly, checkered with light, and she saw the tall man crossing one of these apertures, throwing a long, crooked shadow ahead of him on the paving. He held a heavy bag of groceries in each arm. He was no more stooped than before—the curvature of his spine seemed set—but the bags must be heavy, and she pitied him. She drove on, evoking defensively the worlds of difference that lay between them and the chance that he would have misunderstood her kindness had she offered to give him a ride. But when she had completed her defense it seemed so shallow, idle and selfish that she turned the car around in her own driveway and drove back toward Parthenia. Her best instinct was to help him—to make some peace between his figure and her irrational fear of death—and why should she deny herself this? He would have passed the lighted stores by this time, she decided, and she drove slowly up the dark street, looking for his stooped figure. When she saw him she turned the car around and stopped. "Can I help you?" she asked. "Can I give you a ride? You seem to have so much to carry." He turned and looked at the beautiful stranger without quite relaxing his half-grin, and she wondered if he wasn't a deaf-mute as well as weak-minded. Then a look of distrust touched the grin. There was no question about what he was feeling. She was from that world that had gulled him, pelted him with snowballs and rifled his lunchbox. His mother had told him to beware of strangers and here was a beautiful stranger, perhaps the most dangerous of all. "No!" he said. "No, no!" She drove on, wondering what was at the bottom of her impulse; wondering, in the end, why she should scrutinize a simple attempt at kindness.

On Thursday the maid was off, and Melissa took care of the baby. He slept after lunch, and she woke him at four, lifting him out of his crib and letting the blankets fall. They were alone. The house was quiet. She carried him into the kitchen, put him in his highchair and opened a can of figs. Sleepy and docile and pale, he followed her with his eyes, and smiled sweetly when their eyes met. His shirt was stained and wet, and she wore a wrapper. She sat by him at the table, with her face only a few inches from his, and they spooned the figs out of the can. He shuddered now and then with what seemed to be pleasure. The quiet house, the still kitchen, the pale and docile boy in his stained shirt, her round white arms on the table, the comfortable slovenliness of eating from a can were all part of an intimacy so intense and yet so tranquil that it seemed to her as if she and the baby were the same flesh and blood, subjects of the same heart, all mingled and at ease. What a comfort, she thought, is one's skin. . . . But it was time then to change the boy, time to dress herself, time to take up cheerfully the other side of her life. Carrying the child through the living room she saw, out of the window, the stooped figure with his rubbers and umbrella.

A wind was blowing and he moved indifferently through a diagonal fall of yellow leaves, craning his neck like an adder, his back bent under its impossible burden. She held the baby's head against her breast, foolishly, instinctively, as if to protect his eyes from some communicable evil. She turned away from the window, and shortly afterward there was a loud pounding on the back door. How had he found where she lived, and what did he want? He might have recognized her car in the driveway; he might have asked who she was, the village was that small. He had not come to thank her for attempted kindness. She felt sure of that. He had come—in his foolishness—to accuse her of something. Was he dangerous? Was there any danger left in Proxmire Manor? She put the boy down and went toward the back door, summoning her self-respect. When she opened it, there was Mr. Narobi's good-looking grocery boy. He made it all seem laughable—came in beaming and with a kind of radiance that seemed to liberate her from this absurd chain of anxieties.

"You're new?" she asked.

"Yes."

"I don't know your name."

"Emile. It's a funny name. My father was French."

"Did he come from France?"

"Oh, no, Quebec. French Canadian."

"What does he do?"

"When people used to ask me that, I used to say, 'He plays the harp!' He's dead. He died when I was little. My mother works at the florist's—Barnum's—on Green Street. Maybe you know her?"

"I don't think I do. Would you like a beer?"

"Sure. Why not? It's my last stop."

She asked if he wanted something to eat, and got him some crackers and cheese. "I'm always hungry," he said.

She brought the baby into the kitchen and they all three sat at the table while he ate and drank. Stuffing his mouth with cheese, he seemed to be a child. His gaze was clear and disarming. She couldn't meet it without a stir in her blood. And was this sluttishness? Was she worse than Mrs. Lockhart? Would she be dragged figuratively out of Proxmire Manor at the tail of a cart? She didn't care.

"Nobody ever gave me a beer before," he said. "They give me Cokes, sometimes. I guess they don't think I'm old enough. But I drink. Martinis, whisky, everything."

"How old are you?"

"Nineteen. Now I have to go."

"Please don't go," she said.

He stood at the table, covering her with his wide gaze, and she wondered what would happen if she reached out to him. Would he run out of the kitchen? Would he shout, "Unhand me!"? He seemed ripe; he seemed ready for the picking; and yet there was something else in the corner of his eyes—reserve, wariness. He perhaps had a vision of something better, and if he had, she would encourage him with all her heart. Go and love the drum majorette, the girl next door.

"Oh, I'd like to stay," he said. "It's nice here. But it's Thursday, and I have to take my mother shopping. Thank you very much."

He went to the house three or four times a week. Melissa was usually alone in the late afternoons and he timed his visits. Sometimes she seemed to be waiting for him. No one had ever been so attentive. She seemed interested in all the facts of his life—that his father had been a surveyor, that he drove a secondhand Buick, that he had done well at school. She usually gave him a beer and sat with him in the kitchen. Her company excited him. It made him feel that he might do well. Some of her worldliness, some of her finesse, would rub off on him and get him out of the grocery business. Suddenly, one afternoon, she said quite shyly, "You know, you're divine."

He wondered if she hadn't lost her marbles. He had heard that women sometimes did. Had he been wasting his time? He didn't want to fool around with a woman who had lost her marbles. He knew he wasn't divine. If he was, someone would have said so before and if he had been divine and had been convinced of this, he would have

concealed it—not through modesty but through an instinct
of self-preservation. "Sometimes I think I'm good-looking,"
he said earnestly to try and modify her praise. He finished
his beer. "Now I have to get back to the store."

CHAPTER XI

Melissa went shopping in New York a few days later. She
stood on the platform with her neighbor, Gertrude Bender,
waiting for the midmorning train. As the train came around
the curve the station agent pushed out on a wagon one of
those yellow wooden boxes that are used for transporting
coffins. This simple fact of life came as a blow to Melissa's
high spirits. "It must be Gertrude Lockhart," her friend
whispered. "They're sending her back to Indiana."

"I didn't know she was dead," Melissa said.

"She hung herself in the garage," her friend said, still
whispering, and they boarded the train.

Now it was not true that nothing happened in Proxmire
Manor; the truth was that eventfulness in the community
took such eccentric curves that it was difficult to compre-
hend. It was not a force of discreetness that kept Melissa
from knowing Gertrude Lockhart's story; it was that the
story was more easily forgotten than understood. She had
been, considering her widespread reputation for licentious-
ness, a singularly winsome woman; light-boned, quick, a
little nervous. Her skin was very white. This was not a
point of beauty, a stirring pallor. She just happened to have
a white skin. Her hair was ash-blond but it had lost its
shine. Her eyes were bright, small, dark and set close
together. Her ears were too big, a fact that made her seem
basically unserious. At the fourth- or fifth-string boarding
school she had attended she had been known as Dirty
Gertie. She was married, happily enough to Pete Lockhart

and had three small children. Her downfall began not with immortal longings but with an uncommonly severe winter when the main soil line from their house to the septic tank froze. The toilets backed up into the bathtubs and sinks. Nothing drained. Her husband went off to work. Her children caught the school bus. At half-past eight she found herself alone in a house that had, in a sense, ceased to function. The place was not luxurious but it appeared to be civilized; it appeared to promise something better than relieving herself in a bucket. At nine o'clock she took a drink of whisky and began to call the plumbers of Parthenia. There were seven and they were all busy. She kept repeating that her case was an emergency. One firm offered, as a favor, to stir up for her a retired plumber and presently an old man in an old car came to the house. He looked sadly at the mess in the bathtubs and the sinks and told her that he was a plumber, not a ditchdigger, and that she would have to find someone to dig a trench before he could repair the drain. She had another drink, put on some lipstick and drove into Parthenia.

She went first to the state employment office where eighteen or twenty men were sitting around looking for work but none of them was willing to dig a ditch and she saw as one of the facts of her life, her time, that standards of self-esteem had advanced to a point where no one was able to dig a hole. She went to the liquor store to get some whisky and told the clerk her problems. He said he thought he could get someone to help. He made a telephone call. "I've got you somebody," he said. "He's not as bad as he sounds. Give him two dollars an hour and all the whisky he can drink. His father-in-law fired him out of the house a couple of weeks ago and he's on the bum, but he's a nice guy." She went home and had another drink. Sometime later the doorbell rang. She had expected an old man with the shakes but what she saw was a man in his thirties. He wore tight jeans and a dark pullover and stood on her steps with his hands thrust into his back pockets, his chest pushed forward in a curious way as if this were a gesture of pride, friendship or courtship. His skin was dark, rucked deeply around the mouth like the seams on a boot, and his eyes were brown. His smile was bare amorousness. It was his only smile, but she didn't know this. He would smile amorously at his shovel, amorously into his whisky glass, amorously into the hole he had dug, and when it was time to go home he would smile amorously at the ignition switch on his car. She offered him some whisky but he said he would wait. She showed him where the tools were and he began to dig.

He worked for two hours and uncovered and cleared the frozen drain. She was able to clear out the bathtubs and sinks. When he returned the tools she asked him in for his whisky. She was quite drunk herself by then. He poured himself a water glass of whisky and drank it off. "What I really need," he said, "is a shower. I'm living in a furnished room. You have to take turns at the bathtub." She said he could take a shower, knowing full well what was afoot. He drank off another glass of whisky and she led him upstairs and opened the bathroom door. "I'll just get out of these things," he said, pulling off his sweater and dropping his jeans.

They were still in bed when the children came home. She opened the door and called sweetly down the stairs: "Mummy's resting. There are cookies on top of the icebox. Be sure and take your vitamin pills before you go out to play." When the children went out she gave him ten dollars, kissed him good-bye and slipped him out the back door. She never saw him again.

The old plumber fixed the drain and on the weekend Pete filled in the trench. The weather remained bitter. One morning, a week or ten days later, she was wakened by her husband's huffing and puffing. "There isn't time, darling," she said. She slipped on a wrapper, went downstairs and tried to open a package of bacon. The package promised to seal in the bacon's smoky flavor but she couldn't get the package open. She broke a fingernail. The transparent wrapper that imprisoned the bacon seemed like some immutable transparency in her life, some invisible barrier of frustrations that stood between herself and what she deserved. Pete joined her while she was struggling with the bacon and continued his attack. He was very nearly successful—he had her backed up against the gas range— when they heard the thunder of their children's footsteps in the hall. Pete went off to the train with mixed and turbulent feelings. She got the children some breakfast and watched them eat it with the extraordinary density of a family gathered at a kitchen table on a dark winter morning. When the children had gone off to get the school bus she turned up the thermostat. There was a dull explosion from the furnace room. A cloud of rank smoke came out of the cellar door. She poured herself a glass of whisky to steady her nerves and opened the door. The room was full of smoke but there was no fire. Then she telephoned the oil-burner repairman they employed. "Oh, Charlie isn't here," his wife said brightly. "He's up in Utica with his bowling team. They're in the semi-finals. He won't be back for ten days." She called every oil-burner man in the telephone directory but none of them was free. "But someone must come and help me," she exclaimed to one of the women who answered the phone. "It's zero outside and there's no heat at all. Everything will freeze." "Well, I'm sorry but I won't have a man free until Thursday," the stranger said. "But why don't you buy yourself an electric heater? You can keep the temperature up with those things." She had some more whisky, put on some lipstick and drove to the hardware store in Parthenia where she bought a large electric heater. She plugged it into an outlet in the kitchen and pulled the switch. All the lights in the house went out and she poured herself some more whisky and began to cry.

She cried for her discomforts but she cried more bitterly for their ephemeralness, for the mysterious harm a transparent bacon wrapper and an oil-burner could do to the finest part of her spirit; cried for a world that seemed to be without laws and prophets. She went on crying and drinking. Some repairmen came and patched things up but when the children came home from school she was lying unconscious on the sofa. They took their vitamin pills and went out to play. The next week the washing machine broke down and flooded the kitchen. The first repairman she called had gone to Miami for his vacation. The second would not be able to come for a week. The third had gone to a funeral. She mopped up the kitchen floor but it was two weeks before a repairman came. In the meantime the gas range went and she had to do all the cooking on an electric plate. She could not educate herself in the maintenance and repair of household machinery and felt in herself that tragic obsolescence she had sensed in the unemployed of Parthenia who needed work and money but who could not dig a hole. It was this feeling of obsolescence that pushed her into drunkenness and promiscuity and she was both.

One afternoon when she was very drunk she threw her arms around the milkman. He pushed her away roughly. "Jesus, lady," he said, "what kind of a man do you think I am?" In a blackmailing humor he stuffed the icebox with eggs, milk, orange juice, cottage cheese, vegetable salad and eggnog. She took a bottle of whisky up to her bedroom. At four o'clock the oil burner went out of order. She was back on the telephone again. No one could come for three or four days. It was very cold outside and she watched the winter night approach the house with the horror of an aboriginal. She could feel the cold overtake the rooms. When it got dark she went into the garage and took her life.

They held a little funeral for her in the undertaking parlor in Parthenia. The room where her monumental coffin stood was softly lighted and furnished like a cocktail lounge and the music from the electric organ was virtually what you would have heard in a hotel bar in someplace like Cleveland. She had, it turned out, no friends in Proxmire Manor. The only company her husband was able to muster was a handful of near strangers they had met on various cruise ships. They had taken a two-week Caribbean cruise each winter and the ceremony was attended by the Robinsons from the S.S. *Homeric,* the Howards from S.S. *United States,* the Gravelys from the *Gripsholm* and the Leonards from the *Bergensfjord.* A clergyman said a few trenchant words. (The oil-burner repairmen, electricians, mechanics and plumbers who were guilty of her death did not attend.) During the clergyman's remarks Mrs. Robinson (S.S. *Homeric*) began to cry with a violence and an anguish that had nothing to do with that time or place. She groaned loudly, she rocked in her chair, she sobbed convulsively. Mrs. Howard and Mrs. Leonard and then the men began to sob and wail. They did not cry over

the loss of her person; they scarcely knew her. They cried
at the realization of how bitterly disappointing her life had
been. Melissa knew none of this, of course, traveling that
morning on the same train that carried Mrs. Lockhart's
remains on the first leg of their trip back to Indiana.

Gertrude Bender, with whom Melissa sat, had silver-gilt
hair skinned back in a chignon with such preciseness and
skill that Melissa wondered how it had been accomplished.
She had matching silver-gilt furs, and rattled six gold brace-
lets. She was a pretty, shallow woman who wielded the inarguable powers of great wealth and whose voice was shrill.
She talked about her daughter Betty. "She's worried about
her schoolwork but I tell her, 'Betty,' I tell her, "don't you
worry about your schoolwork. Do you think what I learned
in school got me where I am today? Develop a good figure
and learn the forks. That's all that matters.' "

In the seat in front of Melissa there was an old lady
whose head was bowed under the weight of a hat covered
with cloth roses. A family occupied the facing seats across
the aisle—a mother and three children. They were poor.
Their clothing was cheap and threadbare, and the woman's
face was worn. One of her children was sick and lay cross
her lap, sucking his thumb. He was two or three years old,
but it was hard to guess his age, he was so pale and thin.
There were sores on his forehead and sores on his thin legs.
The lines around his mouth were as deep as those on the
face of a man. He seemed sick and miserable, but stubborn
and obdurate at the same time, as if he held in his fist a
promise to something bewildering and festive that he would
not relinquish in spite of his sickness and the strangeness
of the train. He sucked his thumb noisily and would not
move from his position in the midst of life. His mother bent
over him as she must have done when she nursed him,
and sang him a lullaby as they passed Parthenia, Gates-
bridge, Tuxon Valley and Tokinsville.

Gertrude said, "I don't understand people who lose their
looks when they don't have to. I mean what's the point of
going through life looking like an old laundry bag? Now
take Molly Singleton. She goes up to the Club on Saturday
nights wearing those thick eyeglasses and an ugly dress
and wonders why she doesn't have a good time. There's

no point in going to parties if you're going to depress everyone. I'm no girl and I know it, but I still have all the partners I want and I like to give the boys a thrill. I like to see them perk up. It's amazing what you can do. Why, one of the grocery boys wrote me a love letter. I wouldn't tell Charlie—I wouldn't tell anyone, because the poor kid might lose his job—but what's the sense of living if you don't generate a little excitement once in a while?"

Melissa was jealous. That the rush of feeling she suffered was plainly ridiculous didn't diminish its power. She seemed, unknowingly, to have convinced herself of the fact that Emile worshiped her, and the possibility that he worshiped them all, that she might be at the bottom of his list of attractions, was a shock. It was all absurd, and it was all true. She seemed to have rearranged all of her values around his image; to have come unthinkingly to depend upon his admiration. The fact that she cared at all about his philandering was painfully humiliating, but it remained painful.

She left New York in the middle of the afternoon and called Narobi's when she got back. She ordered a loaf of bread, garlic salt, endives—nothing she needed. He was there fifteen or twenty minutes later.

"Emile?" she asked.

"Yes."

"Did you ever write a letter to Mrs. Bender?"

"Mrs. who?"

"Mrs. Bender."

"I haven't written a letter since last Christmas. My uncle sent me ten dollars and I wrote a letter and thanked him."

"Emile, you must know who Mrs. Bender is."

"No, I don't. She probably buys her groceries somewhere else."

"Are you telling the truth, Emile?"

"Sure."

"Oh, I'm making such a damn fool of myself," she said, and began to cry.

"Don't be sad," he said. "Please don't! I like you very much, I think you're fascinating, but I wouldn't want to make you sad."

"Emile, I'm going to Nantucket on Saturday, to close up the house there. Would you like to come with me?"

"Oh, gee, Mrs. Wapshot," he said. "I couldn't do that. I mean I don't know." He knocked over a chair on his way out.

Melissa had never seen Mrs. Cranmer. She could not imagine what the woman looked like. She then got into the car and drove to the florist shop on Green Street. There was a bell attached to the door and, inside, the smell of flowers. Mrs. Cranmer came out of the back, taking a pencil from her bleached hair and smiling like a child.

Emile's mother was one of those widows who keep themselves in a continuous state of readiness for some call, some invitation, some meeting that will never take place because the lover is dead. You find them answering the telephone in the back-street cab stands of little towns, their hair freshly bleached, their nails painted, their high-arched shoes ready for dancing with someone who cannot come. They sell nightgowns, flowers, stationery and candy, and the lowest in their ranks sell movie tickets. They are always in a state of readiness, they have all known the love of a good man, and it is in his memory that they struggle through the snow and the mud in high heels. Mrs. Cranmer's face was painted brightly, her dress was silk, and there were bows on her high-heeled pumps. She was a small, plump woman, with her waist cinctured in sternly, like a cushion with a noose around it. She looked like a figure that had stepped from a comic book, although there was nothing comic about her.

Melissa ordered some roses, and Mrs. Cranmer passed the order on to someone in the back and said, "They'll be ready in a minute." The doorbell rang and another customer came in—a thick-featured man with a white plastic button in his right ear that was connected by an electrical cord to his vest. He spoke heavily. "I want something for a deceased," he said. Mrs. Cranmer was diplomatic, and through a series of delicate indirections tried to discover his relationship to the corpse. Would he like a blanket of flowers, at perhaps forty dollars, or something a little less expensive? He gave his information readily, but only in reply to direct questions. The corpse was his sister. Her children were scattered. "I guess I'm the closest she has left," he said confusedly, and Melissa, waiting for her roses, felt a premonition of death. She must die—she must be the subject of some such discussion in a flowershop, and close her eyes forever on a world that distracted her with its beauty. The image, hackneyed and poignant, that came to her was of life as a diversion, a festival from which she was summoned by the secret police of extinction, when the dancing and the music were at their best. I do not want to leave, she thought. I do not ever want to leave. Mrs. Cranmer gave her the roses, and she went home.

CHAPTER XII

❧ ❦

The Moonlite Drive-In was divided into three magnificent parts. There was the golf links, the roller rink and the vast amphitheater itself, where thousands of darkened cars were arranged in the form of an ancient arena, spread out beneath the tree of night. Above the deep thunder from the rink and the noise from the screen, you could hear—high in the air and so like the sea that a blind man would be deceived—the noise of traffic on the great Northern Expressway that flows southward from Montreal to the Shenandoah, engorging in its clover leaves and brilliantly engineered gradings the green playing fields, rose gardens, barns, farms, meadows, trout streams, forests, homesteads and churches of a golden past. The population of this highway gathered for their meals in a string of identical restaurants, where the murals, the urinals, the menus and the machines for vending sacred medals were uniform. It was some touching part of the autumn night and the hazards of the road that so many of these travelers pleaded for the special protection of gentle St. Christopher and the blessings of the Holy Virgin.

An exit (Exit 307) curved away from the Northern Expressway down toward the Moonlite, and here was everything a man might need: the means for swift travel, food, exercise, skill (the golf links), and in the dark cars of the amphitheater a place to perform the rites of spring —or, in this case, the rites of autumn. It was an autumn night, and the air was full of pollen and decay. Emile sat on the back seat with Louise Mecker. Charlie Putney, his best friend, was in the front seat with Doris Pierce. They were all drinking whisky out of paper cups, and they were all in various stages of undress. On the screen a woman exclaimed, "I want to put on innocence, like a bright, new dress. I want to feel clean again!" Then she slammed a door.

Emile was proud of his skin, but the mention of cleanliness aroused his doubts and misgivings. He blushed. These parties were a commonplace of his generation, and if he hadn't participated in them he would have gotten himself a reputation as a prude and faggot. Four boys in his high school class had been arrested for selling pornography and heroin. They had approached him, but the thought of using narcotics and obscene pictures disgusted him. His sitting undressed in the back seat of a car might be accounted for by the fact that the music he danced to and the movies he watched dealt less and less with the heart and more and more with overt sexuality, as if the rose gardens and playing fields buried under the Expressway were enjoying a revenge. What is the grade-crossing tender standing in the autumn sun thinking of? Why has the postmaster such a dreamy look? Why does the judge presiding at General Sessions seem so restless? Why does the cab driver frown and sigh? What is the shoeshine boy thinking of as he stares out into the rain? What darkens the mind and torments the flesh of the truck driver on the Expressway? What are the thoughts of the old gardener dusting his roses, the garage mechanic on his back under the Chevrolet, the idle lawyer, the sailor waiting for the fog to lift, the drunkard, the soldier? The times were venereal, and Emile was a child of the times.

Louise Mecker was a tomato, but her looseness seemed only to be one aspect of a cheerful disposition. She did what she was expected to do to get along, and this was part of it. And yet in her readiness she sometimes seemed to debase and ridicule the seat of desire, toward which he still preserved some vague and tender feelings. When the lilac under his bedroom window bloomed in the spring and he could smell its fragrance as he lay in bed, some feeling, as strong as ambition but without a name, moved him. Oh, I want— I want to do so well, he thought, sitting naked at the Moonlite. But what did he want to do? Be a jet pilot? Discover a waterfall in Africa? Manage a supermarket? Whatever it was, he wanted something that would correspond to his sense that life was imposing; something that would confirm his feeling that, as he stood at the window of Narobi's grocery store watching the men and women on the sidewalk and the stream of clouds in the sky, the procession he saw was a majestic one.

He thought of Melissa, who by giving him a beer had penetrated into his considerations. In the last six or eight months he had been bewildered by the sudden interest men and women took in his company. They seemed to want something from him and to want it ardently, and although he was not an innocent or a fool, he was genuinely uncertain about what it was they wanted. His own desires were violent. While he was shaving in the morning, a seizure of sexual need doubled him up with pain and made him groan. "Cut yourself, dear?" his mother asked. Now he thought of Melissa. He thought of her—oddly enough —as a tragic figure, frail, lonely and misunderstood. Her husband, whoever he was, would be obtuse, stupid and clumsy. Weren't all men his age? She was a fair prisoner in a tower.

Halfway through the feature, they got dressed and, with the cutout open and the radio blaring "Take It Easy, Greasy," roared out of the Moonlite onto the Expressway, jeopardizing their lives and the lives in every car they passed (men, women and children in arms), but gentle St. Christopher or the mercies of the Holy Virgin spared them, and they got Emile safely home. He climbed the stairs, kissed his mother good night—she was studying an article in *Reader's Digest* about the pancreas—and went to bed. Lying in bed, he decided, quite innocently, that he was tired of tomatoes, movies and paper cups, and that he would go to Nantucket.

CHAPTER XIII

Melissa had bought the plane tickets and made all the arrangements, and she asked Emile not to speak to her on the plane. He wore new shoes and a new pair of pants, and walked with a bounce in order to feel the thickness of the new soles and to feel the nice play of muscle as it worked up his legs and back into his shoulders. He had never been on a plane before, and he was disappointed to find that it was not so sleek as the planes in magazine advertisements and that the fuselage was dented and stained with smoke. He got a window seat and watched the activity on the field, feeling that as soon as the plane was airborne he would begin a new life of motion, comfort and freedom. Hadn't he always dreamed of going here and there and making friends in different places and being easily accepted as a man of strength and intelligence and not a grocery boy without a future or a destiny, and had he ever doubted that his dreams would come true? Melissa was the last one to get on, and was wearing a fur coat, and the dark skins made her appear to him like a visitor from another continent where everything was beautiful, orderly and luxurious. She didn't look in his direction. A drunken sailor took the seat beside Emile and fell asleep. Emile was disappointed. Watching the planes that passed over Parthenia and Proxmire Manor, he had assumed that the people who traveled in them were of a high order. In a little while they were off the ground.

It was charming. At the distance of a few hundred

feet, all the confused and mistaken works of man seemed orderly. He smiled down broadly at the earth and its population. The sensation he had looked forward to, of being airborne, was not what he had anticipated, and it seemed to him that the engines of the plane were struggling to resist gravity and hold them in their place among the thin clouds. The sea they were crossing was dark and colorless, and as they lost sight of land he felt in himself a corresponding sense of loss, as if at this point some sustaining bond with his green past had been cut. The island, when he saw it below them on the sea, with a cuff of foam on its northeast edge, looked so small and flat that he wondered why anyone should want to go there. When he left the plane she was waiting for him by the steps and they walked through the airport and got a cab. She told the driver, "First I want to go into the village and get some groceries, and then I want to go to Madamquid."

"What do you want to go to Madamquid for?" the driver asked. "There's nobody out there now."

"I have a cottage out there," she said.

They drove across a bleak landscape but one so closely associated with her youth and her happiness that the bleakness escaped her. In the village, they stopped at the grocery store where she had always traded, and she asked Emile to wait outside. When she had bought the groceries, a boy wearing the white apron and bent in exactly the same attitude as Emile was when she first saw him carried them out to the taxi. She gave him a tip and looked up and down the street for Emile. He was standing in front of the drugstore with some other young men his age.

Her courage left her then. The society of the bored and the disappointed, from which she had hoped to escape, seemed battlemented, implacable and splendid—a creation useful to concert halls, hospitals, bridges and courthouses, and one that she was not fit to enter. She had wanted to bring into her life the freshness of a journey and had achieved nothing but a galling sense of moral shabbiness. "You want me to get your boyfriend?" the cab driver asked.

"He's not my boyfriend," Melissa said. "He's just come out to help me move some things."

Emile saw her then, and crossed the street, and they
started for Madamquid. She felt so desperate that she took
his hand, not expecting him to support her, but he turned
to her with wonderful largess, a smile so strong and tender
that she felt the blood pour back into her heart. They were
heading out to the point where there was nothing to see but
the cream-colored dunes, with their scalp locks of knife
grass, and the dark autumn ocean. He was perplexed by
this. One of the several divisions in his world was that
group of people who went away for the summer—who
closed their houses in June and bought no more groceries
until September—and never having enjoyed any such
migratory privileges himself, he had imagined the places
where they went as having golden sands and purple seas,
the houses palatial and pink-walled, with patios and
swimming pools, like the houses he saw in the movies.
There was nothing like that here, and he couldn't believe
that even in the long, hot days of summer this place would
look less of a wilderness. Were there fleets of sailboats,
deck chairs and beach umbrellas? There was no trace of
summery furniture now. She pointed out the house to him
and he saw a big, shingled building on a bluff. He could
see that it was big—it was big all right—but if you were
going to build a summer house why not build something
neat and compact, something that would be nice to look
at? But maybe he was wrong, maybe there was something
to be learned here; she seemed so pleased at the sight of the
old place that he was willing to suspend judgment. She
paid off the cab driver and tried to open the front door, but
the lock had rusted in the salt air and he had to help. He
finally got the door open, and she went in and he carried in
the bags and then, of course, the groceries.

She knew well enough that the place was homely—it
was meant to be—but the lemony smell of the matchboard
walls seemed to her like the fragrance of the lives that
had been spent there in the sunny months. Her sister's old
violin music, her brother's German textbooks, the water
color of a thistle her aunt had painted seemed like the
essence of their lives. And while she had quarreled with
her brother and her sister and they no longer communi-
cated with each other, all her memories now were kind

and gentle. "I've always been happy here," she said. "I've always been terribly happy here. That's why I wanted to come back. It's cold now, of course, but we can light some fires." She noticed then, on the wall at her left, the pencil markings where each Fourth of July her uncle had stood them up against the matchboard and recorded their growth. Afraid that he might see this incriminating evidence of her age, she said, "Let's put the groceries in the icebox."

"That's a funny word, icebox," he said. "I never heard it before. It's a funny thing to call a frigidaire. But you speak differently, you know—people like you. You say lots of different things. Now, you say divine—you say lots of things are divine, but, you know, my mother, she wouldn't ever use that word, excepting when she was speaking of God."

Frightened by the chart in the hallway, she wondered if there was anything else incriminating in the house, and remembered the gallery of family photographs in the upstairs hall. Here were pictures of her in school uniforms, in catboats, and many pictures of her playing on the beach with her son. While he put the groceries away, she went upstairs and hid the pictures in a closet. Then they walked down the bluff to the beach.

It was surprisingly warm for that time of year. The wind was southerly; in the night it would probably change around to the southwest, bringing rain. All along the beach, the waves from Portugal rolled in. There was the noise of a detonation, the roar of furling water, and then the glistening discharge fanned out on the sand, faded and sank. Ahead of her, at the high-water mark, she saw a sealed bottle with a note inside and ran to pick it up. What did she expect? The secret of the Spada treasure, or a proposal of marriage from a French sailor? She handed Emile the bottle and he broke it open on a stone. The note was written in pencil. "To whomever in the whole wide world may read this I am a 18 yr old college boy, sitting on the beach at Madamquid on Sept. 8. . . ." His sense of the act of setting his name and address adrift on the tide was rhapsodic, but the bottle must have returned to where he stood a little while after he had walked away.

Emile asked if he could go swimming, and then bent down to unlace his new shoes. One of the laces knotted and his face got red. She dropped to her knees and undid it herself. He got out of his clothes hurriedly in order to display his youth and his brawn, but he asked her earnestly if she minded if he took off his underpants. He stood with his back to her while he did this, and then walked off into the sea. It was colder than he had expected. His shoulders and his buttocks tightened and his head shook. Naked and shivering, he seemed pitiful, vain and fair—a common young man trying to find some pleasure and adventure in his life. He dove into a wave and then came lunging back to where she stood. His teeth were chattering. She threw her coat over him and they went back to the house.

She had been right about the wind. After midnight or later, it came out of the southwest, spouting rain, and as she had done ever since she was a child, she got out of bed and crossed the room to close the windows. He woke and heard the sound of her bare feet on the wooden floor. He couldn't see her in the dark, but as she came back toward the bed her step sounded heavy and old.

It rained in the morning. They walked on the beach, and Melissa cooked a chicken. Looking for a bottle of wine, she found a long-necked green bottle of Moselle, like the bottle she had set out in her dream of the picnic and the ruined castle. Emile ate most of the chicken. At four they took a cab to the airport, and flew back to New York. In the train out to Proxmire Manor he sat several seats ahead of her, reading the paper.

Moses met her at the station and was pleased to have her back. The baby was awake; and Melissa sat in a chair in their bedroom singing, "Sleep, my little one, sleep. Thy father guards the sheep. . . ." She sang until both the baby and Moses were asleep.

CHAPTER XIV

In the meantime things at the Wapshots' in Talifer were
very gloomy. There were no checks from Boston and no
explanation and Betsey was complaining. One Sunday
afternoon after Coverly had cooked some lunch and
washed the dishes Betsey returned to her television set.
Their little son had been crying since before lunch. Coverly
asked the boy why he cried but he only went on crying.
Would he like to take a walk, would he like a lollipop,
could Coverly build him a house of blocks? "Oh, leave
him alone," Betsey said and turned up the volume. "He can
watch TV with me." The boy, still sobbing, went to his
mother and Coverly put on a jacket and went out. He took
a bus to the computer center and walked across the fields
to the farmland. It was late in the season, purple asters
bloomed along the path and the air was so heavy with pollen that it gave him a not unpleasant irritation in his
nostrils; the whole world smelled like some worn and
brilliant carpet. The maples and beeches had turned and
the moving lights of that afternoon among the trees made
the path ahead of him seem like a chain of corridors and
chambers, yellow and gold consistories and vaticans, but
in spite of this show of light he seemed still to hear the
music from the television, to see the lines at Betsey's mouth
and to hear the crying of his little son. He had failed. He
had failed at everything. Poor Coverly will never amount
to anything. He had heard it said often enough by his
aunts from behind the parlor door. He will marry a bony
woman and beget a morbid child. He will never succeed at
anything. He will never pay his debts. He stooped to
tighten a shoelace and at that exact moment a hunting

<u>arrow</u> whistled over his head and sank into the trunk of a tree on his right.

"Hey," Coverly shouted, "hey. You damned near killed me." There was no reply. The archer was concealed by a screen of yellow leaves and why should he confess to his nearly murderous mistake? "Where are you," Coverly shouted, "where the hell are you?" He ran into the brush beside the path and in the distance saw an archer, all dressed in red, climbing a stone wall. He looked exactly like the devil. "You, you," Coverly called after him but the distance was too great for him to catch the brute. There was no reply, no echo. He startled a pair of crows who flew off toward the gantries. That the arrow would have killed him had he not stopped to tighten his shoelace exploded in his consciousness, accelerated the beating of his heart and made his tongue swell. But he was alive, he had missed death at this chance turning as he had missed it at a thousand others and suddenly the color, fragrance and shape of the day seemed to stir themselves and surround him with great force and clarity.

He saw nothing unearthly, heard no voices, came at the experience through a single fact—the deathly arrow—and yet it seemed the most volcanic, the most like a turning point, in his life. He felt a sense of himself, his uniqueness, a raptness that he had never felt before. The syllables of his name, the coloring of his hair and eyes, the power in his thighs seemed intensified into something like ecstasy. The voices of his detractors behind the parlor door—and he had listened to them earnestly all the years of his life—now seemed transparently covetous and harmful, the voices of people loving enough but whose happiness would best be served if he did not make any discoveries of himself. His place in the autumn afternoon and the world seemed indisputable, and with such a feeling of resilience, how could anything harm him? The sense was not that he was inviolate but headstrong and that had the arrow struck him he would have fallen with the brilliance of that day in his eyes. He was not the victim of an emotional and a genetic tragedy; he had the supreme privileges of a changeling and he would make something illustrious of his life. He examined the arrow and tried to pull it out of the tree but

the shaft broke. The feathers were crimson and he thought
that if he gave the broken arrow to his son the boy might
stop crying, and when the boy saw the crimson feathers
he did.

Coverly's resolve to do something illustrious settled on
a plan to diagnose the vocabulary of John Keats, a project
that in turn depended upon a friend named Griza. Most
of the employees lunched in the subterranean cafeteria but
Coverly usually took the elevator up and ate a sandwich
in the sunlight. This choice was odd enough to serve as
the basis for a friendship. One of the technicians in the
computer room also ate a sandwich in the sun, and this
and the fact that they both came from Massachusetts made
them fast friends. In the spring they threw a baseball; in
the autumn they spiraled a football back and forth with a
conspicuous sense of simpler things than the gantry line on
the horizon. Griza was the son of a Polish immigrant
but he had been raised in Lowell and his wife was the
granddaughter of a Yankee farmer. He was one of the
technicians who serviced the big computer and might have
been recognized as one. There were no mandates for dress
in the computation center and no established hierarchies
but over the months the outlines of a society and a list of
sumptuary laws had begun to emerge, expressing, it
seemed, an inner love of caste. The physicists wore cashmere pullovers. The senior programmers wore tweeds
and colored shirts. Coverly's rank wore business suits and
the technicians seemed to have settled on a uniform that
included white shirts and dark ties. They were separated
from the rest of the center by the privilege of manipulating
the console and by the greater privilege of technical
knowledge and limited responsibility. If a program failed
repeatedly, they could be sure it was not their fault, and
this gave them all the briskness and levity that you sometimes see in the deck hands on a ferry boat. Griza had
never been to sea but he walked as if he walked on a
moving deck and looked somehow as if he slept in a bunk,
kept watches and did his own laundry. He was a slight
man with less than a stomach—that whole area seemed
limber and concave; he used a fixative on his hair and
combed it in a careful cross-hatch at the nape of his neck,

a style that had been popular with street boys ten years earlier. Thus he seemed to have one foot in the immediate past. Coverly expected him, sooner or later, to confess to some eccentric ambition. Was he building a raft in his cellar for a trip down the Mississippi? Was he perfecting a machine for compressing empty beer cans? A simplified contraceptive? A chemical solvent for autumn leaves? A project like this seemed necessary to settle the lines of his character, but Coverly was mistaken. Griza hoped to work at the site until the retirement age, when he planned to invest his savings in a parking lot in Florida or California.

From his position at the computer Griza seemed to know a great deal about the politics at the site. He did not seem to have the disposition of a gossip and yet Coverly came away from their lunch hours each day with a wealth of information. The receptionist at the security center was pregnant. Cameron, the director of the site, wouldn't last six weeks. The top brass were bitterly divided in their opinions. They quarreled over whether or not coherent radio signals had been received from Tau Ceti and Epsilon Eridani, they disputed the existence of other civilizations in the solar system, they challenged the intelligence of dolphins. Griza passed along his news indifferently but there was always plenty of it. Coverly cultivated Griza with the hope that Griza might help him. He wanted Griza to put the vocabulary of Keats through the computer. Griza seemed undecided but he did invite Coverly to come home with him for supper one night.

When they finished work they took a bus to the end of the line and began to walk. It was a part of the site that Coverly had never seen. "We're in the emergency housing section," Griza explained. It was a trailer camp although most of the trailers stood on cement block foundations. Some of them were massive and had two levels. There were street lights, gardens, picket fences and inevitably a pair of painted wagon wheels, a talisman of the rural and mythical past. Coverly wondered if they had come from the farm near the computation center. Griza stopped at the door of one of the more modest trailers, opened the door and let Coverly in.

There was one long and pleasant room that seemed to

serve a number of purposes. Griza's mother was standing at the stove. His wife was putting a fresh diaper on their daughter. Old Mrs. Griza was a heavy, gray-haired woman who wore a Christmas tree ornament on her dress. Christmas was far away and this ornament had the appeal of those farmhouses you pass, coming down from the ski trails in the north where the colored Christmas lights burn way past Epiphany and are sometimes not dismantled until the snow melts, as if Christmas had been unself-consciously enlarged to embrace the winter. Her face was broad and kindly. Young Mrs. Griza wore a torn man's shirt and a pair of tartan slacks that she had outgrown. Her face was large, her long hair pretty and disheveled, her eyes were beautiful when they were open wide, which they seldom were that evening. The cast of her eyes and her mouth was downward, suggesting sullenness, and it was this sullenness, so swiftly contradicted by the light and authority of her smile, that made her face compelling. Gentling and dressing the baby she seemed nearly imperious. Griza opened two cans of beer and he and Coverly sat down at the end of the room farthest from the stove.

"We're a little crowded in here now," the old lady said. "Oh, I wish you could have seen the house we had in Lowell! Twelve rooms. Oh, it was a lovely house; but we had rats. Oh, those rats. Once I went down cellar to get a stick of wood for the stove and this big man rat jumped at me, jumped right at me! Well, he missed me, thank God, went right over my shoulder but ever after that I was afraid of them. I mean when I saw how fearless they was. We used to have a nice centerpiece in the dining room. Fruit, you know, or wax flowers, but I come down one morning and there was this nice centerpiece all chewed up. Rats. It broke my heart. I mean it made me feel I didn't have anything I could call my own. Mice too. We had mice. They used to get into the pantry. One year I made a big batch of jelly and the mice chewed right through the wax tops and spoiled the jelly. But the mice was nothing compared to the termites. I always noticed the living-room floor was kind of springy and one morning when I was pushing the vacuum cleaner a whole section of the floor give way and sagged into the cellar. Termites. Termites and carpenter ants. It was a combination. The termites ate the under-pinnings of the house and the carpenter ants ate the porch. But the worst was bedbugs. When my cousin Harry died he left me this big bed. I didn't think anything about it. I felt funny in the night, you know, but I'd never seen a bedbug in my life and I couldn't imagine what it was. Well, one night I turned on the light good and quick and there they were. There they were! Well, by this time they'd spread all over the house. Bedbugs everywhere. We had to have everything sprayed and, oh, my, the smell was dread-ful. Fleas too. We had fleas. We had this old dog named Spotty. Well, he had fleas and the fleas got off him into the rugs and it was a damp house, the fleas bred in the rugs and you know there was one rug there when you stepped onto it there would be a cloud of fleas, thick as smoke, fleas all over you. Well, supper's ready."

They ate frozen meat, frozen fried potatoes and frozen peas. Blindfolded one could not have identified the peas, and the only flavor the potatoes had was the flavor of soap. It was the monotonous fare of the besieged, it would be served everywhere on the site that night, but where were the walls, the battering rams, where was the enemy that could be accounted for this tasteless porridge? Coverly was happy there and they talked about New England during the meal. While the women washed the dishes Coverly and Griza spoke about running the Keats vocabulary through the computer. Griza's invitation to dinner seemed to have been a gesture of trust or assent and he agreed to run the vocabulary through the hardware if Coverly would make the preparations. They drank a glass of whisky and ginger ale and Coverly went home.

On the next night Coverly arranged his life along these lines. He left the computation center at five, cooked sup-per, bathed and put his son to bed. Then he returned to the computation center with his soft leather copy of Keats and began to translate this, on an electrical typewriter, into binary digits. "I stood tip-toe upon a little hill," he began, "the air was cooling, and so very still. . . ." It took him three weeks to get through it all including *King Stephen*. It was half-past eleven one night when he typed: "To feel

forever its soft fall and swell,/Awake for ever in a sweet
unrest,/Still, still to hear her tender-taken breath,/And so
live ever——or else swoon to death."

CHAPTER XV

☙ ɜ❧

Griza said that if everything went on schedule he would run
the tape through late on a Saturday afternoon. He telephoned Coverly on Friday night and told him to come in
at four. The tape was stored in Coverly's office and at four
he brought it up to the room where the console stood. He
was very excited. He and Griza seemed to be alone in the
center. Somewhere an unanswered telephone was ringing.
His instructions, converted into binary digits, asked the
machine to count the words in the poetry, count the vocabulary and then list those words most frequently used in
the order of their usage. Griza put the instructions and the
tape into a pair of towers and pulled some switches on the
console. He was in that environment where he felt most
like himself and swaggered around like a deck hand. Coverly was sweating with excitement. To make some conversation he asked Griza about his mother and his wife but
Griza, ennobled by the presence of the console, did not
reply. The typewriter began loudly to clatter and Coverly
turned. When the machine stopped Griza tore the paper off
its rack and passed it to Coverly. The number of words in
the poetry came to fifteen thousand three hundred and
fifty-seven. The vocabulary was eight thousand five hundred and three and the words in the order of their frequency were: "Silence blendeth grief's awakened fall/The
golden realms of death take all/Love's bitterness exceeds
its grace/That bestial scar on the angelic face/Marks
heaven with gall."

"My God," Coverly said. "It rhymes. It's poetry."

Griza was going around turning off the lights. He didn't reply.

"But it's poetry, Griza," Coverly said. "Isn't that wonderful? I mean there's poetry within the poetry."

Griza's indifference was implacable. "Yuh, yuh," he said. "We better get out of here. I don't want to get caught."

"But you see, don't you," Coverly said, "that within the poetry of Keats there is some other poetry." It was possible to imagine that some numerical harmony underlay the composition of the universe, but that this harmony embraced poetry was a bewildering possibility and Coverly then felt himself to be a citizen of the world that was emerging; a part of it. Life was filled with newness; there was newness everywhere! "I guess I'd better tell somebody," Coverly said. "It's a discovery, you know."

"Keep cool," Griza said. "You tell somebody, they'll know I was using the console on off hours and I'll get my arse reamed." He had turned off all the lights and they moved into the corridor. Then at the end of the corridor a door opened and Dr. Lemuel Cameron, director of the site, came toward them.

Cameron was a short man. He walked with a stoop. His ruthlessness and his brilliance were legendary and Griza and Coverly were frightened. Cameron's hair was a lusterless black, cut so long that a curl hung over his forehead. His skin was dark and sallow with a fine flush of red at the cheek. His eyes were mournful but it was their brows, their awnings, their hairy settings, that made his appearance seem distinguished and formidable. His brows were an inch thick, brindled with gray and tufted like the pelt of a beast. They looked like structural beams, raised into a position that would support the weight of his knowledge and his authority. We know that heavy eyebrows support nothing, not even thin air, nor are they rooted in the intellect or the heart, but it was his brows that intimidated the two men.

"What's your name?" he asked. The question was directed at Coverly.

"Wapshot," he said.

If Cameron had been a recipient of Lorenzo's bounty, he showed no signs of it.

"What are you doing here?" he asked.

"We've just made a word-count of the vocabulary of John Keats," Coverly said in his most earnest manner.

"Ah, yes," Cameron said. "I'm interested in poetry myself although it's not commonly known." Then, raising his face and giving them a smile that was either gassy or insincere, he recited with practiced expression:

> How many worlds around their suns
> Have woven night and day,
> For countless thinking things like men,
> Now deep in stone or clay!
> Their story caught in light now comes
> To us, unskilled to know
> The comedy, the tragedy, the glint of friend or foe.
> In that faint and cryptic message
> From afar and long ago.

Coverly said nothing and Cameron looked at him narrowly.

"I've seen you before?" he asked.

"Yes, sir."

"Where."

"On the mountain."

"Come to my office on Monday," he said. "What time is it?"

"Quarter to seven," Coverly said.

"Have I eaten?" he asked.

"I don't know, sir," said Coverly.

"I wonder," he said, "I wonder." He went up on the elevator alone.

CHAPTER XVI

ઓ ૈ

Coverly reported to Cameron's office on Monday morning.
He clearly recalled his first encounter with the old genius.
This had been in the mountains, three hundred miles north
of Talifer, where Coverly had gone skiing one weekend
with some other men from the office. They reached the
place late in the afternoon and would have time for only
one run before dark. They were waiting for the chair lift
when they were asked to step aside. It was Cameron.

He was with two generals and a colonel. They were all
much bigger and younger than he. There was an appreciable stir at his arrival but he was, after all, a legendary
skier. His contribution to the theory of thermal heat had
been worked out from his observation of the molecular
action on the base of his skis. He wore fine ski clothes and
had a scarlet headband above his famous eyebrows. His
eyes were brilliant that afternoon and he moved toward
the lift with the preciseness and grace (Coverly thought)
of someone who enjoys unchallenged authority. He went
up the mountain, followed by his retinue and then by
Coverly and his friends. There was a hut or refuge at the
summit where they stopped to smoke. There was no fire in
the refuge. It was very cold. When Coverly had adjusted
his bindings he found that he and Cameron were alone.
The others had gone down. The presence of Cameron
made Coverly uneasy. Without speaking, without making a
sound, he seemed to project around him something as palpable as an electromagnetic field. It was late, it would be
dark very soon but all the mountain peaks, all of them
buried in snow, still stood in the canted light of day like
the gulfs and trenches of an ancient sea bed. What moved
Coverly in the scene was its vitality. Here was a display of

the inestimable energies of the planet; here in the last light was a sense of its immense history. Coverly knew enough not to speak of this to the doctor. It was Cameron who spoke. His voice was harsh and youthful. "Isn't it remarkable," he said, "to think that only two years ago it was generally thought that the heterosphere was divided into two regions."

"Yes," Coverly said.

"First of course we have the homosphere," the doctor explained. He spoke with the forced courtesy of some professors. "Within the homosphere the primary components of air are uniformly mixed in their standard proportions by weight of 76 percent nitrogen, 23 percent oxygen and one percent argon, apart from water vapor." Coverly turned to see him. His face was drawn by the intense cold. His breath smoked. His habit of explanation seemed impervious to the majesty of their circumstances. Coverly felt that he barely saw the light and the mountains. "We have within the homosphere," he went on, "the troposphere, the stratosphere and the mesosphere with, beyond the mesopause, oxygen and nitric acid, ionized by Lyman Beta components and above this oxygen and some nitric oxide, ionized by short ultraviolet ray. The electronic density above the mesopause is 100,000 a cubic centimeter. Above this it rises to 200,000 and then to a million. Then the gross density of atoms becomes so low that the electron density diminishes. . . ."

"I think we'd better go down," Coverly said. "It's getting dark. Would you like to go first?"

Cameron refused and called good luck to Coverly as Coverly poled off. He made the first turn and the second but the third turn was already dark and he took a spill. He was not hurt but, getting to his feet, he happened to look overhead and saw Dr. Cameron descending sedately in the chair lift.

Coverly met his friends below the chair-lift station and went on to an inn where they had a drink in the bar. Cameron and his retinue came in a few minutes later and took a table in a corner. It was no trouble to hear what Cameron was saying. It seemed that he could not control the penetrativeness of his voice. He was talking about running the trail and talking about it in detail; the hairpin turns, the long stretch of washboard, the icy schusses and the drifted snow. Here was a man responsible in a sense for the security of the nation, who could not be counted upon to tell the truth about his skiing. He was notorious for his insistence upon demonstrable truths and yet in this matter was a consummate liar. Coverly was fascinated. Had he brought another and a finer sense of truth to the face of the mountain? Had he judged from the chair lift that the trail was too steep and swift for his strength? Had he guessed that if he admitted to judicious timidity he might have impaired the respectfulness of his team? Had his disregard for the common truth involved some larger sense of truth? Coverly didn't know whether or not he had been seen from the chair lift.

A secretary led Coverly into Cameron's office that morning. "Your interest in poetry," the old man began at once, "is my principal reason for asking you here, for what could be more poetic than those hundred thousand million suns that make up the glittering jewelry of our galaxy? This vastness of power is utterly beyond our comprehension. It seems certain that we are receiving light from more than a hundred billion billion suns. It is conservatively estimated that one star in a thousand carries a planet hospitable to some form of life. Even if this estimate should prove a million times too big there would still be a hundred billion such planets in the known universe. Would you like to work for me?" the doctor asked.

"I don't think you understand, Dr. Cameron," Coverly said. "You see, my only training is in taping and preprogramming. When I was transferred from Remsen the machine made a slip-up and I ended in public relations; but I don't think you understand that—"

"Don't you tell me what I understand and what I don't understand," Cameron shouted. "If what you're trying to tell me is that your ignorance is limpid and abysmal, you're trying to tell me something I already know. You're a blockhead. I know it. That's why I want you. Blockheads are difficult to find these days. On your way out tell Miss Knowland to have you transferred to my staff. Write me a twenty-minute commencement address along the lines of

what I've just said and plan to leave with me for Atlantic
City next week. What time is it?"

"Quarter to ten," Coverly said.

"Hear that bird?" the doctor asked.

"Yes," Coverly said.

"What is he saying?" the doctor asked.

"I'm not sure," Coverly said.

"He's calling my name," said Cameron, a little angrily.
"Can't you hear it? He's calling my name. Cameron, Cameron, Cameron."

"It does sound like that," said Coverly.

"Do you know the constellation Pernacia?"

"Yes," said Coverly.

"Did you ever notice that it contains my initials?"

"I'd never thought of it that way," Coverly said. "I see
now, I see it now."

"How long can you hold your breath?" Cameron asked.

"I don't know," Coverly said.

"Well, try." Coverly took a deep breath and Cameron
looked at his wristwatch. He held his breath for a minute
and eight seconds. "Not bad," Cameron said. "Now get
out of here."

CHAPTER XVII

&ᴥ ᴥ⅝

We are born between two states of consciousness; we spend
our lives between the darkness and the light, and to climb
in the mountains of another country, phrase our thoughts
in another language or admire the color of another sky
draws us deeper into the mystery of our condition. Travel
has lost the attributes of privilege and fashion. We are no
longer dealing with midnight sailings on three-stacked
liners, twelve-day crossings, Vuitton trunks and the glittering lobbies of Grand Hotels. The travelers who board

the jet at Orly carry paper bags and sleeping babies, and might be going home from a hard day's work at the mill. We can have supper in Paris and, God willing, breakfast at home, and here is a whole new creation of self-knowledge, new images for love and death and the insubstantiality and the importance of our affairs. Most of us travel to improve on the knowledge we have of ourselves, but none of this was true for Cousin Honora. She went to Europe as a fugitive.

She had developed, over the years, a conviction that St. Botolphs was the fairest creation on the face of the earth. Oh, it was not magnificent, she well knew; it was nothing like the postcards of Karnak and Athens that her Uncle Lorenzo had sent her when she was a child. But she had no taste for magnificence. Where else in the world were there such stands of lilac, such lambent winds and brilliant skies, such fresh fish? She had lived out her life there, and each act was a variation on some other act, each sensation she experienced was linked to a similar sensation, reaching in a chain back through the years of her long life to when she had been a fair and intractable child, unlacing her skates, long after dark, at the edge of Parson's Pond, when all the other skaters had gone home and the barking of Peter Howland's collies sounded menacing and clear as the bitter cold gave to the dark sky the acoustics of a shell. The fragrant smoke from her fire mingled with the smoke from all the fires of her life. Some of the roses she pruned had been planted before she was born. Her dear uncle had lectured her on the ties that bound her world to Renaissance Europe, but she had always disbelieved him. What person who had seen the cataracts in the New Hampshire mountains could care about the waterworks of kings? What person who had smelled the rich brew of the North Atlantic could care about the dirty Bay of Naples? She did not want to leave her home and move on into an element where her sensations would seem rootless, where roses and the smell of smoke would only remind her of the horrible distances that stood between herself and her own garden.

She went alone to New York on a train, slept restlessly in a hotel bedroom, and one morning she boarded a ship for Europe. In her cabin she found that the old judge had

sent her an orchid. She detested orchids, and she detested
improvidence, and the gaudy flower was both. Her first
impulse was to fire it out of the porthole, but the porthole
wouldn't open, and on second thought it seemed to her
that perhaps a flower was a necessary part of a traveler's
costume, a sign of parting, a proof that one was leaving
friends behind. There was loud laughter, and talk, and the
noise of drinking. Only she, it seemed, was alone.

Removed from the scrutiny of the world, she could seem
a little foolish—she spent some time trying to find a place
to hide the canvas money belt in which she kept her cash
and documents. Under the sofa? Behind the picture? In the
empty flower vase or the medicine cabinet? A corner of the
carpet was loose and she hid her money belt there. Then she
stepped out into the corridor. She wore black clothes and a
tricorne hat, and looked a little as George Washington
might have looked had he lived to be so old.

The festivities in the crowded staterooms had moved out
into the corridor, where men and women stood drinking
and talking. She couldn't deny that it would have been
pleasanter if a few friends had come down to put a social
blessing on her departure. Without the orchid on her
shoulder, how could these strangers guess that in her own
home she was a celebrated woman, known to everyone and
famous for her good works? Mightn't they, glancing at
her as she passed, mistake her for one of those cussed old
women who wander over the face of the earth trying to
conceal or palliate that bitter loneliness that is the fitting
reward for their contrary and selfish ways? She felt painfully disarmed and seemed to have only the fewest proofs
of her identity. What she wanted then was some common
room, where she could sit down and watch things.

She found a common room, but it was crowded and all
the seats were taken. People were drinking and talking and
crying, and in one corner a grown man stood saying good-
bye to a little girl. His face was wet with tears. Honora
had never seen or dreamed of such mortal turmoil. The
go-ashore was being sounded, and while many of the fare-
wells were cheerful and lighthearted, many of them were
not. The sight of a man parting from his little daughter—
it must be his little daughter, separated from him by some

evil turn of events—upset Honora terribly. Suddenly the man got to his knees and took the child in his arms. He concealed his face in her thin shoulder, but his back could be seen shaking with sobs, while the public-address system kept repeating that the hour, the moment, had come. She felt the tears form in her own eyes, but the only way she could think of to cheer the little girl was to give her the orchid, and by now the corridors were too crowded for Honora to make her way back to her stateroom. She stepped over the high brass sill onto a deck.

The gangways were thronged with visitors leaving the ship. The stir was tremendous. Below her she could see a strip of dirty harbor water, and overhead there were gulls. People were calling to one another over this short distance, this still unaccomplished separation, and now all but one of the gangways were up, and the band began to play what seemed to her to be circus music. The loosening of gigantic hemp lines was followed by the stunning thunder of the whistle, so loud it must ruffle the angels in Heaven. Everyone was calling, everyone was waving—everyone but her. Of all the people standing on the deck, only she had no one to part with, only her going was lonely and meaningless. In simple pride, she took a handkerchief out of her pocketbook and began to wave it to the faces that were so swiftly losing their outline and their appeal. "Good-bye, good-bye, my dear, dear friend," she called to no one. "Thank you. . . . Thank you for everything. . . . Good-bye and thank you. . . . Thank you and good-bye."

At seven o'clock she put on her best clothes and went up to dinner. She shared a table with a Mr. and Mrs. Sheffield, from Rochester, who were going abroad for the second time. They were traveling with orlon wardrobes. During dinner they told Honora about their earlier trip to Europe. They went first to Paris, where they had nice weather— nice drying weather, that is. Each night, they took turns washing their clothes in the bathtub and hanging them out to dry. Going down the Loire they ran into rain and were not able to do any wash for nearly a week, but once they reached the sea the weather was sunny and dry, and they washed everything. They flew to Munich on a sunny day and did their wash in the Regina Palast, but in the middle

of the night there was a thunderstorm and all their clothing, hung out on a balcony, got soaked. They had to pack
their wardrobes wet for the trip to Innsbruck, but they
reached Innsbruck on a clear and starry night and hung
everything out to dry again. There was another thunderstorm in Innsbruck, and they had to spend a day in their
hotel room, waiting for their clothes to dry. Venice was a
wonderful place for laundry. They had very little trouble in
Italy, and during their Papal audience Mrs. Sheffield convinced herself that the Pope's vestments were made of
orlon. They remembered Geneva for its rainy weather,
and London was very disappointing. They had theater
tickets, but nothing would dry, and they had to spend two
days in their room. Edinburgh was even worse, but in
Skye the clouds lifted and the sun shone, and they took a
plane home from Prestwick with everything clean and dry.
The sum of their experience was to warn Honora against
planning to do much wash in Bavaria, Austria, Switzerland
and the British Isles.

Toward the end of this account, Honora's face got very
red, and suddenly she leaned across the table and said,
"Why don't you stay home and do your wash? Why do
you travel halfway around the world, making a spectacle
of yourself in front of the waiters and chambermaids of
Austria and France? I've never owned a stitch of orlon, or
whatever you call it, but I expect I'll find laundries and
dry cleaners in Europe just as at home, and I'm sure I'd
never travel for the pleasure of hanging out a clothesline."

The Sheffields were shocked and embarrassed. Honora's
voice carried, and passengers at the nearby tables had
turned to stare at her. She tried to extricate herself by calling a waiter. "Check," she called. "Check. Will you please
bring me my check?"

"There is no check, madam," the waiter said.

"Oh, yes," she said, "I forgot," and limped out of the
room.

She was too angry at the Sheffields to be remorseful, but
she was faced again with the fact that her short temper was
one of her worst qualities. She wandered around the decks
to cool off, admiring the yellowish shroud lights and thinking how like a second set of stars they were. She was stand-

ing on the stern deck, watching the wake, when a young
man in a pin-striped suit joined her. They had a pleasant
conversation about the stars, and then she went to bed and
slept soundly.

In the morning, after a hearty breakfast, Honora arranged for a deck chair on the leeward side. She then settled herself with a novel (*Middlemarch*) and prepared to
relax and enjoy the healthfulness of the sea air. Nine quiet
days would conserve her strength and perhaps even
lengthen her life. It was the first time that she had ever
planned a rest. Sometimes after lunch on a hot day she
would shut her eyes for five minutes but never for longer.
In the mountain hotels where she went for a change of air
she had always been an early riser, a marathon chair
rocker and a tireless bridge player. Up until now there
had always been things to do, there had always been demands on her time, but now her old heart was weary and
she should rest. She pressed her head against the chair
cushion and drew the blanket over her legs. She had seen
thousands of travel advertisements in which people her
age stretched out in deck chairs, watching the sea. She had
always wondered what pleasant reveries passed through
their minds. Now she waited for this enviable tranquillity
to steal over her. She shut her eyes, but she shut them
emphatically; she drummed her fingers on the wooden
armrest and wriggled her feet. She counseled herself to
wait, to wait, to wait for repose to overtake her. She
waited perhaps ten minutes before she sat up impatiently
and angrily. She had never learned to sit still, and, as with
so much else in life, it seemed too late now for her to
learn.

Her sense of life was a sense of motion and embroil-
ments, and even if to move gave her a keen pain in the
heart, she had no choice but to move. To be stretched out
in a deck chair that early in the day made her feel idle,
immoral, worthless and—what was most painful of all—
like a ghost, neither living nor dead; like some bitterly un-
willing bystander. To tramp around the decks might tire
her, but to be stretched out under a blanket like a corpse
was a hundred times worse. Life seemed like a chain of
brilliant reflections on water, unrelated perhaps to the mo-

tion of the water itself but completely absorbing in their color and shine. Might she kill herself with her love of things? Were the forces of life and death identical? And would the thrill of rising on a fine day be the violence that ruptured the vessels of her heart? The need to move, to talk, to make friends and enemies, to involve herself was irresistible, and she struggled to get to her feet, but her lameness, her heaviness, the age of her body and the shape of the deck chair made this impossible. She was stuck. She grasped the armrests and struggled to raise herself, but she fell back helplessly. Again she struggled to get up. She fell back again. There was a sudden sharp pain in her heart, and her face was flushed. Then she thought that she would die in another few minutes—die on her first day at sea, be sewn into an American flag and dropped overboard, her soul descending into Hell.

But why should she go to Hell? She knew well enough. It was because she had been all her life a food thief. As a child, she had waited and watched until the kitchen was empty and had then opened the massive icebox doors, grabbed a drumstick off the cold chicken and dipped her fingers into the hard sauce. Left alone in the house, she had climbed to the top pantry shelf on an arrangement of chairs and stools and eaten all the lump sugar in the silver bowl. She had stolen candy from the highboy, where it was saved for Sunday. She had, when the cook's back was turned, ripped a piece of skin off the Thanksgiving turkey before grace was said. She had stolen cold roast potatoes, doughnuts set out to cool, beef bones, lobster claws and wedges of pie. Her vice had not been cured by her maturity, and when, as a young woman, she invited the altar guild to tea, she ate half the sandwiches before they arrived. Even as an old woman leaning on a stick, she had gone down to the pantry in the middle of the night and stuffed herself with cheese and apples. Now the time had come to answer for her gluttony. She turned desperately to the man in the deck chair on her left. "I beg your pardon," she said, "but I wonder if . . ." He seemed to be asleep. The deck chair on her right was empty. She shut her eyes and called on the angels. A second later, the moment after her prayers had gone up, a young officer stopped to wish her good morning and to extend an invitation from the captain to join him on the bridge. He pulled her out of her chair.

On the bridge she shot the sun with a hand sextant and reminisced. "When I was nine years old, my Uncle Lorenzo bought me a twelve-foot sloop," she said, "and for the next three years there wasn't a fisherman at Travertine I couldn't outsail." The captain asked her for cocktails. At lunch the steward seated her with a twelve-year-old Italian boy who spoke no English. They got along by smiling at one another and making signs. In the afternoon she played cards until it was time to go down and get ready for the captain's cocktail party. She went to her stateroom and took out of her suitcase a rusty curling iron that had served her faithfully for thirty-five years or more. She plugged this into an outlet in the bathroom. All the lights in the cabin went off, and she yanked out the plug.

A moment later, there were sounds of running in the corridors, and people called confusedly to one another in Italian and English. She hid her curling iron in the bottom of her suitcase and drank a glass of port. She was an honest woman, but she was too stunned, at the moment, to confess to the captain that she had blown a fuse.

She seemed to have done much more. Opening the door to her stateroom, she found the corridor dark. A steward ran by, carrying a lamp. She closed the door again and looked out of her porthole. Slowly, slowly, the ship was losing way. The high white crest at the bow slacked off.

In the corridors and on the decks there were more calls and sounds of running. Honora sat miserably on the edge of her berth, having, through her own clumsiness, her own stupidity, halted this great ship in its passage across the sea. What would they do next? Take to the boats and row to some deserted island, rationing their biscuits and water? It was all her fault. The children would suffer. She would give them her water ration and share her biscuits, but she did not think she had the strength to confess. They might put her in the brig or drop her overboard.

The sea was calm. The ship drifted with the swell, and had begun to roll a little. The voices of men, women and children echoed off the corridors and over the water. "It's the generators," she heard someone say. "Both generators have blown." She began to cry.

She dried her tears and stood by the porthole, watching the sunset. She could hear the orchestra playing in the ballroom, and she wondered if people were dancing in the dark. Way below her, in the crew's quarters, someone had put out a fishing line. They must be fishing for cod. She wished she had a line herself, but she didn't dare ask for one, because they might then discover that she had stopped the ship.

A few minutes before dark, all the lights went on, there was a cheer from the deck, and the ship took up its course. Honora watched the white crest at the bow form and rise as they headed once more for Europe. She didn't dare go up to the dining room, and made a supper of Saltines and port wine. Later she took a turn around the decks, and the young man in the pin-striped suit asked if he could join her. She was happy to have his company and the support of his arm. He said that he was traveling to get away from things, and she guessed that he was a successful young businessman who wanted, quite naturally, to see the world before he settled down with a wife and children. She wished, fleetingly, that she had a daughter he could marry. Then she could find him a nice position in St. Botolphs, and they could live in one of the new houses in the east end of the village and come and visit her, with their children, on Sundays. When she tired, she was quite lame. He helped her down to her cabin and said good night. He had excellent manners.

She looked for him in the dining room the next day, and she wondered if he was traveling in some other class, or belonged to the fast set that didn't come down for lunch but instead ate sandwiches in the bar. He joined her on deck at dusk that night, when she was waiting for the dinner chimes to ring.

"I don't see you in the dining room," she said.

"I spend most of my time in my cabin," he said.

"But you shouldn't be so unsociable," she said. "You ought to make friends—an attractive young man like you."

"I don't think you'd like me," he said, "if you knew the truth."

"Well, I don't know what you're talking about," she said. "If you're a member of the working class or something like that, it wouldn't make any difference to me. I went up to Jaffrey last summer for a rest, you know, and I met this very nice lady and befriended her, and she said the same thing to me. 'I don't think you'd like me,' she said, 'if you knew who I was.' So then I asked her who she was, and she said she was a cook. Well, she was a very nice woman, and I continued to play cards with her, and it didn't make any difference to me that she was a cook. I'm not stuck-up. Mr. Haworth, the ashman, is one of my best friends, and often comes into the house for a cup of tea."

"I'm a stowaway," the young man said.

She took a deep breath of sea air. The news was a blow. Oh, why should life appear to be a series of mysteries? She had imagined him to be prosperous and successful, and he was merely a lawless outcast. "Where do you sleep?" she asked. "Where do you eat?"

"I sleep in the heads," he said. "I haven't eaten for two days."

"But you must eat."

"I know," he said wistfully. "I know. You see, what I thought I might do is to confide in someone—a passenger —and then, if they were friendly, they could order dinner in their stateroom and I could share it."

For a second she was wary. He seemed importunate. He had moved too swiftly. Then his stomach gave a loud rumble, and the thought of the hunger pangs he must be suffering annihilated her suspicions. "What's your name?" she asked.

"Gus."

"Well, I'm in Cabin 12 on B Deck," she said. "You come down there in a few minutes, and I'll see that you get some supper."

When she got to her cabin, she rang for the waiter and ordered a six-course meal. The young man arrived and hid in the bathroom. When the table was set with covered dishes, he came out of hiding, and it did her heart good to see him eat.

When he had finished his dinner, he took out a package of cigarettes and offered it to her as if she was not an old lady but a dear friend and companion. She wondered if, under the beneficial influence of the sea air, her appearance had grown more youthful. She accepted a cigarette and blew out four matches trying to get it lighted. When it was finally ignited, the smoke cut her throat like a rusty razor. She had a paroxysm of coughing, and scattered embers down the front of her dress. He did not seem to notice this loss of dignity—he was telling her the story of his life —and she held the cigarette elegantly between her fingers until the fire died. Smoking a cigarette definitely made her feel younger. He was married, he told her. He had two little children—Heidi and Peter—but his wife ran away with a sailor and took the children to Canada. He didn't know where they were. He worked as a file clerk for an insurance office and led a life that was so lonely and empty that he had boarded the ship one day during his lunch hour and stayed aboard when she sailed. What was there to lose? He would at least see a little of the world, even if he was sent home in the brig. "I miss the kiddies," he said. "That's the main thing. You know what I did last Christmas? I bought one of those little trees you get in the five-and-ten, and I decorated it, in this room where I live, and I bought presents for the kiddies, and then on Christmas Day I just pretended that they came to see me. Of course, it was all make-believe, but I opened the presents and everything, just as if they were there."

After dinner Honora taught him to play backgammon. He picked up the game very quickly, she thought, and was a remarkably intelligent young man. It seemed a great shame to her that he should waste his youth and his intelligence in loneliness, sorrow and boredom. He was not handsome; his face was too changeable, and his grin was a little foolish. But he was really just a boy, she thought, and with experience and kindness his face would change. They played backgammon until eleven, and, to tell the truth, she had not felt so happy, or at least at ease, since she had begun her travels. When they said good night, he lingered at the door, and seemed, with his inward and foolish—or was it sly?—grin, to be implying that she might let him sleep in the spare berth in her cabin. Enough was enough, and she closed the door in his face.

He did not appear the next day, and she wondered where in the great ship he was hidden, hungry and alone. The bouillon and sandwiches that were passed on the promenade deck only reminded her of the cruel inequalities of life, and she did not enjoy her lunch. She spent most of the afternoon in her cabin, in case he should need her help. Just before the dinner chimes rang, there was a soft knock at the door, and he came in. After dinner she got out the backgammon board, but he seemed restless, and she won every game. She pointed out that he needed a haircut, and when he said that he didn't have any money, she gave him five dollars. He said good night at ten, and she invited him to return the next evening for his dinner.

He didn't come. When the dinner chimes rang at seven, she called a waiter and ordered dinner so that it would be ready for him, but he didn't come. She was sure then that he had been caught and thrown into the brig, and she thought of going to the captain, as the young man's advocate, and explaining the loneliness and the emptiness of his life. She decided, however, not to act until morning, and she went to bed. In the morning, as she was admiring the ocean, she saw him on the main deck, laughing and talking with Mrs. Sheffield.

She was indignant. She was jealous, although she tried to rationalize this weakening of her position as a sensible fear that if he confided in Mrs. Sheffield, Mrs. Sheffield would betray him. He saw Honora, clearly enough—he waved to her—but he went on talking gaily with Mrs. Sheffield. Honora was angry. She even seemed to be in pain, stripped as she was of that sense of ease and comfort she had enjoyed while they played backgammon in her cabin, stripped of a sense of her unique usefulness, her indispensability. She went around the bow to the leeward side of the ship, to admire the waves from there. She noticed that, with her feelings unsettled, the massive, agate-colored seas, veined with white, seemed mightier. She heard footsteps on the deck and wondered was it he? Had he come at last, to apologize for talking with Mrs. Sheffield and to thank her for her generosity? She was sure of one thing: Mrs. Sheffield wouldn't take a stowaway into her cabin and give him supper. The footsteps passed, and so did some others, but the intenseness of her anticipation did not. Would he never come? Then someone stopped at her back and said, "Good morning, darling."

"Don't call me 'darling,' " she said, turning around.

"But you are 'darling' to me."

"You haven't got your hair cut."

"I lost your money on the horse races."

"Where were you last night?"

"A nice man in the bar treated me to sandwiches and drinks."

"What were you telling Mrs. Sheffield?"

"I wasn't telling her anything. She was telling me about her orlon wardrobe, but she's asked me to have drinks with them before lunch."

"Very well, then, they can give you lunch."

"But they don't know I'm a stowaway, darling. You're the only one who knows. I wouldn't trust anyone else."

"Well, if you want some lunch," she said, "I might be in my cabin at noon."

"You'd better make it half-past one or two. I don't know when I'll get away from the Sheffields," he said, and walked off.

At half-past twelve she went down to her cabin to wait for him—for, like many of the old, she traveled with her clocks fifteen or twenty minutes fast, and was a half-hour early for all her engagements, sitting empty-handed in waiting rooms and lobbies and corridors, feeling quite clearly that her time was running out. He blew in a little after two, and he refused at first to hide in the bathroom. "If you want me to go to the captain and tell him there's a stowaway aboard, I'll do it," she said. "If that's what you want, I'll do it. There's no point in having the news percolate up to him from the kitchens, and it will if the waiter sees you here." In the end, he hid in the bathroom and she ordered lunch. After lunch he stretched out on the sofa and fell asleep. She sat in a chair, watching him, tapping her foot on the carpet and drumming her nails on the arm of her chair. He snored. He muttered in his sleep.

She saw then that he was not young. His face was lined and sallow; there was gray in his hair. She saw that his youthfulness was a ruse, an imposture calculated to appeal to some old fool like herself, although she was doubtless not the only dupe. Asleep, he looked aged, sinful and cunning, and she felt that his story of the two children and the lonely Christmas had been a lie. There was no innocence in him beyond the naïveness with which he would count upon preying on the lonely. He seemed a fraud, a shabby fraud, and yet she could not inform on him; she could not even bring herself to wake him. He slept until four, woke, pierced all of her skepticism with one of his most youthful and engaging grins, said that he was late and went out. The next time she saw him, it was three in the morning and he was taking her money belt out from under the carpet.

He had hit something, made some noise that waked her. She was terrified—not by him but by the possibilities of evil in the world; by the fear that her sense of reality, her saneness, was no more inviolable than the doors and windows that sheltered her. She was too angry to be afraid of him.

She had turned on the light switch nearest to the bed. This lit a single bulb in the ceiling, a feeble and sorry light that made this scene of robbery and treachery in the darkest hour and the vastness of the ocean seem like a nausea fantasy. He turned on her his sliest grin, his look of a long-lost loving son. "I'm sorry I woke you up, darling," he said.

"You put that money back."

"Now, now, darling," he said.

"You put that money back this instant."

"Now, now, darling, don't get excited."

"That's my money," she said, "and you put it back where you found it." She pulled a wrapper over her shoulders and swung her feet onto the floor.

"Now, listen, darling," he said, "stay where you are. I don't want to hurt you."

"Oh, you don't, do you?" she said, and she picked up a brass lamp and struck him full on the skull.

His eyes rolled upward and his smile faded. He weaved to the left and the right and then fell in a heap, striking his head on the arm of a chair. She seized the money belt and then spoke to him. She shook him by the shoulders. She felt his pulse. He seemed to have none. "He's dead," she said to herself. She didn't know his last name, and since she didn't believe what he had told her about himself, she knew nothing about the man she had killed. His name wasn't on the passenger list, he had no legitimacy. Even the part he played in her life had been an imposture. If she shoved his body out the porthole into the sea, who would ever know? But this was the wrong thing to do. The right thing was to get the doctor, whatever the consequences, and she went into the bathroom and dressed hastily. Then she stepped into the deserted corridor. The purser's and doctor's offices were locked and dark. She climbed a flight of stairs to the main deck, but the ballroom and the bar and the lounges were all empty. An old man in his pajamas stepped out of the darkness and came toward her. "I can't sleep either, sister," he said. "Gin knits up the raveled sleeve of care. You know how old I am? I'm seven days younger than Herbert Hoover and one hundred and five days older than Winston Churchill. I don't like young people. They make too much noise. I have three grand-children and I can stand them for ten minutes. Not a second more. My daughter married a prince. Last year I gave them fifteen thousand. This year he must have twenty-five. It's the way he asks me for the money that burns me up. 'It is very painful for me to ask you for twenty-five thousand,' he says. 'It is very painful and humiliating.' My little grandchildren can't speak English. They call me Nonno. . . . Take a load off your feet, sister. Sit down and talk with me and help to pass the time."

"I'm looking for the doctor," Honora said.

"I have an unfortunate habit of quoting Shakespeare," the old man said, "but I will spare you. I know a lot of Milton, too. Also Gray's 'Elegy,' and Arnold's 'The Scholar Gypsy.' How far away those streams and meadows seem! My conscience is uneasy. I've killed a man."

"You did?" Honora asked.

"Yes. I had a fuel-oil business in Albany. That's my home. I did a gross business of over two million a year. Fuel, oil and maintenance. One night a man called and said his burner was making a funny noise. I told him noth-ing could be done until morning. I could have got him a serviceman, or I could have gone there myself, but I was drinking with friends, and why should I go out on a cold night? Half an hour later, the house burned down, cause undetermined. . . . It was a man, his wife and three little children. Five coffins in all. I often think about them."

Honora remembered then that she had left her cabin door open and that the corpse could be seen by anyone who passed. "Sit down. Sit down, sister," the old man said, but she waved him away and limped back down the stairs. Her cabin door stood open, but the corpse was gone. What had happened? Had someone come and disposed of the body? Were they now searching the ship for her? She listened, but there was no sound of footsteps—nothing but the titanic, respiratory noise of the sea, and somewhere a door banging as the ship heeled a little. She closed and locked her door and poured herself some port. If they were going to come and get her, she wanted to be fully dressed, and anyhow she couldn't sleep.

She stayed in her cabin until noon, when her telephone rang and the purser asked if she would come to his office. He only wanted to know if she wouldn't like to have her bags shipped from Naples to Rome. Having prepared herself for an entirely different set of questions and answers, she seemed very absent-minded. But what had happened? Did she have some accomplice aboard who had pushed the stowaway's body out the porthole? Almost everyone smiled at her, but how much did they know? Had he picked himself up off the floor of her cabin, and was he now nursing his wounds somewhere? The enormousness of the ship and its thousands of doors discouraged her from trying to find him. She looked for him in the bar and the ballroom, and she investigated the broom closet at the end of her corridor. Passing an open cabin door, she thought she heard him laughing, but when she stopped, the laughter stopped, and someone shut the door. She examined the lifeboats—a traditional sanctuary, she knew, for stowaways—but all the lifeboat covers were fast. She would have felt less miserable if she had had some familiar work to do, such as raking and burning leaves, and she even thought of asking the stewardess if she couldn't sweep the corridor, but she perceived the impropriety of this.

She did not see the stowaway again until the day they were to dock in Naples. The sky and the sea were gray.

The air was moist and dispiritingly humid. It was one of those timeless days, she thought, so unlike the stunning best of spring and autumn—one of those gloomy days of which the year, after all, is forged. He came swinging down the deck late in the afternoon with a woman on his arm. The woman was not young, and she had a bad complexion, but they were looking into one another's eyes like lovers and laughing. As he passed Honora, he spoke to her. "Excuse me," he said.

This final cheapness infuriated her. She went down to her cabin. Everything was packed—her book and her mending—and she had nothing to distract her. What she then did is hard to explain. She was not an absent-minded or a thoughtless woman, but she had been raised in gaslight and candlelight and had never made her peace with electrical appliances or other kinds of domestic machinery. They seemed to her mysterious and at times capricious, and because she came at them hastily and in total ignorance they often broke, backfired or exploded in her face. She could never imagine that she was to blame, and felt instead that an obscure veil hung between her and the world of machinery. This indifference to engines, along with her impetuousness and her anger at the stowaway, may have accounted for what she then did. She looked at herself in the mirror, found her appearance lacking, took her old curling iron out of the bottom of the suitcase, and plugged it in again.

They drifted into the Bay of Naples without a light showing. Powerless, helmless, they floated stern foremost on the ebb tide. Two tugs came out from the port to tow them in, and a portable generator on the dock was connected to the ship's lines so that there was light enough to disembark. Honora was one of the first to go ashore. The noise of Neapolitan voices sounded to her like a wilderness, and, stepping onto the Old World, she felt in her bones the thrill of that voyage her forefathers had made how many hundreds of years ago, coming forth upon another continent to found a new nation.

PART
TWO

Transgressus
of
science

CHAPTER XVIII

The cast of characters in the Nuclear Revolution changed so swiftly that Dr. Cameron has long since been forgotten excepting for a few disorders he incited. A crucifix hung on the wall behind his desk. The figure of Christ was silver or leaden and it was the kind of thing tourists pick up in the back streets of Rome and carry to the Vatican for a Papal blessing. It had no value or beauty and its only usefulness was to state that the doctor was a convert, a sinful one perforce, since he was known to believe in neither the divine nor scientific ecology of nature, but the priest who had given him instruction had stressed the mercifulness of Our Lord and the old man believed passionately that there was some blessedness in the nature of things although his transgressions were repeated and spectacular. He believed, and said so publicly, that matrimony was not an adequate means of genetic selection. He had administered, for the Air Force, some experiments in the manipulation of chromosomal structures for the production of what we call courage. He believed in sperm banks and, for the immediate future, a clear command of the chemistry of personality. He loosely embraced his belief in blessedness, his science and his own unquiet nature by thinking of himself as a frontiersman, approaching a future in which he would be obsolete. He was a gourmet and knew the foolishness of stuffing himself with snails, beef filets, sauces and wines but he classed his interest in good food as a mark of obsolescence. He similarly classified as obsolete his own sexual drives—that nagging inquietude in his middle. His wife had been dead for twenty years and he had kept a series of mistresses and housekeepers, but the older and more pow-

erful he grew, the more discretion was demanded of him
and he had not been safely able to enjoy a relationship
with anyone in the United States.

He was one of those blameless old men who had found
that lasciviousness was his best means of clinging to life. In
the act of love his heart sent up a percussive beating like a
gallows drum in the street, but lewdness was his best sense
of forgetfulness, his best way of grappling with the unhappy
facts of time. With age his desires had grown more irresistible as his fear of death and corruption mounted. Once,
lying in bed with Luciana, his mistress, a fly had come in
at the window and buzzed around her white shoulders.
The fly had, to his old man's mind, seemed like a singular
reminder of corruption and he had got out of bed, bare as
a jay bird, and raced and jumped around the room with a
rolled-up copy of *La Corriere della Sera* trying, unsuccess-
fully, to kill the pest but when he got back to bed there
was the fly, still buzzing around her breasts.

It was in the arms of his mistress that he felt the chill of
death go off his bones; it was in the arms of his mistress
that he felt himself invincible. She lived in Rome and he
met her there about once a month. There was a legitimate
side to these trips—the Vatican wanted a missile—and a
side more clandestine than his erotic sport. It was in Rome
that he met with those sheiks and maharajas who wanted
a rocket of their own. The commands from one part of his
body to another would begin with a ticklish sensation that
in a day or two, depending upon how hard he drove himself, would become irresistible. Then he would take a jet to
Italy and return a few days later in a most relaxed and
magnanimous frame of mind. Thus he flew one afternoon
from Talifer to New York and spent the night at the Plaza.
His need for Luciana mounted hour by hour like some
simple impulse of hunger and lying in his hotel bed he
granted himself the privilege of putting her together—lips,
breasts, arms and legs. Oh, the wind and the rain and to
hold in one's arms a willing love! He was suffering, as he
would put it, from a common inflammation.

In the morning it was foggy and leaving the hotel he listened for the sound of planes to discover if the airport was
closed but it was impossible to hear anything above the

clash of traffic. He took a taxi to Idlewild and waited in turn to pick up his ticket. Some mistake had been made and he was booked on a tourist flight. "I would like this changed to first class," he said.

"I'm sorry, sir," the girl said, "but there is no first-class space." She did not look at him and went on filing papers.

"I have made thirty-three flights on this line in the last year," the doctor said, "and I think I am entitled to a little preferential treatment."

"We do not give preferential treatment," the girl said. "It is against the law." She had obviously never seen him on television and was unimpressed by the bulk of his eyebrows.

"Now you listen to me, young lady . . ." His voice sawed, soared, made enemies for him everywhere within earshot. "I am Dr. Lemuel Cameron. I am traveling on government business and if I should report your attitude to your superiors—"

"I am very sorry, sir," she said, "but things are backed up because of the fog. The only available first-class space we have is for the evening flight next Thursday if you wish to wait."

Her imperviousness to his importance, her indifference or overt dislike flustered him and he remembered all the others who had looked at him with skepticism or even antagonism as if his whole brilliant career had been a fatuous self-delusion. It was especially her kind, the girls in uniform with overseas caps, their hair dyed, their skirts tight, who seemed as remote to him as a generation of leaves. Where did they go when the flight was over, the office shut? They seemed to bang down a shutter between himself and them, they seemed made of different ingredients than the men and women of his day, they seemed supremely indifferent to his appearance of wisdom and authority.

"I must explain," he said, speaking softly, "that I have a top priority and that I can demand a seat if necessary."

"Your flight is loading at gate eight," she said. "If you wish to wait until Thursday evening I can get you first-class space."

He went down a long corridor to where a shabby-looking

huddle of men and women were waiting to board the plane. They were mostly Italians, mostly working class, waiters and maids going home for a month to see Mamma and show off their ready-made clothes. He liked to stretch his legs in first class, sip his first-class wine and admire the caves of heaven from a first-class port as they traveled swiftly toward Rome but the tourist flight was very different from what he was accustomed to and reminded him of the early days of aviation. When he found his seat he beckoned to the hostess, another impermeable young woman with a brilliant smile, a tight skirt and hair dyed silver and gold. "I've been promised first-class space if there's a cancellation," he said, partly to acquaint her with the facts, partly to make clear to this motley group around him that he was not one of them. "I'm very sorry, sir," she said with a smile that was dazzling in its insincerity, "but there is no first-class space on this flight." Then she kindly ushered into the seats beside him a sickly-looking Italian boy and his mother, who had a baby in her arms. He smiled at them fleetingly and asked if they were going to Rome. "Sí," the woman said wearily, "ma non speaka the English." As soon as they were seated she took a bottle of medicine out of a brown paper bag and offered it to her son. The boy didn't want the medicine. He put his hands over his mouth and turned toward Cameron. *"Si deve, si deve,"* the mother said. *"No, mamma, no, mamma,"* the boy pleaded but she forced him to drink. A little of the medicine spilled onto his clothing and it had a vile and sulphurous smell. The stewardess closed the cabin door and the pilot announced in Italian and then in English that the ceiling was zero and that they had not received their clearance but that it was expected that the fog, the *nebbia,* would lift.

Cameron's legs were cramped and to lift himself out of these unpleasant surroundings he thought about Luciana. He went over her points, her features, as if he were describing them to an acquaintance. He explained the fact that while she was Tuscan she was not heavy, not even in the buttocks, and that if it hadn't been for her walk, that marvelous Roman walk, she could have passed for a Parisienne. She was fine, he pointed out to his acquaintance. She had a fineness that you seldom find in Italian beauties; fine wrists, fine hands, slim, round arms. Oh, the wind and the rain and to hold in one's arms a willing love! That span of blood that leaps from the groin to the brain had made its passage and he was again committed to a painful inflammation. He recalled, in some detail, a piece of erotic slapstick that he had performed on his last visit. His inflammation mounted and mounting with it was a curb of self-disgust, a stubborn love of decency that kept abreast of his unruly flesh. That his body was a fool was well known to him; that it should demand instantaneous requital in a public airplane cabin with his nearest companions a sickly boy and his mother was a measure of its foolishness, but his conscience, clutching at its vision of decency, seemed even more foolish. Then the little boy on his left turned and vomited the medicine his mother had made him drink. The vomit had a bitter smell, bitter as flower water.

Cameron was shocked out of his venereal reverie by this ugly fact of life. The boy's sickness instantly cooled the lewdness of his thinking. He helped the stewardess wipe up the mess with paper towels and courteously accepted the apologies of the mother. He was himself again, judicious, commanding, enlightened. Then the pilot announced in two languages that they were taking the plane into a hangar to wait for their clearance. The ceiling was still zero but they expected a change in the wind and a clearing within the hour.

They drove into a hangar, where there was nothing to watch. A few of the passengers stretched their legs in the aisle. No one complained, except laughingly, and most of them spoke in Italian. Cameron closed his eyes and tried to rest but Luciana stepped trippingly into his reveries. He urged her to go, to leave him in peace, but she only laughed and undid her clothing. He opened his eyes to clear his head with a view of the world. The baby was crying. The stewardess brought the baby a bottle and the captain announced that the fog was general. In a few minutes they would be transported by bus to a New York hotel and would wait for their clearance there. They would be served a courtesy meal by the airline and the flight was scheduled for four that afternoon.

The doctor groaned. Why couldn't they be put up at the International Hotel? he asked the stewardess. She explained that all planes were grounded and the airport hotels were full. A bus drove into the hangar and they boarded it with perfect passivity and returned to the city, where they were received in what was very definitely a third-class hotel. It was nearly noon and Cameron went into the bar and ordered a drink and lunch. "Are you with flight seven?" the waitress asked. He said that he was. "Well, I'm very sorry," she said, "but passengers for flight seven have to eat in the dining room where they serve the *plat du jour*."

"I will pay for my lunch," Cameron said. "And please bring me a drink."

"The courtesy of cocktails is not extended to tourist passengers," the waitress said.

"I will pay for my drink and I will pay for my lunch," Cameron said.

"That won't be necessary," the waitress said, "if you go into the other dining room."

"Does it look to you as if I couldn't pay for my lunch?" Cameron asked.

"I am just trying to explain to you," the waitress said, "that the airline is responsible for your meals."

"I understand," said Cameron. "Now please bring me what I have ordered."

After lunch he watched a television play in his hotel room and rang for a bottle of whisky at four. At six the airline called to say that the flight was scheduled for midnight and that they would board the bus in front of the hotel at eight o'clock. He ate some supper in a restaurant around the corner and joined the other passengers, whom he had begun to detest. They boarded the plane at half-past eleven and were airborne on schedule but the plane was old and noisy and flew so low that he could clearly see the lights of Nantucket when they passed the island. He had his whisky bottle with him and he sipped at this until he fell asleep to suffer an excruciating dream about Luciana. When he woke it was dawn and they were coming in for a landing but it was not Rome; it was Shannon, where they made an unscheduled stop for motor repairs. He cabled Luciana from Shannon but it was five before they took off again and they didn't reach Rome until a little after dawn the next day.

The airport bar and restaurant were shut. He telephoned Luciana. She was asleep, of course, and cross at being waked. She had not received his cable. She could not see him until evening. She would meet him at Quinterella's at eight. He pleaded with her to let him see her sooner— to let him come to her then. "Please, my darling, please," he groaned. She broke the connection. He took a cab into Rome and got a room at the Eden. It was still early in the morning and the people on the streets were dressed for work and hurrying, with that international sameness of people hurrying to work on a hot morning anywhere. He took a shower and lay down on his bed to rest, yearning for her and cursing her but his anger did nothing to palliate his need and the crudeness of his thinking seemed like one of the realities of hell. Oh, the wind and the rain and to hold in one's arms a willing love!

There was the day to kill. He had never seen the Sistine Chapel or any of the other sights of the city and he thought he could do that. It might clear his head. He dressed and went out onto the street looking for one of those famous museums or churches about which one heard so much. Presently he came to a square where there were three churches that looked old. The doors of the first and the second were locked but the third was open and he stepped into a dark place that smelled heavily of spices. There were four women in a front pew and a priest in soiled lace was celebrating mass. He looked around him, anxious to appreciate the art treasures, but there seemed to be a roof leak above the chapel on his right and while he guessed that the painting there must be valuable and beautiful it was cracked and stained with water like the wall of any furnished room. The next chapel was decorated with naked men blowing on trumpets and the next was so dark that he could see nothing. There was a sign in English saying that if you put ten lire in the slot the lights would go on and he did this, revealing a large and bloody picture of a man in the death agonies of being crucified upside down. He did not ever like to be reminded of the susceptibilities of his flesh to pain and he quickly left the church for the smashing light and heat of the square. There was a café with an awning and he sat there and drank a *campari*. A young woman, crossing the street, reminded him of Luciana, but even if she was a tart it was Luciana and not her he wanted. Luciana was a tart but she was his tart and somewhere in the crudeness of his drives was a touching strain of romance. Luciana, he thought, was the kind of woman who could make the simple act of stepping into her pumps seem as if she had slammed a door on time.

Oh, the wind and the rain and to hold in one's arms a willing love! Why should life seem so pitilessly to harry him, why should the only reality seem to be obscene? He thought of the quantum theory, of Mittledorf's Constant, of the discovery of helium in the tetrasphere, but they had no bearing on his sorrow. Are we all unmercifully imbedded in time, insensate, purblind, vain, cold to the appeals of love and reason and stripped of our gifts for reflection and self-assessment? Had the time come for him, and was his only reminder of reasonableness, of the stalwart he had been, a smell of vomit? He had seen brilliant colleagues orbit off into impermeable foolishness and vanity, claiming discoveries they had not discovered, discarding useful men for sycophants, running for Congress, circulating petitions and uncovering international and imaginary networks of enemies. He was no less interested in cleanliness and decency than he had ever been, but he seemed less well equipped to honor these interests. His thinking had the disgusting crudeness of pornography. He seemed to see some image of himself, separate and distant like a figure in a movie, forlorn and unredeemable, going about some self-destructive business in the rainy back streets of a strange city. Where was his goodness, his excellence, his common sense? I used to be a good man, he thought piteously. He shut his eyes in pain and in that movie that played interminably across the fine skin of his eyelids he saw himself stumbling over wet cobblestones under old-fashioned street lamps, falling, falling, falling from usefulness into foolishness, from high spirits into crudeness. Then he was tormented by that cretinous and sordid cylinder in the head or mind on which are inscribed old hymns and dance tunes, the musical junkyard, that territory where campfire songs, singing commercials, marches and fox trots gather and fester in their idiotic repetitiousness and appear at will, their puerile verses and their vulgar melodies in a state of perfect preservation. "Got those racetrack blues," sang this chamber of his mind. It was a tune he had heard forty years ago on a crank-up phonograph and yet he could not stop the singing:

> Got those racetrack blues,
> I'm feelin' blue all the time.
> Got those racetrack blues,
> With all my dough on the line.

He left the café and started back to the Eden but his mind went on caroling:

> But the track is muddy, and I don't mean maybe,
> And I'll never get the money to buy shoes for baby.

He climbed up the Via Sistina and the song went on:

> I've got those racetrack blues,
> I'm feelin' blue all the time. . . .

A young man was waiting for him in the lobby; one of those elegantly barbered youths who hang around the Pincio. He introduced himself as Luciana's brother and said she must pay her dressmaker for the costume she would wear that evening. He took an envelope from his pocket and presented Cameron with a note in Luciana's hand and a bill for a hundred thousand lire. Cameron returned it to the stranger and said he would pay the bill that evening. "Shesa no comea if you don'ta paya," the youth said. "Tell her to call me," Cameron said. He took the elevator up and the telephone was ringing when he entered his room. She was herself. He could imagine her twisting the telephone cord in her fingers. "You paya the bill," she said, "or I no see you. You givea him the money." For a second he thought of breaking the connection, breaking off the affair, but the noise of Roman traffic in the Roman streets reminded him of how far he was from home, that in fact he had no home, no friends, and that an ocean lay between him and his usefulness. He had come too far, he had come too far. Conduct and time were linear and serial; one was hurled through life with the bitch of remorse nipping at one's hocks. No power of reason or justice or virtue could bring him to his senses.

There was a soft knock on the door and her soft-eyed agent stepped into the room. Cameron made him wait but the noises outside his window spelled his doom. After an hour with her he would be his high-minded and magnanimous self again but in order to achieve this he must be swindled, humiliated and gulled. She had jockeyed him into a position of helplessness. "All right," he said, and they walked through the heat down to the Banco di Santo Spirito, where he cashed a draft for three hundred thousand lire and gave the boy his money. Then, and it was the only kind of disdain or self-expression left to him, he walked past the youth and out of the bank.

The day passed miserably. He took a shower at seven and went out to the Via Veneto for a *campari*. She was always late, he had never known a woman who wasn't, and it would probably be nine before she got to Quinterella's. She might, for once, play it safe; she might guess that his patience was not inexhaustible and that he had a mind of his own. But had he? If she asked him to drop to his knees and bark like a dog would he dare to refuse? He stayed at the café until eight and then started down the hill. His feelings were heavy—lustful and melancholy—and it dismayed him that in thinking of Luciana his mind could display such foulness. He started across the Piazza del Popolo. Somewhere a church bell rang. The discordant iron bells of Rome had always surprised him, carrying on, with their contemporaries the fountains, a losing battle against the noise of traffic. Then from the hills there was a peal of thunder. The explosion seemed to ring back from the excitements of his youth, and what a strong, fine youth he had been. A second later the air of Rome was filled with a dense, gray rain. It seemed to fall with a wicked vehemence.

He was stuck by the fountain in the middle of the square. By the time there was a halt in the traffic he was as wet as if he had plunged into the fountain; but he ran across the square to the shelter of a church porch. The porch was crowded with Romans and he had to push to find a place among them. There was no delicacy or shyness in the way in which the crowd jostled one another but he held himself with as much probity as he could muster. When the rain let up, and it let up as suddenly as it had fallen, he stepped back into the *piazza* and looked down at his clothes. His shirt clung to his skin, his tie had lost its shape, there was no press left in his pants and when he pulled the folds of his jacket away from his shoulders he saw that his pocket had been picked.

This was a blow. It stopped him short. What he felt was too violent for indignation. It was the enormous sadness of having lost some lights or vitals—six inches of intestine, a gall bladder or a group of back teeth—the melancholy and enfeebling shock of surgery. His wallet could be replaced, there was plenty of money where that had come from, but for a moment the loss seemed stinging and irreplaceable and he felt guilty. Neither absent-mindedness or drunkenness nor any other fault of his had helped the thief and yet he felt gulled and foolish, an old idiot who had come into a time of life when he would begin to mislay his possessions, lose his tickets and money and become a burden to the world. Somewhere a bell struck the half-hour and the crude iron note reminded him of Luciana, of the crudeness and fitness of the bounding act of love. The thought of her overtook his feeling of loss, he straightened up in spite of his wet clothing. Oh, the wind and the rain and to hold in one's arms a willing love! He stepped into a large pile of dog manure.

It took him nearly five minutes to scrape this off his shoe and like the boy's sickness on the plane it had a tonic effect on his feelings; it aroused some momentary misgivings. It was the sum of obstacles—the delayed flight, the sick child, the thunderstorm—that might in the end cure his ardor. But the restaurant was only a step away and in a few minutes he would be with his swan, his swan who would lead him off to a paradise all laced with green and gold. He strode up to the door of the restaurant, but it was locked. Why were the windows dark? Why did the place seem abandoned? Then on the door he saw a photograph

of Enrico Quinterella framed in a boxwood wreath with a
bow, who, that very afternoon somewhere in Rome, surrounded by his wife and children had received extreme
unction and departed this life.

Death had shut up the place; put out the light. Signore
Quinterella was dead. Then he felt an exalting surge of
deliverance, a return to himself; his mind seemed to fill
with the astringency of all decent things. Luciana was a
slut, her bed a pit and he was free to live sensibly, free
to judge right from wrong. Here was a sense of pureness
without the force of repression and his gratitude to the
contingencies that had liberated him was pious. He walked
back to the Eden like a new man, slept deeply and felt in
the depths of sleep that he had been granted some bounty.
He took a New York plane in the morning and was back
in Talifer that afternoon, convinced that there was some
blessedness in the nature of things.

CHAPTER XIX

❧ ❧

Coverly, without having been given a clue to his usefulness,
packed and left for Atlantic City one evening with Cameron and his team. The ambiguity of his position was
embarrassing. One of the team told Coverly that Cameron
was to speak to a conference of scientists on a detonative
force that was a million times the force of terrestrial
lightning and that could be produced inexpensively. It was
all that Coverly was able to grasp. Cameron sat apart from
the others and read a paper-back which, Coverly saw, by
craning his neck, was called *Cimarron: Rose of the South
West*. It was the first time that Coverly had associated with
men of this echelon and he was naturally inquisitive but
he couldn't understand their point of view, indeed he
couldn't understand their language. They talked about

thermal runions, tolopters, strabometers, trenchions and podules. It was another language and one that seemed to him with the bleakest origins. You couldn't trace here the elisions and changes worked by a mountain range, a great river or the nearness of the sea. Coverly supposed that the palest of them could smite a mountain but they were the most unlikely people to imagine as being armed with the powers of doom-crack. They spoke of lightning in their synthetic language but with the voices of men—strained from time to time with nervousness, broken with coughing and laughter, shaded and colored a little with regional differences. One of them was an aggressive pederast and Coverly wondered if this sexual cynicism had anything to do with his attitude as a scientist. One of them wore a suit coat that bunched around his shoulders. One of them—Brunner—wore a necktie painted with a horseshoe. One of them had a nervous habit of pulling at his eyebrows and they were all heavy smokers. They were men born of women and subject to all the ravening caprices of the flesh. They could destroy a great city inexpensively, but had they made any progress in solving the clash between night and day, between the head and the groin? Were the persuasions of lust, anger and pain any less in their case? Were they spared toothaches, nagging erections and fatigue?

They checked into the Haddon Hall, where Coverly was given a room of his own. Brunner, who was friendly, suggested that Coverly might like to attend some of the open lectures and so he did. The first was by a Chinese on the legal problems of interstellar space. The Chinese spoke in French and a simultaneous translation was broadcast through transistor radios. The legal vocabulary was familiar but Coverly couldn't grasp its application to the cosmos. He could not easily apply phrases like National Sovereignty to the moon. The following lecture dealt with experiments in sending a man into space in a sack filled with fluid. The difficulty presented was that men immersed in fluid suffered a grave and sometimes incurable loss of memory. Coverly wanted to approach the scene with his best seriousness—with a complete absence of humor—but how could he square the image of a man in a sack with the small New

England village where he had been raised and where his character had been formed? It seemed, in this stage of the Nuclear Revolution, that the world around him was changing with incomprehensible velocity but if these changes were truly incomprehensible what attitude could he take, what counsel could he give his son? Had his basic apparatus for judging true and false become obsolete? Leaving the lecture hall he ran into Brunner and asked him to lunch. His motive was curiosity. Compared to Brunner's high-minded scientific probity the rhythms of his own nature seemed wayward and sentimental. Brunner's composure challenged his own disciplines and his own usefulness and he wondered if his pleasure in the unscientific landscape of the Atlantic City boardwalk was obsolete. On his right were the singing waves and on his left a generous show of that mysterious culture that springs up at the edges of the sea and that, with its overt concern with mystery—seers, palmists, fortunetellers, gambling games and tea-leaf diviners—seems like a product of the thunderous discourse between the ocean and the continent. Seers seemed to thrive in the salty air. He wondered what Brunner made of the scene. Did the smell of fried pork excite his memory or what he called his playback? Would the sighing of the waves present him with a romantic vision of the possibilities of adventure? Coverly looked at his companion but Brunner stared out so flatly, so impassively at the scene that Coverly didn't ask his question. He guessed that Brunner saw what was to be seen—brine, a boardwalk, some store fronts—and that if he went beyond the moment, which seemed unlikely, he would have seen the store fronts demolished and replaced by public playgrounds, ball fields and picnic groves. But who was wrong? The possibility that Coverly was wrong made him very uncomfortable. Brunner said that he had never eaten a lobster and so they went into an old matchboard lobster palace at a turn in the walk.

Coverly ordered a bourbon. Brunner sipped a beer and whistled loudly at the prices. He had a very large head and a heavy but not a dark beard. He must have shaved that morning, perhaps carelessly, but the outlines of his brown beard were, by noon, clearly defined. He was pale and his pallor seemed heightened by the largeness and the redness of his ears. The redness stopped abruptly at the point where his ears joined his head. The rest of him was all pallor, it was not a Levantine or a Mediterranean pallor—it was probably an inherited characteristic or the product of a bad diet—but it was, to give him credit, a virile pallor, thick-skinned and lit by those flaming ears. He had his charms, they all had, and it was Coverly's feeling that these were based on the possession of a vision of surmountable barriers, a sense of the future, a means for expressing his natural zeal for progress and change. He drank his beer as if he expected it to incapacitate him and here was another difference. With a single exception they were all temperate men. Coverly was not temperate but his intemperance was his best sense of the abundance of life.

"You live in Talifer?" Coverly asked. He knew that Brunner did.

"Yes. I have a little pad on the west side. I live alone. I was married but that was no go."

"I'm sorry," Coverly said.

"There's nothing to be sorry about. The marriage was no go. We couldn't optimize." He tackled his salad.

"You live alone?" Coverly asked.

"Yes." He spoke with his mouth full.

"How do you spend your evenings?" Coverly asked. "I mean, do you go to the theater?"

Brunner laughed kindly. "No, I don't go to the theater. Some of the team have outside interests but I can't say that I have."

"But if you don't have any outside interests what do you do in the evenings?" *science*

"I study. I sleep. Sometimes I go to a restaurant on Route 27 where you can get all the chicken you can eat for two-fifty. I'm keen on chicken and when I get my appetite dialed up I can put away a very satisfactory payload."

"You go with friends?"

"Nope," he said with dignity. "I go alone."

"Do you have any children?" Coverly asked.

"Nope. That's one of the reasons my wife and I couldn't finalize. She wanted children. I didn't. I had a bad time when I was a kid and I didn't want to put anybody else through that."

"What do you mean?"

"Well, my mother died when I was about two and Dad and Grandma brought me up. Dad was a free-lance engineer but he couldn't hold a job for long. He was a terrible alcoholic. You see, I felt more than most people, I think I felt more than most people that I had to get away. Nobody understood me. I mean, my name didn't mean anything but the name of an old drunk. I had to make my name mean something. So when this lightning thing turned up I felt better, I began to feel better. Now my name means something, at least to some people it does."

Here then was the lightning, a pure force of energy, veined when one saw it in the clouds as all the world is veined—the leaf and the wave—and here was a lonely man, familiar with blisters and indigestion, whose humble motives in inventing a detonative force that could despoil the world were the same as the child actress, the eccentric inventor, the small-town politician. "I only wanted my name to mean something." He must have been forced more than most men to include in the mystery of death the incineration of the planet. Waked by a peal of thunder he must have wondered more than most if this wasn't the end, hastened in some way by his wish to possess a name.

The waitress brought their lobsters then and Coverly ended his interrogation.

When Coverly got back to the hotel there was a note for him in Cameron's hand. He was to meet Cameron outside a conference room on the third floor at five o'clock and drive him to the airport. He guessed from this that he had been attached to Cameron's staff as a chauffeur. He spent the afternoon in the hotel swimming pool and went up to the third floor at five. The door to the conference room was locked and sealed with wire and two secret servicemen in plain clothes waited in the corridor. When the meeting ended it was announced to them by telephone and they broke the seals and unlocked the door. The scene inside was disorderly and bizarre. The doors and windows of the room had been draped, as a security precaution, with blankets. Physicists and scientists were standing on chairs and tables, removing these. The air was cloudy with smoke. It was a moment before Coverly realized that no one was speaking. It was like the close of an especially gruesome funeral. Coverly said hello to Brunner but his lunch companion didn't reply. His face was green, his mouth set in a look of bitterness and revulsion. Could the tragedy and horror of what Cameron had told them account for this silence? Were these the faces of men who had just been told the facts of the millennium? Had they been told, Coverly wondered, that the planet was uninhabitable; and if they had, what was there to cling to in this hotel corridor with its memories of call girls, honeymoon couples and old people down for a long weekend to take the sea air? Coverly looked confusedly from these pale, these obviously terrified faces down to the dark cabbage roses that bloomed on the rug. Cameron, like the others, passed Coverly without speaking and Coverly followed him obediently out to the car. Cameron said nothing on the trip to the airport nor did he say good-bye. He boarded a small Beechcraft —he was going on to Washington—and when the plane had taken off Coverly noticed that he had forgotten his briefcase.

The responsibilities attached to this simple object were frightening. It must contain the gist of what he had said that afternoon and from the faces of his audience Coverly guessed that what he had said concerned the end of the world. He decided to return to the hotel at once and unload the briefcase on one of the team. He drove back to the city with the briefcase in his lap. He asked at the desk for Brunner and was told that Brunner had checked out. So had all the others. Looking around him at the shady or at least heterogeneous faces in the lobby he wondered if any of them were foreign agents. To behave inconspicuously seemed to be his best course of action and he went into the dining room and had some dinner. He kept the briefcase on his lap. Toward the end of his dinner there was a series of percussive explosions from outside the hotel and he thought that the end had come until the waitress explained that it was a display of fireworks put on for the entertainment of a convention of gift-shop proprietors.

With the briefcase secured under his armpit he stepped

out of the hotel to see the fireworks. It seemed fitting to him that a meeting that had dealt with detonative powers should end with such a spendthrift, charming and utterly harmless display. Folding chairs had been set up on the boardwalk for the audience. The display was fired from a set of mortars on the beach. He heard the sound of a projectile dropped into a shell, followed its trajectory by a light trail of cinders as it mounted up past the evening star. There was a blast of white light—it took the sound a moment to reach them—and then there was a confusion of gold streamers, arced like stems, ending in silent balls of colored fire. All this was reflected in the windowpanes of the hotels, and the faces of the gift-shop proprietors, turned up to admire this ingenuous show, seemed excellent and simple. There was a scattering of applause, a touching show of politeness and enthusiasm, the sort of clapping one hears when the dance music ends. The black smoke could be seen clearly against the twilight, changing shapes as it drifted off to sea. Coverly sat down to enjoy himself, to hear the walls of the mortar shell ring again, to follow the trajectory of cinders, the arc of stars, the blooming colors, the sighs of hundreds and the decencies of applause. The show ended with a barrage, a gentle mockery of warfare, demonic drumming and all the thousands of hotel windows flashing white fire. The last explosion shook the boardwalk harmlessly, there was a shower of dancing-school applause and he started back for his hotel. When he entered his room he wondered if it hadn't been rifled. All the drawers were open and clothing was scattered over the chairs; but he had to measure this chaos against the fact that he was not a neat traveler. He slept with the briefcase in his arms.

In the morning Coverly, carrying the briefcase against his chest the way girls carry their schoolbooks, flew from Atlantic City to an International Airport where he waited for a plane to the west. There was, on one hand, the railroad station in St. Botolphs, with its rich aura of arrivals and departures, its smells of coal gas, floor oil and toilets, and its dark waiting room, where some force of magnification seemed brought to bear on the lives of the passengers waiting for their train to arrive; and on the other hand, this loft or palace, its glass walls open to the overcast sky, where spaciousness, efficiency and the smell of artificial leather seemed not to magnify but to diminish the knowledge the passengers had of one another. Coverly's plane was due to leave at two, but at quarter to three they still waited at the gate. A few of the passengers were grumbling, and two or three of them had copies of an afternoon paper that reported a jet crash in Colorado with a death list of seventy-three. Was the jet that had crashed the one they were waiting for? Had they, standing in the dim sunlight, received some singular mercy? Had their lives been saved? Coverly went to the information desk to ask about his flight. The question was certainly legitimate, but the clerk reacted sullenly, as if the purchase of a plane ticket was a contract to walk humbly and in darkness. "There is some delay," he said, unwillingly. "There may be some motor trouble or the connecting flight from Europe may be delayed. You won't board until half-past three." Coverly thanked him for this favor and went up some stairs to a bar. On a gilt easel at the right of the door was a photograph of a pretty singer in evening clothes, a delegate of all those thousands who beam at us from the thresholds of bars and hotel dining rooms; but she didn't go on until nine and would probably be asleep or taking her wash out to the laundromat.

Inside, there was piped-in music and the bartender wore military livery. Coverly took a stool and ordered a beer. The man beside him was swaying comfortably on his stool. "Where you going?" he asked.

"Denver."

"Me, too," the stranger exclaimed, striking Coverly on the back. "I've been going to Denver for three days."

"That's right," the bartender said. "He missed eight flights now. Isn't it eight?"

"Eight," the stranger said. "It's because I love my wife. My wife's in Denver, and I love her so much I can't get on the plane."

"It's good for business," the barkeeper said.

In the gloom at the end of the bar two conspicuous homosexuals with dyed yellow hair were drinking rum.

A family sat at a table eating lunch and conversing in advertising slogans. It seemed to be a family joke.

"My!" the mother exclaimed. "Taste those bite-sized chunks of white Idaho turkey meat, reinforced with riboflavin, for added zest."

"I like the crispy, crunchy potato chips," the boy said. "Toasted to a golden brown in health-giving infrared ovens and topped with imported salt."

"I like the spotless rest rooms," said the girl, "operated under the supervision of a trained nurse and hygienically sealed for our comfort, convenience and peace of mind."

"Winstons taste good," piped the baby in his high chair, "like a cigarette should. Winstons have *flavor*."

The dark bar had the authority of a creation, but it was a creation evolved independently from the iconography of the universe. With the exception of the labels on the bottles there was nothing familiar in the place. Its light were cavernous, its walls were dark mirrors. There was not even a truncated piece of driftwood or a coaster shaped like a leaf to remind him of the world outside. That beauty of sameness that makes the star and the shell, the sea and the clouds all seem to have come from the same hand was lost. The music was interrupted for the announcement that Coverly's flight was boarding, and he paid for his beer and grabbed his briefcase. He stopped in the men's room, where someone had written something exceedingly human on the wall, and then followed the lighted numbers down the long corridor to his gate. There was still no plane in sight, but none of the passengers had been moved by the delay or the news of the crash to change their plans. They stood there passively as if the sullen clerk had in fact sold them humility with their tickets. Coverly's topcoat was too warm for that climate, but most of the other passengers had come from places that were colder or warmer than here. From a duct directly overhead, the continuous music poured gently into their ears. "It's going to be all right," an old lady beside Coverly whispered to an even older companion. "It isn't dangerous. It isn't any more dangerous than the trains. They carry millions of passengers every year. It's going to be all right." The fingers of the older, knobbed like driftwood, touched her cheeks, and in her eyes was

the fear of death. Death was what the scene meant to her—
the frisky mechanics in their white coveralls, the numbered
runways, the noise of an incoming 707. A baby cried. A
man ran a comb through his hair. The objects and sounds
around Coverly seemed to group themselves into some
immutable statement. These were the facts—this music, the
fear of death endured by the old stranger, the flatness of
the field, and way in the distance the roofs of some houses.

The plane came in, they boarded, and the stewardess
seated Coverly between the old lady and a man whose
breath smelled of whisky. The stewardess wore high-heeled
shoes, a raincoat and dark glasses. Coverly saw under her
raincoat the skirts of a red silk dress. As soon as she had
closed the plane, she went to the toilet and reappeared in
the gray skirt and white silk blouse of her profession. Her
eyes, when she took off her glasses, were haggard, and she
peered out of them in pain. "Joe Burner," said the man on
Coverly's right, and Coverly shook his hand and introduced himself. "I'm pleased to meet you, Cove," the
stranger said. "I have a little present here I'd like to give
you." He took a small box from his pocket, and when
Coverly opened it he found a gilt tie clip. "I travel a lot,"
the stranger explained, "and I give away these tie clips
wherever I go. I have them manufactured for me in Providence. That's the jewelry capital of the United States. I
give away two or three thousand clips a year. It's a nice
way of making friends. Everybody can use a tie clip."

"Thank you very much," Coverly said.

"I knit socks for astronauts," said the old lady on
Coverly's left. "Oh, I know it's silly of me, but I love those
boys, and I can't bear to think of them having cold feet.
I've sent ten pairs of socks down to Canaveral in the last
six weeks. They don't thank me, it's true, but they've never
returned them, and I like to think that they use them."

"I'm taking a few days off, to see an old friend who's
dying of cancer," said Joe Burner. "I have at this date
twenty-seven friends who are dying of cancer. Some of
them know it. Some of them don't. But not a one of them
has more than a year to live."

They were wrapped then in a heard and unheard con-
vulsion of sound and pushed roughly back against their

seats by the force of gravity as the plane went down the strip and began its strenuous push for altitude. A large panel fell out of the ceiling and crashed into the aisle, and the glasses and bottles in the pantry rattled noisily. When they had risen above the scattered clouds, the passengers unbuckled their seat belts and resumed their lives, their habits. "Good afternoon," said the loudspeaker. "This is Captain MacPherson welcoming you to Flight 73, nonstop to Denver. We have reports of a little turbulence in the mountains but we expect it to clear by scheduled landing time. We are sorry about the delay, and wish to take this occasion to thank you all for your patience in not doing nothing about it." The speaker clicked off.

Coverly could not see that anyone else was perplexed. Was he mistaken in assuming that navigational competence implied a rudimentary grasp of English? Joe Burner had begun to tell Coverly the story of his life. His style was nearly bardic. He began with the characters of his parents. He described his birthplace. Then he told Coverly about his two older brothers, his interest in sandlot baseball, his odd jobs, the schools he had attended, the wonderful buttermilk pancakes that his mother used to make and the friends that he had won and lost. He told Coverly his annual grosses, the size of his office staff, the nature of his three operations, the wonderfulness of his wife and the amount of money it had cost him to landscape his seven-room, two-bath house on Long Island. "I have something very unique," he said. "I have this lighthouse on my front lawn. Four, five years ago, this big estate on Sands Point was auctioned off for taxes, and Mother and I went down there to see if there was anything we could use. Well, they had this little lake with a lighthouse on it—just ornamental, of course—and when it came time to buy the lighthouse, the bidding was very slow. Well, I bid thirty-five dollars, just for the heck of it, and you know what? That lighthouse was mine. Well, I have this friend in the trucking business—you have to know the right people—and he went down there and got it off the lake. I don't know to this day how he did it. Well, I've got this other friend in the electric business, and he wired it up for me, and now I've got this lighthouse right on my front lawn. It makes the place look real nice. Of course, some of the neighbors complain—you find clinkers in every gang—so I don't turn it on every night, but when we have people in to play cards or watch the television, I turn it on, and it looks beautiful."

The sky by then was the dark blue of high altitudes, and the atmosphere in the plane was as genial as a saloon. The white blouse the hostess wore came loose whenever she bent over to serve a cocktail. She tucked it in each time she straightened up. The seat backs were as high as the walls of an old box pew, and the passengers had a limited degree of privacy and a limited view of one another. Then the bulkhead door opened, and Coverly saw the captain come down the aisle. His color was bad, and his eyes were as haggard as the eyes of the stewardess. Perhaps he was a friend of the pilot and crew who had crashed a few hours earlier in Colorado. Would he, would anyone else, have the fortitude to face this disaster calmly? Would the charred bones of seventy-three bodies mean any less to him than they did to the rest of the world? He nodded to the stewardess, who followed him aft to the pantry. They did not exchange a word, but she put some ice into a paper cup and poured whisky into it. He carried his drink forward and closed the door. The old lady was dozing, and Joe Burner, having finished with his autobiography, had begun to tell his stock of jokes. Without any warning, the plane dropped about two thousand feet.

The confusion was horrible. Most of the drinks hit the ceiling, men and women were thrown into the aisles, children were screaming. "Attention, attention," said the public-address system. "Hear this, everyone."

"Oh, my God," the stewardess said, and she went aft and strapped herself in. "Attention, attention," said the amplified voice, and Coverly wondered then if this might be the last voice that he heard. Once, when he was being prepared for a critical operation, he had looked out of his hospital window into the window of an apartment house across the street, where a fat woman was dusting a grand piano. He had already been given Sodium Pentothal and was swiftly losing consciousness, but he resisted the drug long enough to feel resentment at the fact that the last he might see of the beloved world was a fat woman dusting a grand piano.

"Attention, attention," the voice said. The plane had leveled off in the heart of a dark cloud. "This is not your captain. Your captain is tied up in the head. Please do not move, please do not move from your seats, or I will cut off your oxygen supply. We are traveling at five hundred miles an hour, at an altitude of forty-two thousand feet, and any disturbance you create will only add to your danger. I have logged nearly a million air miles and am disqualified as a pilot only because of my political opinions. This is a robbery. In a few minutes my accomplice will enter the cabin by the forward bulkhead, and you will give him your wallets, purses, jewelry and any other valuables that you have. Do not create any disturbance. You are helpless. I repeat: You are helpless."

"Talk to me, talk to me," the old lady asked. "Please just say something, anything."

Coverly turned and nodded to her, but his tongue was so swollen with fear that he could not make a sound. He worked it around desperately in his mouth to stir up some lubrication. The other passengers were still, and on they rocketed through the dark—sixty-five or seventy strangers, their noses pressed against the turmoil of death. What would be its mode? Fire? Should they, like the martyrs, inhale the flames to shorten the agony? Would they be truncated, beheaded, mutilated and scattered over three miles of farmland? Would they be ejaculated into the darkness and yet not lose consciousness during the dreadful fall to earth? Would they be drowned, and while drowning display their last talent for inhumanity in trampling one another at the flooding bulkheads? It was the darkness that gave him most pain. The shadow of a bridge or a building can fall across our spirit with all the weight of a piece of bad news, and it was the darkness that seemed to compromise his spirit. All he wanted then was to see some light, a patch of blue sky. A woman, sitting forward, began to sing "Nearer, My God, to Thee." It was a common church soprano, feminine, decent, raised once a week in the company of her neighbors. "E'en though it be a cross that raiseth me," she sang, "still all my song shall be, nearer, my God, to Thee. . . ."

A man across the aisle took up the hymn, joined quickly by several others, and when Coverly remembered the words, he sang:

> Though like a wanderer,
> Weary and lone,
> Darkness comes over me,
> My rest a stone. . . .

Joe Burner and the old lady were singing, and those who didn't know the words came in strong on the refrain. The bulkhead door opened, and there was the thief. He wore a felt hat and a black handkerchief tied over his face with holes cut for the eyes. It was, except for the felt hat, the ancient mask of the headsman. He wore black rubber gloves and carried a plastic wastebasket to collect their valuables. Coverly roared:

> There let my way appear,
> Steps into heaven,
> All that Thou sendest me
> In mercy given. . . . .

They sang more in rebelliousness than in piety; they sang because it was something to do. And merely in having found something to do they had confounded the claim that they were helpless. They had found themselves, and this accounted for the extraordinary force and volume of their voices. Coverly stripped off his wristwatch and dropped his wallet into the basket. Then the thief, with his black-gloved hands, lifted the briefcase out of Coverly's lap. Coverly let out a groan of dismay and might have grabbed at the case had not Burner and the old lady turned on him faces so contorted with horror that he fell back into his seat. When the thief had robbed the last of them, he turned back to the bulkhead, staggering a little against the motion of the plane —a disadvantage that made his figure seem familiar and harmless. They sang:

> Then with my waking thoughts,
> Bright with Thy praise,

Out of my stormy griefs,
Altars I'll raise. . . .

"Thank you for your cooperation," said the public-
address system. "We will make an unscheduled landing in
West Franklin in about eleven minutes. Please fasten your
seat belts and observe the no-smoking signal."

The clouds outside the ports began to lighten, to turn
from gray to white, and then they sailed free into the blue
sky of late afternoon. The old lady dried her tears and
smiled. To lessen the pain of his confusion Coverly suddenly concluded that the briefcase had contained an electric toothbrush and a pair of silk pajamas. Joe Burner
made the sign of the cross. The plane was losing altitude
rapidly, and then below them they could see the roofs of
a city that seemed like the handiwork of a marvelously
humble people going about useful tasks and raising their
children in goodness and charity. The moment when they
ceased to be airborne passed with a thump and a roar of
the reverse jets, and out of the ports they could see that
international wilderness that hedges airstrips. Scrub grass
and weeds, a vegetable slum, struggled in the sandy bottom
soil that formed the banks of an oily creek. Someone
shouted, "There they *go!*" Two passengers opened the
bulkhead. There were confused voices, and when someone
asked for information, the complexity of human relation-
ships so swiftly re-established itself that those who knew
what was going on pridefully refused to communicate with
those who didn't and the first man into the forward cabin
spoke to them with condescension. "If you'll quiet down
for a minute," said he, "I'll tell you what we know. We've
released the crew and the captain has made radio contact
with the police. The thieves got away. That's all I can tell
you now."

Then faintly, faintly, they heard the sirens approaching
over the airstrip. The first to come was a fire crew, who
put a ladder up against the door and got it open. Next to
come were the police, who told them they were all under
arrest. "You're going to be let off in lots of ten," one of the
policemen said. "You're going to be questioned." He was
gruff, but they were magnanimous. They were alive, and no

incivility could disturb them. The police then began to count them off in lots. The ladder of the fire truck was the only way of getting down from the plane, and the older passengers mounted this querulously, their faces working with pain. Those who waited seemed immersed in the passivity of some military process; seemed to suffer that suspense of discernment and responsibility that overtakes any line of soldiers. Coverly was No. 7 in the last lot. A gust of dusty wind blew against his clothing as he went down the ladder. A policeman took him by the arm, a touch he bitterly and instantly resented, and it was all he could do to keep from flinging the man's arm off. He was put with his group into a closed police van with barred windows.

A policeman took him again by the arm when he left the van and again he had to struggle to control himself. What was this testiness of his flesh? he wondered. Why did he loathe this stranger's touch? Rising before him was the Central Police Headquarters—a yellow-brick building with a few halfhearted architectural flourishes and a few declarations of innocent love written in chalk on the walls. The wind blew dust and papers around his feet. Inside he found himself in the alarming and dreary atmosphere of wrongdoing. It was a passage into a world to which he had been granted merely a squint—that area of violence he glimpsed when he spread newspapers on the porch floor before he painted the screens. Roslyn man shoots wife and five children. . . . Murdered child found in furnace. . . . They had all been here, and had left in the air a palpable smell of their bewilderment and dismay, their claims of innocence. He was led to an elevator and taken up six flights. The policeman said nothing. He was breathing heavily. Asthma? Coverly wondered. Excitement? Haste?

"Do you have asthma?" he asked.

"You answer the questions," the policeman said.

He led Coverly down a corridor like the corridor in some depressing schoolhouse and put him in a room no bigger than a closet, where there was a wooden table, a chair, a glass of water and a questionnaire. The policeman shut the door, and Coverly sat down and looked at the questions.

Are you the head of a household? he was asked. Are you divorced? Widowed? Separated? How many television sets do you own? How many cars? Do you have a current passport? How often do you take a bath? Are you a college graduate? High school? Grammar school? Do you know the meaning of "marsupial"; "seditious"; "recondite"; "dialectical materialism"? Is your house heated by oil? Gas? Coal? How many rooms? If you were forced to debase the American flag or the Holy Bible, what would be your choice? Are you in favor of the federal income tax? Do you believe in the International Communist Conspiracy? Do you love your mother? Are you afraid of lightning? Are you for the continuation of atmospheric testing? Do you have a savings account? Checking account? What is your total indebtedness? Do you own a mortgage? If you are a man, would you classify your sexual organs as being size 1, 2, 3 or 4? What is your religious affiliation? Do you believe John Foster Dulles is in Heaven? Hell? Limbo? Do you often entertain? Are you often entertained? Do you consider yourself to be liked? Well liked? Popular? Are the following men living or dead: John Maynard Keynes. Norman Vincent Peale. Karl Marx. Oscar Wilde. Jack Dempsey. Do you say your prayers each night? . . .

Coverly attacked these questions—and there were thousands of them—with the intentness of a guilty sinner. He had given his watch to the thief, and had no idea of how long it took him to fill out the questionnaire. When he was done, he shouted, "Hullo. I'm finished. Let me out of here." He tried the door and found it open. The corridor was empty. It was night, and the window at the end of the hall showed a dark sky. He carried his questionnaire to the elevator and rang. As he stepped out of the elevator on the street floor, he saw a policeman sitting at a desk. "I lost something very valuable, very important," Coverly said.

"That's what they all say," the policeman said.

"What do I do now?" asked Coverly. "I've answered all the questions. What do I do now?"

"Go home," the policeman said. "I suppose you want some money?"

"I do," Coverly said.

"You're all getting a hundred from the insurance company," the policeman said. "You can put in a claim later if you've lost more." He counted out ten ten-dollar bills and looked at his watch. "The Chicago train comes through in about twenty minutes. There's a cab stand at the corner. I don't suppose you'll want to fly again for a while. None of the others did."

"Have they all finished?" Coverly asked.

"We're holding a few," the man said.

"Well, thank you," Coverly said, and walked out of the building into a dark street in the town of West Franklin, feeling in its dust, heat, distant noise and anonymity of its colored lights the essence of his loneliness. There was a newsstand at the corner, and a cab parked there. He bought a paper. "Disqualified Pilot Robs Jet In Midair," he read. "A Great Plane Robbery took place at 4:16 this afternoon over the Rockies . . ." He got into the cab and said, "You know, I was in that plane robbery this afternoon."

"You're the sixth fare who's told me that," the driver said. "Where to?"

"The station," Coverly said.

CHAPTER XX

It was late the next afternoon when Coverly finally made his way from Chicago back to Talifer. He went to Cameron's office at once but he was kept waiting nearly an hour. Now and then he could hear the old man's voice, through the closed door, raised in anger. "You'll never get a Goddamned man on the Goddamned moon," he was shouting. When Coverly was finally let in, Cameron was alone. "I've lost your briefcase," Coverly said.

"Oh, yes," the doctor said. He smiled his unfortunate smile. Then it was a toothbrush and some pajamas, Coverly thought. It was nothing, after all!

"There was a robbery on the plane coming West," Coverly said.

"I don't understand," Cameron said. The light of his smile was undiminished.

"I have a newspaper here," Coverly said. He showed Cameron the paper he had bought in West Franklin. "They took everything. Our watches, wallets, your briefcase."

"Who took it?" Cameron asked. His smile seemed to brighten.

"The thieves, the robbers. I suppose you might call them pirates."

"Where did they take it?"

"I don't know, sir."

Cameron left his desk and went to the window, putting his back to Coverly. Was he laughing? Coverly thought so. He had duped the enemy. The briefcase had been empty! Then Coverly saw that he was not laughing at all. These were the painful convulsions of bewilderment and misery; but what did he cry for? His reputation, his absent-mindedness, his position; for the world itself that he could see outside his window, the ruined farm and the gantry line? Coverly had no means of consoling him and stood in a keen agony of his own, watching Cameron, who seemed then small and old, racked by these uncontrollable muscular spasms. "I'm sorry, sir," Coverly said. "Get the hell out of here," Cameron muttered and Coverly left.

It was closing time and the bus he took home was crowded. He tried to judge himself along traditional lines. Had he refused to yield up the briefcase he might have wrecked the plane and killed them all; but mightn't this have been for the best? What could he anticipate or what could he look back upon with any calm? When he went back to work in the morning what office would he report to? What had Cameron wanted of him in the first place? What sense could he make of the old man sobbing at his window? Would Betsey, when he got home, be watching TV? Would his little son be in tears? Would there be any supper? Some vision of St. Botolphs in the light of a summer evening appeared to him. It was that hour when the housewives called their children in for supper with those small bells that used to be used for summoning servants

to the table. Silver or not, they all had a silvery note and
Coverly recalled this silvery ringing now from all the back
stoops of Boat Street and River Street, calling children in
from the banks of the river.

His own place was brightly lighted. Betsey ran into his
arms when he entered the house. "I just been hoping and
praying, sweetie, that you'd get home for supper," she said,
"and now my prayers are answered, my prayers are answered. We've been asked out to dinner!" Coverly could
not work this in with anything that had happened in the
last twenty-four hours and he settled for a mode of emotional and intellectual improvisation. He was tired but it
would have been cruel to frustrate Betsey's only invitation.
He kissed his son, tossed him into the air a few times and
made a strong drink. "This nice woman," Betsey said, "her
name is Winifred Brinkley, well, she came to the house
collecting money for the Heart Drive and I told her, I just
told her that I thought this was the lonesomest place on the
face of the earth. I just didn't care who knew it. She then
told me she thought it was lonesome too and that wouldn't
we like to come to a little dinner party at her house tonight.
So then I told her you were in Atlantic City and I didn't
know when you would return but I just prayed and prayed
that you'd get back in time and here you are!"

Coverly took a bath and changed while Betsey transported a high school boy who was going to stay with
Binxey. The Brinkleys lived in the neighborhood and they
walked there, arm in arm. Now and then Coverly bent his
long neck and gave Betsey a kiss. Mrs. Brinkley was a thin,
spritely woman, brilliantly made up and loaded down with
beads. She kept saying "Crap." Mr. Brinkley had an uncommonly receding forehead, a lack or infirmity that was
accentuated by the fact that his gray, curly hair was arranged in loops over this receding feature like the curtains
in some parlor. He seemed gallantly to be combating an
air of fatigue and inconsequence by wearing a gold collar
pin, a gold tie clip, a large bloodstone ring and a pair of
blue-enamel cuff links that flashed like semaphores when
he poured the sherry. Sherry was what they drank but
they drank it like water. There were two other guests—
the Cranstons from the neighboring city of Waterford. "I

just had to ask somebody from out of town," Mrs. Brinkley said, "so we wouldn't have to listen to all that crap about Talifer."

"One thing I know, one thing I've learned," Mr. Cranston said, "and that is that you've got to have balls. That's what matters in the end. Balls." He wore a crimson hunting shirt and had yellow curls and a face that seemed both cherubic and menacing. His gray-haired wife seemed much older and more intelligent than he and in spite of his talk it was easiest to imagine him, not in the bouncing act of love, but in some attitude of bewilderment and despair while his wife stroked his curls and said: "You'll find another job, honey. Don't worry. Something better is bound to come along." Mrs. Brinkley's youngest child had just returned from a tonsillitis operation at the government hospital and during sherry they all talked about their tonsils and adenoids. Betsey positively shone. Coverly had never had his tonsils or adenoids removed and he was a little out of things until he brought up appendicitis. This carried them to the dinner table, where they then talked about dentistry. The dinner was the usual, washed down with sparkling Burgundy. After dinner Mr. Cranston told a dirty story and then got up to leave. "I hate to rush," he said, "but you know it takes us an hour and a half to get back and I have to work in the morning."

"Well, it shouldn't take you an hour and a half," Mr. Brinkley said. "How do you go?"

"We take the Speedway," Mr. Cranston said.

"Well, if you get outside Talifer before you take the Speedway," Mr. Brinkley said, "you'll save about fifteen minutes. Maybe twenty. You go back to the shopping center and turn right at the second traffic light."

"Oh, I wouldn't do it that way," Mrs. Brinkley said. "I'd go straight out past the computation center and take the clover leaf just before you get to the restricted area."

"Oh, you would, would you," said Mr. Brinkley. "That way you'd run right into a lot of construction. Just do what I say. Go back to the shopping center and turn right at the second traffic light."

"If they go back to the shopping center," Mrs. Brinkley said, "they'll get stuck in all that traffic at Fermi Circle. If they don't want to go out by the computation center, they could head straight for the gantries and then turn right at the road block."

"My God, woman," Mr. Brinkley said, "will you shut your big damned mouth?"

"Aw, crap," said Mrs. Brinkley.

"Well, thanks a lot," said the Cranstons, heading for the door. "I guess we'll just take the Speedway the way we used to." They were gone.

"Now you got them all mixed up," Mr. Brinkley said. "I don't know what makes you think you can give directions. You can't even find your way around the house."

"If they'd gone the way I told them in the beginning," Mrs. Brinkley said fiercely, "they would have been perfectly all right. There isn't any construction out by the restricted area. You just made that up."

"I did not," Mr. Brinkley said. "I was out there Thursday. That whole place is torn up."

"You were in bed with a cold on Thursday," Mrs. Brinkley said. "I had to keep bringing you trays."

"Well, I guess we'd better go," Coverly said. "It was awfully nice and thank you very much."

"If you would just learn to shut your mouth," Mr. Brinkley shouted at his wife, "the whole world would be very grateful. You shouldn't be allowed to drive a car, let alone give people directions."

"Thank you," said Betsey shyly at the door.

"Who smashed up the car last year?" Mrs. Brinkley screamed. "Who was the one who smashed up the car? Please tell me that."

They walked home, stopping now and then to exchange a kiss, and that journey ended like any other.

CHAPTER XXI

⊷ఈ ఇ⊶

Coverly had not seen Cameron again. He killed some days
at his desk, revising his commencement address about the
jewelry of heaven. He was ordered, one morning, to report
to security. He guessed that he would be charged with the
loss of the briefcase and wondered if he would be arrested.
Coverly was one of those men who labor under a preter-
naturally large sense of guilt that, like some enormous
bruise, concealed by his clothing, could be carried pain-
lessly until it was touched; but once it was touched it would
threaten to unnerve him with its pain. He was a model of
provincial virtues—truthful, punctual, cleanly and cour-
ageous—but once he was accused of wrongdoing by some
powerful arm of society his self-esteem collapsed in a heap.
Yes, yes, he was a sinner. It was he who had butchered
the ambassador, hocked the jewelry and sold the blue-
prints to the enemy. He approached the security offices
feeling deeply guilty. There was a long corridor painted
buttercup yellow and eight or ten men and women were
ahead of him. It seemed like a doctor's or a dentist's anteroom, a consular anteroom, a courthouse corridor, an employment office; it seemed, this scene for waiting, to be an
astonishingly large part of the world. One by one the other
men and women were called by name and let in at a door
at the end of the yellow corridor. None of them returned so
there must have been another way out but their disappearance seemed to Coverly ominous. Finally his name was
called and a pretty secretary, her face composed in a
censorious scowl, ushered him into a large office that
looked like an old-fashioned courtroom. There was an
elevated bench behind which sat a colonel and two men
in civilian clothes. A recording clerk sat below the bench.

On the left was an American flag in a standard. The flag was heavy silk with a gold fringe and would never have left its stand, not even for a fine parade in auspicious weather.

"Coverly Wapshot?" the colonel asked.

"Yes, sir."

"Could I please have your security card?"

"Yes, sir." Coverly passed over his security card.

"You know a Miss Honora Wapshot of Boag Street, St. Botolphs?"

"It's Boat Street, sir."

"You know this lady?"

"Yes, sir, I've known her all my life. She's my cousin."

"Why didn't you report to this office the fact of her criminal indictment?"

"Her what?" What could she have done? Arson? Been caught shoplifting at the five-and-dime? Bought a car and run it into a crowd? "I don't know anything about her criminal indictment," Coverly said. "She's been writing me about a holly tree that grows behind her house. It has some kind of rust and she wants it sprayed. That's all I know about her. Could you tell me what she was charged with?"

"No. I can tell you that your security clearance has been suspended."

"But, Colonel, I don't understand any of this. She's an old lady and I can't be held responsible for what she does. Is there any appeal, is there any way I can appeal this?"

"You can appeal through Cameron's office."

"But I can't go anywhere, sir, without a security clearance. I can't even go to the men's room."

The clerk filled out a slip that looked like a fishing license and passed it to Coverly. It was, he read, a limited security clearance with a ten-day expiration. He thanked the clerk and went out a side door as another suspect was let in.

Coverly went at once to Cameron's office, where the receptionist said that the old man was out of town and would be gone at least two weeks. Coverly then asked to see Brunner, the scientist who had lunched with him in Atlantic City, and the girl cleared him through to Brunner's office. Brunner wore the cashmere pullover of his caste and sat in

front of a colored writing board covered with equations
and a note saying: "Buy sneakers." There was a wax rose
in a vase on his desk. Coverly told Brunner his problems
and Brunner listened to him sympathetically. "You never
see any classified material, do you?" he asked. "It's the
kind of thing the old man likes to fight. Last year they
fired a janitor in the computation center because it appears
that his mother worked briefly as a prostitute during the
Second World War." He excused himself and returned
with another member of the team. Cameron was in Washington and was going from there to New Delhi. The two
scientists suggested that Coverly go down to Washington
and catch the old man there. "He seems to like you,"
Brunner said, "and if you spoke to him, he could at least
extend your temporary clearance until he returns. He's up
for a Congressional hearing at ten tomorrow morning. It's
in Room 763." Brunner wrote the number down and
passed it to Coverly. "If you get there early perhaps you
could speak to him before he goes on. I don't think there'll
be many spectators. This is the seventeenth time he's been
grilled this year and there has been a certain loss of interest."

CHAPTER XXII

ᴇᴈ ʚᴈ

Whether or not Cameron would speak to Coverly after
their last interview was highly questionable; but it appeared
to be Coverly's only chance and he decided to take it,
moved mostly by his indignation at the capriciousness of
the security officers who could confuse his old cousin's
eccentricities with national security. He flew to Washington
that night and went to Room 763 in the morning. His
temporary security clearance served and he had no trouble
getting in. There were very few spectators. Cameron came

in at another door at quarter after ten and went directly to the witness stand. He was carrying what appeared to be a violin case. The chairman began to question him at once and Coverly admired the quality of his composure and the density of his eyebrows.

"Dr. Cameron?"

"Yes, sir." His voice was much the best in the room; the most commanding, the most virile.

"Are you familiar with the name Bracciani?"

"I have answered this question before. My answer is on record."

"The records of previous hearings have nothing to do with us today. I have requested the records of earlier hearings but my colleagues have refused them. Are you familiar with the name Bracciani?"

"I see no reason why I should come to Washington repeatedly to answer the same questions," the doctor said.

"You are familiar with the name Bracciani?"

"Yes."

"In what connection?"

"Bracciani was my name. It was changed to Cameron by Judge Southerland in Cleveland, Ohio, in 1932."

"Bracciani was your father's name?"

"Yes."

"Your father was an immigrant?"

"All of this is known to you."

"I have already told you, Dr. Cameron, that my colleagues have withheld the records of earlier hearings."

"My father was an immigrant."

"Was there anything in his past that would have encouraged you to disown his name?"

"My father was an excellent man."

"If there was nothing embarrassing, disloyal or subversive in your father's past, why did you feel obliged to disown his name?"

"I changed my name," the doctor said, "for a variety of reasons. It was difficult to spell, it was difficult to pronounce, it was difficult to identify myself efficiently. I also changed my name because there are some parts of this country and some people who still suspect anything foreign. A foreign name is inefficient. I changed my name as in going from one country to another one changes one's currency."

A second senator was recognized; a younger man. "Isn't it true, Dr. Cameron," he asked, "that you are opposed to any investigation beyond our own solar system and that you have refused money, cooperation and technical assistance to anyone who has challenged your opinions?"

"I am not interested in interstellar travel," he said quietly, "if that's what you meant to ask me. The idea is absurd and my opinion is based on fundamental properties such as time, acceleration, power, mass and energy. However, I would like to make it clear that I do not assume our civilization to be the one intelligent civilization in the universe." That fleeting smile pressed over his face, a jewel of forced and insincere patience, and he leaned forward a little in his chair. "I feel that life and intelligence will have developed at about the same speed as on earth wherever the proper surroundings and the needed time have been provided. Present data—and these are extremely limited—suggest that life may have developed on the planets of about six percent of all stars. I feel myself that the spectrum of light reflected from the dark areas of Mars shows characteristics that prove the presence of plant life. As I've said, I think the possibilities of interstellar travel absurd; but interstellar communication is something else again.

"The number of civilizations with whom we might possibly communicate depends upon six factors. One: The rate at which stars like our sun are being formed. Two: The fraction of such stars that have planets. Three: The fraction of such planets that can sustain life. Four: The fraction of livable planets upon which life has arisen. Five: The fraction of the latter that have produced beings with a technology adequate for interstellar communication. Six: The longevity of this high technology. About one in three million stars has the probability of a civilization in orbit. However, this could still mean millions of such civilizations within our galaxy alone and, as you gentlemen all know, there are billions of galaxies." The hypocritical smile again passed over his face. Gas? Coverly wondered. "It seems unlikely to me," he went on, "that technologies would develop on a planet covered with water. Some of my col-leagues are enthusiastic about the intelligence of the dolphin but it seems to me that the dolphin is not likely to develop an interest in interstellar space." He waited for the hesitant and scattered laughter to abate. "The twenty-one-centimeter band—that is, one thousand four hundred and twenty megacycles—emitted by the colliding atoms of hydrogen throughout space has produced some interesting signals, especially from Tau Ceti, but I am very skeptical about their coherence. I do believe that scientists in every advanced civilization will have discovered that the energy value of each unit or quantum of radiation, whether in the form of light or radio waves, equals its frequency times a value known to us, and perhaps to some of you, as Planck's Constant.

"Optical masers appear to be our most promising means of interstellar communication." Now he was deep in his classroom manner and nothing would stop him until he had inflicted on them all the tedium, excitement and pain of a lecture period. "The optical version of these masers can produce a beam of light so intense and narrow that, if transmitted from the earth, it would illuminate a small portion of the moon." Again there was the fleeting, the sugary smile. "Extraneous wavelengths are eliminated so that unlike most light beams this one is pure enough to be modulated for voice transmission. A maser system could be detected with our present technology if it were transmitting from a solar system ten light years away. We must study the spectra of light from nearby stars for emission lines of peculiar sharpness and strength. This would be unmis-takable evidence of maser transmissions from a planet or-biting that star. The light signals would be elaborately coded. In the case of a system one thousand light years away it would take two thousand years to ask a question and receive an answer. A superior civilization would load its signal beam with vast amounts of information. A highly advanced civilization, having triumphed over hunger, dis-ease and war, would naturally turn its energies into the search for other worlds. However, a highly advanced civilization might take another direction." Here his voice so grated with censoriousness and reproach that it woke two senators who were dozing. "A highly advanced civilization might well destroy itself with luxury, alcoholism, sexual license, sloth, greed and corruption. I feel that our own civilization is seriously threatened by biological and mental degeneration.

"But to get back to your original question." He used the smile this time to indicate a change of scenery; they were in another part of the forest. "The earth-moon system extends its influence for a considerable distance into space. The earth's gravity, magnetism and reflected radiation have no appreciable influence. At the climax of the sunspot cycle the sun erupts, putting clouds of gas into space. Magnetic storms of great violence usually break out on earth a day or so later. But the nature of interplanetary space is absolutely unknown. We know nothing about the shape, composition and magnetic characteristics of the clouds from the sun. We don't even know whether they follow a spiraling or a direct path. Mapping the solar system is virtually impossible because of the uncertainty as to the precise distance between the planets and the sun."

"Dr. Cameron?" Another senator had been recognized. "Yes."

"We have some sworn testimony here on the subject of what some of your colleagues have described as an ungovernable temper. Dr. Pewters testified that on August 14th, during a discussion of the feasibility of moon travel, you tore down the Venetian blinds in his office and stamped on them." Cameron smiled indulgently. "Hugh Tompkins, an enlisted man and a driver from the motor pool, claims that when he was delayed, through no fault of his own, in reaching your office, you slapped him several times in the face, ripped the buttons off his uniform and used obscene language. Miss Helen Eckert, a stewardess for Pan-American Airlines, states that when your flight from Europe was forced to land in Chicago rather than in New York you created such a disturbance that you seriously threatened the safety of the flight. Dr. Winslow Turner states that during a symposium on interstellar travel you threw a heavy glass ashtray at him, cutting his face severely. There is a deposition here, from the doctor who stitched up the cut."

"I plead guilty to all these offenses," the doctor said charmingly.

"Dr. Cameron?" asked another senator.

"Yes."

"Critics of your administration at Talifer state that you have neither terminated, suspended nor reduced experiments that have so far cost the government six hundred million dollars and that appear to be fruitless. They state that a total of four hundred and seventeen million has been spent on abortive missiles and another fifty-six million on inoperative tracking experiments. They state that your administration has been characterized by mismanagement, waste and duplication."

"I don't, in this instance, know what you mean by fruitless, abortive and inoperative, Senator," Cameron said. "Talifer is an experimental station and our work cannot be reduced to linear mathematics. All my decisions, viewed in the full light of all factors, seem to me to have been proper at the time and I assume full responsibility for them all."

"Dr. Cameron?" The next senator to be recognized was a stout man and seemed oddly shy for a politician.

"Yes."

"My question is perhaps not germane, it involves my constituents, indeed it involves their well-being, their health, but as you know the microbes that breed in missile fuel have been traced to an outbreak of respiratory disease in the vicinity of Talifer."

"I beg your pardon, Senator, but there is absolutely no scientific proof tracing these microbes to the unfortunate outbreak of respiratory disease. No scientific proof at all. We do know that microbes breed in the fuel—a fungus of the genus Loremendrum that produces airborne spores and special mutants. These are no more significant than the microbes that breed in gasoline, kerosene and jet fuel. In volumes so large a concentration of contaminants can quickly become a troublesome amount of residue."

"Dr. Cameron?" One saw this time an old man, slim and with the extraordinary pallor of an uncommonly long life span. Indeed, he seemed more dead than alive. At a little distance his shaking hands appeared to be bone. He

wore a piped vest and a well-cut suit and had the stance
of a dandy, a dandy's air of self-esteem. His nose was
enormous and purple and hooked to the bridge was a
pince-nez from which depended a long, black ribbon. His
voice was not feeble but he spoke with that helplessness
before emotion of the very old and now and then dried,
with a broad linen handkerchief, a trickle of saliva that ran
down his chin.

"Yes," the doctor said.

"I was born in a small town, Dr. Cameron," the old man
said. "I think the difference between this noisy and public
world in which we now live and the world I remember is
quite real, quite real." There was an embarrassing pause as
he seemed to wait for his heart to pump enough blood for
his brain to carry on. "Men of my age, I know, are inclined
to think sentimentally of the past and yet even after dis-
counting these deplorable sentiments I think I can find
much in the past that is genuinely praiseworthy. However
. . ." He seemed again to have forgotten what he planned
to say; seemed again to be waiting for the blood to rise.
"However, I have lived through five wars, all of them
bloody, crushing, costly and unjust, and I think inescapable, but in spite of this evidence of man's inability to live
peacefully with his kind I do hope that the world, with all
its manifest imperfections, will be preserved." He dried his
cheeks with his handkerchief. "I am told that you are
famous, that you are great, that you are esteemed and
honored everywhere and I respect your honors unequivo-
cally but at the same time I find in your thinking some nar-
rowness, some unwillingness, I should say, to acknowledge
those simple ties that bind us to one another and to the
gardens of the earth." He dried his tears again and his old
shoulders shook with a sob. "We possess Promethean
powers but don't we lack the awe, the humility, that primitive man brought to the sacred fire? Isn't this a time for
uncommon awe, supreme humility? If I should have to
make some final statement, and I shall very soon for I am
nearing the end of my journey, it would be in the nature
of a thanksgiving for stout-hearted friends, lovely women,
blue skies, the bread and wine of life. Please don't destroy

the earth, Dr. Cameron," he sobbed. "Oh, please, please don't destroy the earth."

Cameron courteously overlooked this outburst and the questioning went on.

"Is it true, Dr. Cameron, that you believe in the inevitability of hydrogen warfare?"

"Yes."

"Would you give us an estimate of the number of survivors?"

"I'm sorry, but I can't. It would be the roughest guesswork. I think there will be a substantial number of survivors."

"In the case of reverses, Dr. Cameron, would you be in favor of destroying the planet?"

"Yes," he said. "Yes, I would. If we cannot survive, then we are entitled to destroy the planet."

"Who would decide that we had reached the ultimate point of survival?"

"I do not know."

The old man, having dried his tears, was up on his feet again. "Dr. Cameron, Dr. Cameron," he asked, "don't you think that there might be some bond of warmth amongst the peoples of the earth that has been underestimated?"

"Some what?" Cameron was not discourteous, but he was dry.

"Some bond of human warmth," the old man said.

"Men and women," the doctor said, "are chemical entities, easily assessable, easily altered by the artificial increase or elimination of chromosomal structures, much more predictable, much more malleable, than some plant life and in many cases much less interesting."

"Is it true, Dr. Cameron," the old man went on, "that your reading is confined to *Western Romances*?"

"I think I read as much as most men of my generation," the doctor replied. "I sometimes go to the movies. I watch television."

"But isn't it true, Dr. Cameron," the old man asked, "that the humanities have not been a part of your education?"

"You are talking to a musician," the doctor said.

"Did I understand you to say that you're a musician?"

"Yes, Senator. I am a violinist. You seem to have suggested that my lack of familiarity in the humanities would account for my cool-headedness about the demolition of the planet. This is not true. I love music and music is surely one of the most exalted of the arts."

"Did I understand you to say that you play the violin?"

"Yes, Senator, I play the violin."

He opened the violin case, took out an instrument, which he rosined and turned, and played a Bach air. It was a simple piece of beginner's music and he played it no better than any child but when he finished there was a round of applause. He put the violin away.

"Thank you, Dr. Cameron, thank you." It was the old man who was once more on his feet. "Your music was charming and reminded me of a reverie I often enjoy when some man from another planet who has seen our earth says to his friends: 'Come, come, let us rush to the earth. It is shaped like an egg, covered with fertile seas and continents, warmed and lighted by the sun. It has churches of indescribable beauty raised to gods that have never been seen, cities whose distant roofs and smokestacks will make your heart leap, auditoriums in which people listen to music of the most serious import and thousands of museums where man's drive to celebrate life is recorded and preserved. Oh, let us rush to see this world! They have invented musical instruments to stir the finest aspirations. They have invented games to catch the hearts of the young. They have invented ceremonies to exalt the love of men and women. Oh, let us rush to see this world!'" He sat down.

"Dr. Cameron?" It was the voice of a senator who had just come in. "You have a son?"

"I had a son," the doctor said. There was a splendid edge to his voice.

"You mean to say that your son is dead?"

"My son is in a hospital. He is an incurable invalid."

"What is the nature of his illness?"

"He is suffering from a glandular deficiency."

"What is the name of the hospital?"

"I don't recall."

"Is it the Pennsylvania State Hospital for the Insane?"

The doctor colored, he seemed touched. He was on the defensive for a moment. Then he rallied.

"I don't recall."

"In discussing your son's illness has the subject of your treatment of him ever arisen?"

"All the discussions of my son's illness," the doctor said forcefully, "have unfortunately been confined to psychiatrists. These discussions are not sympathetic to me because psychiatry is not a science. My son is suffering from a glandular deficiency and no idle investigation of his past life will alter this fact."

"Do you recall an incident when your son was four years old and you punished him with a cane?"

"I don't recall any specific incident. I probably punished the boy."

"You admit to punishing the boy?"

"Of course. My life is highly disciplined. I cannot tolerate a hint of disobedience or unreliability in my organization, my associates or myself. My life, my work, involving the security of the planet, would have been impossible if I had relaxed this point of view."

"Is it true that you beat him so cruelly with a cane that he had to be taken to the hospital and kept there for two weeks?"

"As I have said, my life is highly disciplined. If I should relax my disciplines I would expect to be punished. I treat those around me in the same way."

He replied with dignity but the damage had been done.

"Dr. Cameron," the senator asked.

"Yes, sir."

"Do you ever remember employing a housekeeper named Mildred Henning?"

"That's a difficult question." He put a hand to his eyes. "I may have employed this woman."

"Mrs. Henning, will you please come in."

An old, white-haired woman dressed in mourning came through the door and when the formalities of recognition had been established she was asked to testify. Her voice was cracked and faint. "I worked for him six years in California," she said, "and toward the end I just stayed on to try and protect the boy, Philip. He was always after him. Sometimes it seemed like he wanted to kill him."

"Mrs. Henning, will you please describe the incident you mentioned to us earlier."

"Yes. I have the dates here. I had to call the county health officer and so I have the dates. It was the nineteenth of May. He, the doctor, left some change, some silver, on his bureau and the boy helped himself to a twenty-five-cent piece. You couldn't blame him. He never had a penny for himself. When the doctor came home that night he counted his money, he was very methodical. When he seen that he was short some he asked the boy if he took it. Well, he was a good, honest boy and he owned right up to it. So then the doctor took him to his room, the boy had a room at the back of the house and there was a closet and he told him to go into the closet. Then he went into the bathroom and got him a glass of water and he gave him the water and then he locked the closet door. This was about quarter to seven. I didn't say anything because I wanted to help the boy and I knew if I opened my big mouth it would only make things worse for the boy. So I served the doctor his dinner with a straight face and then I listened and I waited but I didn't go near the closet where the poor boy was locked in the dark. So then I went to the closet in my bare feet and I whispered to him but he was crying so, he was so miserable that he couldn't do anything but sob and I told him not to worry, that I was going to lie down there on the floor by the closet and stay all night and I did. I lay there until dawn and then I whispered good-bye to him and I went down and cooked the breakfast. Well, the doctor went to the site at eight and then I tried to unlock the door but it was a good strong lock and none of the keys in the house would open it and still the poor boy was crying so that he couldn't speak hardly and he had drunk his water and had nothing to eat and there was no way of getting any water or food in to him. So when my housework was done I got a chair and sat by the door and talked with him until half-past six when the doctor come home and I thought he'd let the boy out then but he didn't go near the back of the house and ate his supper just as if nothing was wrong. Well, then I waited,

I waited until he started to get ready for bed and then I called the police. He told me to get out of the house, he told me I was fired and when the police come he tried to get them to throw me out but I got the policeman to open the closet and the poor little fellow—oh, he was so sick— come out but I had to go although it broke my heart to leave him alone and I never saw the doctor again until today."

"Do you recall this incident, Dr. Cameron?"

"Do you suppose, with my responsibilities, that I can afford to entertain such recollections?"

"You don't recall punishing the boy?"

"If I punished him I only meant to teach him right from wrong." His voice still had its edge, still soared, but he took no one with him.

"You don't recall locking your son in a closet for two days with nothing to eat or drink?"

"I gave him water."

"Then you do recall the incident?"

"I only wanted to teach him right from wrong."

"Do you visit your son?"

"From time to time." Something was carrying him on, some energy. He smiled.

"Do you remember the last time you visited him?"

"I can't recall."

"Would it have been ten years ago?"

"I can't recall."

"Would you recognize your son?"

"Of course."

"Daddy, Daddy."

The man who spoke from the open door seemed older than his father. His hair was white; his face was swollen. He was crying and he crossed the hearing room, knelt where his father sat, awkwardly for he was not a child, and put his head on the doctor's knee. "Daddy," he cried, "oh, Daddy. It's raining."

"Yes, dear." It was the most eloquent thing he had said. He no longer saw the hearing room or his persecutors. He seemed immersed in some human, some intensely human balance of love and misgiving as if the feelings were a storm with a circumference and an eye and he was in the stillness of the eye. "It's raining, Daddy," the man said. "Stay with me. Don't go out in the rain. Stay with me just once. They tell me you've hurt me but I don't believe them. I love you, Daddy. I'll always love you, Daddy. I write you all the time, Daddy, but you never answer my letters. Why don't you answer my letters, Daddy? Why don't you ever answer my letters?"

"I don't answer your letters because I'm ashamed of them," the doctor said hoarsely but not as if he spoke to someone childish or insane but to an equal, his son. "I send you everything you need. I sent you some nice stationery but you write me on wrapping paper, you write me on laundry lists, you even write me on toilet paper." His voice rose in anger and rang off the marble walls. "How in hell do you expect me to answer letters when you write them on toilet paper? I'm ashamed to receive them, I'm ashamed to see them. They remind me of everything in life I detest."

"Daddy, Daddy," the man cried.

"We'll go now, Philip. We have to go." There was an attendant with him. The attendant took his patient by the arm.

"No, I want to stay with Daddy. It's raining and I want to stay with Daddy."

"Come along, Philip."

"Daddy, Daddy," he cried, all the way to the door, and when it closed he could still be heard as Mrs. Henning must have heard his voice in the closet so many years ago.

"I move," the old man said, "that we propose, if that lies within our power, a suspension of Dr. Cameron's security clearance." The proposal seemed to be within their power. The motion was passed and the meeting was adjourned. Cameron remained in the witness chair and Coverly went out with the others.

CHAPTER XXIII

Emile and Melissa planned to meet in Boston. Melissa told Moses that she had to go north to see her aunt. Her aunt was in Florida but Moses didn't question her explanation.

She and Emile flew in separate planes. He arrived an hour later than she, and went to her room, where they spent the afternoon. Later they went out for a walk. It was very cold, and, looking at the façades and campaniles of Copley Square, she was moved by the thought that Boston had once thought itself the sister city of Florence, that vale of flowers. The wind scored her face. He stopped to look at a ring in a jeweler's window. It was a man's ring, a star sapphire set in gold. The ring did not interest her but it seemed to hold him. She shook with the cold while he admired the stone. "I wonder how much it costs. I'm going in and ask."

"Don't, Emile," she said. "I'm frozen. And anyhow, those things are always terribly expensive."

"I'll just ask. It won't take a minute."

She waited for him in the shelter of the door. "Eight hundred dollars!" he exclaimed when he came out. "Think of that. Eight hundred dollars."

"I told you it would be expensive."

"Eight hundred dollars. But it was pretty, though, wasn't it? And I suppose if you needed money you could always sell it. I mean, they must fix the price on things like that, don't you think? It would be sort of like an investment. You know, if I had eight hundred dollars I might buy a ring like that. I just might. People when they saw the ring, they would always know that you were worth eight hundred dollars. Waiters. Like that. I mean they would respect you when you were wearing a ring like that."

It seemed to her that he was deliberately debasing their relationship and forcing her into the humiliating position of buying him the ring, but she was mistaken; the idea had never occurred to him.

"Do you want me to buy you the ring, Emile?"

"Oh, no, I wasn't thinking about that. It just caught my eye. You know how things catch your eye."

"I'll buy it for you."

"No, no, forget about it."

They had dinner in a restaurant and went to a movie. Walking back to the hotel he bought a newspaper, and he sat reading it in her room while she undressed and brushed her hair. "I'm hungry," he said suddenly. His tone was petulant. "At home I get a bowl of cornflakes or a sandwich, something before I go to bed." He stood up, put his hands on his stomach and shouted, "I'm hungry. I just don't get enough to eat in these restaurants. I'm still growing. I have to have three big meals a day and sometimes something in between!"

"Well, why don't you go down and get something to eat?"

"Well."

"Do you need money?"

"Sort of."

"Here," she said. "Here's some money. Go down and get some supper."

He went out, but he didn't return. At midnight she locked the door and went to sleep. In the morning she dressed, went to the jeweler's and bought the ring. "Oh, I remember you," the clerk said, "I saw you last night. I saw you standing outside the door when your son came in to ask the price." It was a blow, and she supposed she could be seen flinching. She thought that perhaps the winter dark and the pale light in the street had made her seem old. "You're a very generous mother," the clerk said when he took her check and passed her the box. She called Emile's room and when he came down she gave him the ring. His pleasure and gratitude were not, she thought, mercenary and crass but only a natural response to the ancient tokens of love, the immemorial power of stones and fine gold.

It was a foggy afternoon, all the planes were grounded, and they went back on the train, sitting in different cars.

He sat by the window, watching the landscape. Somewhere south of Boston the train passed a suburban tract of houses. They were new, and although the architects and the gardeners had rung a few changes here and there, the effect was monotonous. What interested him was that rising in the center of the development was a large, ugly, loaf-shaped and colorless escarpment of granite. The roads must circumvent it expensively. Its sides were too steep to hold the foundations of a house. It seemed, in its uselessness, triumphantly obdurate and perverse. It was the only form on the landscape that had not succumbed to change. It could not be dynamited. It could not be quarried and carried away piecemeal. It was useless, and it was invincible. Some boys his age were climbing the steep face, and he guessed this was their last refuge.

It was late and it was getting cold, and he could remember the sense of the season and the hour when it was time to leave off playing and go home to study. Near where he lived there was a similar rock, and he had climbed it on winter afternoons, to smoke cigarettes and talk with his friends about the future. He could remember grasping for handholds on the steep face, and how the rough stone pulled at his best school clothes, but what he remembered most clearly was how once his feet were on the ground, he had a sense of awakening to a whole new life, the arrival at a new state of consciousness, as clearly unlike his past as sleep in unlike waking. Standing at the foot of the cliff at that hour and season—about to go home and study but not yet on the path—he would stare at the yards and the tress and the lighted houses with a galvanic sense of discovery. How forceful and interesting the world had seemed in the early winter light! How new it all seemed! He must have been familiar with every window, roof, tree and landmark in the place, but he felt as if he were seeing it all for the first time.

How old he had grown since then.

They met ten days or two weeks later, in a New York hotel. She was there first and ordered some whisky and roast-beef sandwiches. When he came in, she poured herself a drink and made one for him, and he ate both the sandwiches she had ordered. She was wearing a bracelet, made of silver bells, that she had bought long ago in Casablanca. She had been given a Mediterranean cruise as a Christmas present by a rich elderly cousin, and in her travels she had never been able to escape a genuine and oppressive sense of gratitude to the old lady. When she saw Lisbon she thought, Oh, Cousin Martha, I wish you could see Lisbon! When she saw Rhodes she thought, Oh, Cousin Martha, I wish you could see Rhodes! Standing in the Casbah at dusk she thought, Oh, Cousin Martha, I wish you could see how purple the skies are above Africa! Remembering this she gave the silver bells a shake.

"Do you have to wear that bracelet?" he asked.

"Of course not," she said.

"I hate that kind of junky stuff," he said. "You've got lots of nice jewelry—those sapphires. I don't see why you want to wear junk. Those bells are driving me crazy. Every time you move they jingle. They get on my nerves."

"I'm sorry, darling," she said. She took off the bracelet. He seemed ashamed or confused by his harshness; he had never before been harsh or callous with her.

"Sometimes I wonder why it happened to me like this," he said. "I mean, I couldn't have had anything better, I know. You're beautiful and you're fascinating—you're the most fascinating woman I ever saw—but sometimes I wonder—wondered—why it should happen to me this way. I mean, some fellows, right away they get a pretty young girl, she lives next door, their folks are friendly, they go to the same schools, the same dances, they go dancing together, they fall in love and get married. But I guess that's not for poor people. No pretty girls live next door to me. There aren't any pretty girls on my street. Oh, I'm glad it happened to me the way it did, but I can't stop wondering what it would have been like some other way. I mean like in Nantucket that weekend. That was the big football weekend, and I was thinking, there we were, all alone in that gloomy old house—that was a real gloomy place, rainy and everything—while some fellows were driving in convertibles to the football game."

"I must seem terribly old."

"Oh, no. No, you don't. It isn't that. . . . Only once. That was in Nantucket, too. It was raining in the night. It began to rain and you got up to shut the window."

"And I seemed terribly old?"

"Just for a minute. . . . Not really. But you see, you're used to comfort, you're different. Two cars, plenty of clothes. I'm just a poor kid."

"Does it matter?"

"Oh, I know you think it doesn't, but it does. When you go into a restaurant you never look at the prices. Now, your husband, he can buy you all these things. He can buy you anything you want, he's loaded, but I'm just a poor kid. I guess I'm sort of a lone wolf. I guess most poor people are. I'll never live in a house like yours. I'll never get to join a country club. I'll never have a place at the beach. And I'm still hungry," he said, looking at the empty sandwich plate. "I'm still growing, you know. I have to have lunch. I don't want to seem ungrateful or anything but I'm hungry."

"You go down to the dining room, darling," she said, "and get some lunch. Here's five dollars." She kissed him and then as soon as he was gone she left the hotel herself.

CHAPTER XXIV

She wandered around the streets—she had no place to go —wondering what had been the first in the chain of events that had brought her to where she was. The barking of a dog, the dream of a castle or her boredom at Mrs. Wishing's dance. She went home, and regard this lovely woman then, getting off the train in Proxmire Manor. See what she does. See what happens to her.

She wears a mink coat and no hat. Her car is a convertible. She drives up the hill to her house whose whiteness seems to authenticate her purity. How could anyone who lives in such a decorous environment be sinful? How could anyone who has so much Hepplewhite—so much Hepplewhite in good condition—be shaken by unruly lusts? She embraces her only son with tears in her eyes. This love for the boy seems to be one more thing to be crowded into her soul. Alone in her bedroom she doubled over with need and groaned like a bitch in rut. He seemed —his phantom—to cross the room and while she knew the plainness of his mind his skin seemed to shine; he seemed to be some golden Adam. She wanted to forget him. She wanted absolution. She had taken a lover, but was this so revolutionary? She had perhaps been mistaken in her choice, but wasn't this, in the history of things, as common as rain? She thought briefly of confessing to Moses but she knew his pride well enough to know that he would fire her out of the house. She felt herself gored. She had hoped to be a natural woman, sensual but unromantic, able to take a lover cheerfully and to leave him cheerfully when the time came. What had been revealed to her was the force of guilt and lust within her own disposition. She had transgressed the canons of a decorous society and she seemed impaled on the decorum she despised. The pain was unbearable and she went downstairs and poured herself a drink. She would have been ashamed, that early in the day, to ask the cook for ice and she watered the whisky in the bathroom and drank it there.

The drink made her feel better. She quickly had another. She was not able to exorcise the image of Emile but she was able, slowly, and with the help of whisky, to put the image in a different light. He came toward her with his arms out and drew her down but now he seemed evil, he seemed to intend to debase and destroy her. She had been innocent, she had been wronged! That was it. The comfort of attributing evil to him was enormous. He had preyed on her innocence! But now, remembering the trip to Nantucket when she had received from him only the most heartening and gentle lasciviousness, could she claim to be innocent, to have been wronged? The comfort of absolution vanished and she drank some more whisky. By the time Moses came home she was quite drunk.

Moses said nothing. He thought she must have received some bad news. She seemed drowsy, she dropped a lighted cigarette on the rug and going in to dinner she stumbled and nearly fell. When Moses went out to put the cars in the garage she went to the bar and drank some whisky from a bottle. As drunk as she was she could not sleep. Moses did not touch her but as he lay beside her she thought that a small scar in the hair on Emile's belly was more precious to her than the enormousness of all of Moses' love. When Moses went to sleep she went downstairs and poured herself more whisky. She drank until three o'clock but when she went to bed the image of Emile, her golden Adam, was still vivid. To distract herself she planned the renovation of her kitchen. She removed the old range, refrigerator, dishwasher and sink, chose a new linoleum, a new garbage disposal unit, a new color scheme, a new means of lighting. Was this some foolishness of hers or of her time that, caught in the throes of a hopeless love, the only peace of mind that she could find was in imagining new stoves and linoleum?

She went to the doctor for an examination the next afternoon. She stretched out on the examination table, wearing a slip. The room was uncomfortably warm. The doctor touched her, she thought, with a gentleness that was not clinical, although this might, she knew, be the summit of her confused feelings, distorted by lewd dreams, drunkenness and a nearly sleepless night. As he handled her breasts she thought she saw in his face the undisguisable sadness of desire. She turned her face away but now her breathing was deep and tortured and her accumulated frustrations, her sorrow for Moses and her lust for Emile threatened to overwhelm her. What could she do? Discuss the weather? Criticize the Zoning Board? Evoke what seemed to her then to be the fragile and dishonest chain of circumstances that kept them from ruin? He seemed to linger, lasciviously, over the examination and she felt the bonds of her common sense give one by one until her feelings were wild. She reached up and caressed the back of his neck and he made no move to discourage her. When she heard him fumbling with his clothing she closed her eyes. The moment was explosive and instantaneous. She nearly lost consciousness. While he was dressing the telephone rang. "Yes, yes," he said, "but as you know, Ethel, we don't expect her to live through the day." Melissa dressed and put on her furs. "When can I see you again?" the doctor asked. She didn't reply. Six or seven patients were waiting in the front room. One of them, an old man, was groaning in pain. She was in great pain herself, a keener pain, she thought, because his suffering was blameless. She stepped out into the street, into the afternoon. The parking meters ticked. Chopped meat and bacon were on sale. A fountain splashed in the public park. She smiled and waved to a friend who passed in a car. The consummate skill with which she could appear respectable was crushing and she detested impostors. Here was the light of late afternoon—the store fronts seemed lit with fire—and she seemed, by her misery, shut away from the light.

Was she sick? It was the charitable judgment, she knew, that the street and its people would pass on her and she rebelled against it bitterly for if she was sick so was Moses, so was Emile, so was the doctor, so was mankind. The world, the village, would forgive her her sins if she would go to Dr. Herzog, whom she had last seen dancing with a fat woman in a red dress, and unburden herself three times a week for a year or two of her memories and confusions. But wasn't it her detestation of bigotry and anesthesia that had gotten her into trouble, her loathing of mental, sexual and spiritual hygiene? She could not believe that her sorrows might be whitewashed as madness. This was her body, this was her soul, these were her needs.

Her little son came to meet her when she entered the house and she took him most tenderly in her arms. When he had gone back in the kitchen she poured herself a drink in the bathroom to blunt the pain. She then telephoned her minister and asked if she could see him at once. His wife, Mrs. Bascom, answered the telephone and kindly invited Melissa to come. Mrs. Bascom, smelling pleasantly of perfume and sherry, let her into the rectory. She would have spent the afternoon playing bridge. It would be sentimental of her, Melissa knew, to long for a life that centered on bridge parties, but the woman's simplicity and good cheer excited in Melissa a dreadful yearning. Mrs. Bascom's containment seemed as substantial as a well-built house, its windows shining with light, while Melissa felt herself to be cruelly exposed to every inclemency. Mrs. Bascom led her into a parlor where the rector was kneeling by an open fireplace, lighting some paper and kindling with a match. "Good afternoon," he said, "good afternoon, Mrs. Wapshot." For some reason he pronounced her name "Wapshirt." He was a portly man, his hair stained a discouraging gray like the last snows of winter and with a strong, plain face. "I thought we'd have a little fire," he said. "There's nothing like a fire, is there, to stimulate conversation? Sit down, do sit down. I have a confession to make." She flinched at the word. "Mrs. Bascom's bridge club, one of her *three* bridge clubs, met this afternoon and I decided to give myself a vacation and spent the whole afternoon watching television. Now I know a lot of people disapprove of television but during my, shall we say, dissipation this afternoon I saw some very interesting playlets and some splendid acting, some splendid performances. I wouldn't be at all surprised to discover that the standards of acting on television today are a great deal higher than those we find in the theater. I saw one very interesting playlet about a woman who was tempted—tempted, I say, there was nothing at all unsavory—by the monotony of her middle-class life to abandon her family in favor of a business enterprise. She had a most unpleasant mother-in-law. Not really unpleasant, I suppose, but a woman, you might say, whose character had been formed by a series of unfortunate circumstances. She was a possessive woman. She felt that the heroine neglected her husband. Well, the mother-in-law was wealthy and they had every reason to expect a substantial inheritance when she passed away. They took a picnic to a lake—oh, it was very well done—and during a storm the mother-in-law drowned. The next scene was in the lawyer's office where the will was read and where they discovered to their astonishment that they had been cut off with a single dollar. Well, the wife, rather than being disappointed, discovered new sources of strength in herself at this turn of events and was able to rededicate herself— to undergird her dedication, so to speak—to her family once more. It was all very revealing and it seems to me that if we looked at television oftener and saw the sorrows and the problems of others we might be less selfish, less egotistical, less likely to be overwhelmed by our own little problems."

Melissa had come to him for compassion but she felt then that she might better have asked for compassion from a barn door or a stone. For a moment his stupidity, his vulgarity, seemed inviolable. But if he had no compassion for her, wasn't it then her responsibility to extend some compassion to him, to try and understand, to try at least to tolerate the image of a stout and simple man applauding the asininities on television? What touched her, as he leaned toward the fire, was the antiquity of his devotions. No runner would ever come to his door with the news that the head of the vestry had been martyred by the local police and had she used the name of Jesus Christ, out of its liturgical context, she felt that he would have been terribly embarrassed. He was not to blame, he had not chosen this moment of history, he was not alone in having been overwhelmed at the task of giving the passion of Our Lord ardor and reality. He had failed, he seemed sitting by his fire to be a failure as she was and to deserve, like any other failure, compassion. She felt how passionately he would have liked to avoid her troubles; to discuss the church fair, the World Series, the covered-dish supper, the high price of stained glass, the perfidy of Communism, the comfortableness of electric blankets, anything but her trouble.

"I have sinned," Melissa said. "I have sinned and the memory is grievous, the burden is intolerable."

"How have you sinned?"

"I have committed fornication with a boy. He is not twenty-one."

"Has this happened often?"

"Many times."

"And with others?"

"With one other but I feel that I can't trust myself."

He shielded his eyes with his hands and she saw that he was shocked and disgusted. "In matters like this," he said, his eyes still shielded, "I work with Dr. Herzog. I can give

you his telephone number or I'll be happy to call him myself and make an appointment."

"I will not go to Dr. Herzog," Melissa said, weeping. "I
cannot."

She left the rectory and at home telephoned Narobi's.
The cook had ordered the groceries and she asked for a
case of quinine water, a bunch of water cress and a box of
peppercorns. "Your cook had a case of quinine water de-
livered this morning," Mr. Narobi said. He was unpleasant. "Yes, I know," Melissa said. "We're having guests."
Emile came a little while later.

"I'm sorry I left you in New York," Melissa said.

"That's all right." He laughed. "I was just hungry."

"I want to see you."

"Sure," he said. "Where?"

"I don't know."

"Well, there's this shack," he said. "Some of the fellows
and me have this shack down by the cove. I'll check in at
the store and meet you there in half an hour."

"All right."

"You go over the railroad bridge," he said, "down to the
cove. There's a dirt road there by the dump. I'll get there
early and make sure no one's around."

She hardly saw the place beyond the wall near where she
lay. "You know," he said, "for lunch I had the Manhattan
clam chowder and then a hot roast-beef sandwich with two
vegetables and pie with ice cream and I'm still hungry."

CHAPTER XXV

&

Emile and Mrs. Cranmer lived on the second floor of a
two-family frame house. The house was painted a dark
green with white trim—the green turned black in the rain
and was one of a species, gregarious in that one seldom

finds them alone. They appear in the suburbs of Montreal, reappear across the border in Northern lumber and mill towns, flourish in Boston, Baltimore, Cleveland and Chicago and go underground briefly in the wheat states to appear again in the depressed neighborhoods of Sioux City, Wichita and Kansas City, forming an irregular and mighty chain of quasi-nomadic domiciles, that reaches across the entire continent.

On her walk home in the evening from Barnum's Mrs. Cranmer passed the house that had been hers when Mr. Cranmer was alive. It was a large brick and stucco house. Twelve rooms! The dimensions and conveniences of the place returned to her like an incantation. The house had been sold by the bank to an Italian family named Tomasi. In spite of her struggle to accept the doctrines of equality that had been taught to her in school she still felt some bitterness that people from another country, people who had not yet learned the language and the customs of the United States, could possess the house of someone who was native born like herself. The economic facts were inescapable and she knew them but this didn't cure her bitterness. The house still seemed to be hers, still seemed in her custody, still reminded her of the richness of her life with Mr. Cranmer. The Tomasis spent most of their time in the kitchen and the front windows were usually dark but this evening a fringed lamp in one of the windows was lighted and beyond the lamp she could see, hanging on the wall, the enlarged photographs of some foreigners, the men with mustaches and high collars and the women in black. There was a powerful otherness for her in looking into the lighted windows of a house where her life had been centered. On she went in her comic-strip shoes.

The evening paper was in the mailbox. She usually looked at this in the kitchen. The most sensational stories dealt with the covert moral revolution that was being waged by men of Emile's age. They robbed, they pillaged, they drank, they raped and when they were locked up in jail they ripped out the plumbing. She reasoned that their parents were to blame and she sent up to heaven a completely sincere prayer of thanksgiving over the fact that Emile was such a good boy. In her own youth she had seen some wildness but the world had seemed more commodious and forgiving. She had never been able to settle on who was to blame. She feared that the world might have changed too swiftly for her intelligence and her intuition. She had no one to help her sift out the good from the evil. When she had finished with the paper she usually went into her room and unfastened those gallant bindings that signified that she had known the love of a good man. She was never unready, she was never slovenly. She put on clean slippers and a clean cotton dress and then as a rule she cooked the supper. This night she went directly into her bedroom, lay on her bed in the dark and cried.

Driving back from the shack Emile felt that he was discovering in himself a new vein of seriousness, a new aspect of maturity. The kitchen was lighted when he came in but his mother was not at the stove and then he heard her crying in her room. He knew at once why she cried but he was completely unprepared. His heart moved him at once into her dark room, where she looked more desolate, more than ever like a child, dumped by her misery onto the bed, utterly mystified and forsaken. He felt crushed with the force of her grief. "I just can't believe it," she sobbed. "Just can't believe it. I thought you were such a good boy; I thanked God night after night for your goodness and all the time right under my nose you were doing that. Mr. Narobi told me. He came to the store today."

"It isn't true, Mother. Whatever Mr. Narobi said isn't true."

She worked her face in the wet pillow like a child and he felt as if she were a child, his daughter, treated cruelly by some stranger.

"That's what I prayed you'd say, that's what I hoped you'd say but I can't believe anything any more. Mr. Narobi told me all about it and why should he tell me if it wasn't true? He couldn't make that all up."

"It isn't true, Mother."

"But why did he tell me all this then, why did he tell me all these lies? He said there's this woman you've been going off with. He said she's always calling the store when she doesn't need anything and that he knows what's going on."

"It isn't true."

"But why did he tell me these lies then? Perhaps he's jealous," she asked in a reckless hopefulness. "You know the year before last he asked me to marry him. Of course I'll never marry again, but he seemed cross when I said so." She sat up and dried her tears.

"Perhaps that's it."

"He came here one night when I was alone. He brought me a box of candy and asked me to marry him. When I said no he was angry, he said I'd be sorry. Do you think that's what he's trying to do? Make me sorry?"

"Yes, that must be it."

"Isn't that funny? To think that someone should want to do me harm. Isn't that funny? Don't people do the strangest things?"

She washed her face and began to cook supper and Emile went to his room, worried about the sapphire ring, hidden in a drawer. He would feel safer if it was in his pocket. He opened the drawer and was taking the ring out of the box when he turned and saw her standing in the doorway. "Give that to me," she said. "Give that to me, you devil. Whoever put the devil into you, who was it? Give me that ring. Is this how she paid you, you dirty, rotten snake? Don't think I'm going to cry over you. I cried my last true tears at your father's grave. I know what it was to be loved by a good man and nobody can take that away from me. You stay in your room until I tell you to come out."

Moses answered the door the next evening when Mrs. Cranmer rang. She was wearing a hat, gloves and so forth and he couldn't imagine what she wanted. She had no car and must have walked over from the bus stop. He thought at first that she had the wrong address. She might have been a cook or a seamstress, looking for work. To speak to him directly, as she did, seemed to drain her courage and self-esteem.

"You tell your wife to leave my son alone."

"I don't understand."

"You tell your wife to leave my son alone. I don't know how many other men she's after but if I catch her near my boy again I'll scratch her eyes out."

"I don't . . ." She had exhausted her strength and he

closed the door calling: "Melissa, Melissa." Why didn't she answer? Why didn't she answer? He heard her climbing the stairs and he followed. The door stood open and she sat at her dressing table with her face in her hands. He felt the blood of murder run in his veins and as, in desire, he sometimes seemed to feel her body beneath his hands before he had touched her, now he seemed to feel her throat, its cords and muscles, as he put out her life. He was shaking. He came up behind her, put his hands around her neck and when she screamed he strangled the scream but then some fear of Hell rose in him and he threw her onto the floor and went out.

CHAPTER XXVI

What had happened; what had happened to Moses Wapshot? He was the better-looking, the brighter, the more natural of the two men and yet in his early thirties he had aged as if the crises of his time had been much harsher on a simple and impetuous nature like his than on Coverly, who had that long neck, that disgusting habit of cracking his knuckles and who suffered seizures of melancholy and petulance.

Moses arrived suddenly in Talifer one Saturday morning, unannounced. He found his brother washing windows. A mythology that would penetrate with some light the density of the relationship between brothers seems to stop with Cain and Abel and perhaps this is as it should be. The utter delight with which Coverly and Moses greeted one another was seasoned unself-consciously with mayhem. Moses smiled scornfully at his brother's window-washing rags. Coverly noticed that Moses' face was red and swollen. Moses carried a walking stick with a silver handle. As soon as he got into the house he unscrewed the handle and

poured himself a martini from the stock. "It holds a pint,"
he said calmly. "Wouldn't Father have liked one?" He
drank his gin that early in the day as if the memory of his
father and so many other stalwarts had exempted him, as a
Wapshot, from the problems of abstemiousness and self-
discipline. "I'm on my way to San Francisco," he explained. "I thought I'd drop in. There's a plane out at five.
Melissa and the boy are *fine*. They're just bully."

He said this boisterously and with force for like Coverly
—like Melissa—he had developed an adroitness at believ-
ing that what had happened had not happened, that what
was happening was not happening and that which might
happen was impossible. The mystery of Honora was their
first concern. Coverly had telephoned St. Botolphs but no
one had answered. His letters to Honora had been returned. Moses had felt that her letters about the holly tree
might have concealed the fact that she was sick but how
could this fit in with the fact that she had broken some
law? Coverly might have shown his brother the computation center or let him see the gantry line through his binoc-
ulars but instead he drove Moses to the ruined farm and
they walked there in the woods. It was a fine winter's day
in that part of the world and Coverly brought to its brightness and space considerable moodiness. The orchard still
bore some crooked fruit and the sound and fragrance of
windfalls seemed to him as ancient a piece of the world as
its oceans. Paradise must (he thought) have smelled of
windfalls. A few dead leaves coursed along the wind, re-
minding Coverly of the energies that drive the seasons.
Watching the leaves drawn down and along he felt in himself an arousal of aspiration and misgiving. Moses appeared to be concerned principally with his thirst. When
they had walked for a little while he suggested that they
find a liquor store. As they were going back to the car
there seemed to be an abort on the gantry line. There was
a loud explosion from that direction and then there were
signs that an air alert had been sounded. No planes could
be seen in the blue sky but they could be heard roaring like
that most innocent of roarings when a sea shell is held by
some old man to the ear of a child.

They went back to the car and drove to a liquor store

in the outskirts but the place was shut. A sign hung in the glass window: "This store is closed so that our employees can be with their families." Now sporadic and senseless panic sometimes swept Talifer. A handful of men and women would lose their hopefulness and retire to their shelters to pray and get drunk; but this seemed no more significant to Coverly than the Adventists of his childhood who would now and then dress in sheets, climb Parson's Hill and wait for the resurrection of the dead and the life of the world to come. Total disaster seemed to be some part of the universal imagination. They drove on toward the shopping center and found a liquor store that was open. Moses said that he needed cash and the proprietor of the store, on Coverly's endorsement, cashed a check for a hundred dollars. When they got back to the house Moses filled up his walking stick and settled down for some serious drinking. At four Coverly drove his brother to the commercial airport and said good-bye to him at the main entrance; a farewell that seemed to be for both of them a violent mixture of love and combativeness.

Three days later the liquor store called to say that Moses' check had bounced. Coverly stopped there and covered it with a check of his own. On Thursday a motel near the airport called. "I saw your name in the phone book," the stranger said, "and it's such a funny name I thought you might be related. There's a man out here named Moses Wapshot. He's been here since Saturday and just by counting the empties I would guess he's drinking about two quarts a day. He hasn't made a nuisance of himself or nothing but unless he's pouring the stuff down the sink he's heading for trouble. I thought you ought to know if he was a member of your family." Coverly said he would be right out and he drove to the motel but when he got there Moses had gone.

CHAPTER XXVII

᥍᧞ ᥇᧞

It is doubtful that Emile had ever loved Melissa, had ever
experienced a genuine impulse of love for anyone but himself and the ghost of his father. He thought now and then
of Melissa, always concluding that he was blameless; that
whatever suffering she endured was no responsibility of his.
He killed some time after he was fired from Narobi's and
presently went to work at the new supermarket on the hill
—the one with a steeple. He was employed nominally as a
stock boy but when Mr. Freeley, the manager, took him
on, he explained that he would have another mission. The
market had then been open two months but business was
poor and the housewives of the village, like indulged children, were capricious and sometimes ill-tempered from the
lack in their lives of the tonic forces of longing and need.
Mr. Freeley had seen them storm his doors on opening day
and take away the fresh orchid corsage that was given to
each customer, but when the flowers were all gone he had
seen them return with something like heartlessness to their
old friends, the Grand Union and the A & P. They
swarmed like locusts, exhausting his below-cost specials
and buying the rest of their groceries somewhere else. His
market, he thought, was a thing of splendor. The broad
glass doors opened at a beam of light onto a museum of
victuals—galleries and galleries of canned goods, heaps
of frozen poultry and, over by the fish department, a little
lighthouse above a tank of sea water in which lobsters
swam. The air was full of music and soft lights. There
were diversions for the children and delicacies for the
gourmet but nobody—almost nobody—ever came his way.
   The store was one of a chain and the capriciousness of
the spoiled housewives had been calculated by the statisti-

cians in the central office. The ladies were incapable of
fidelity and could be counted upon, sooner or later, to find
their idle way into Mr. Freeley's museum. One only had to
wait and keep the place resplendent. But the ladies delayed longer than the statisticians had expected and Mr.
Freeley was finally given an exploitation package. On
Easter Eve a thousand plastic eggs were to be hidden in the
grass of the village. All of them contained certificates redeemable at the store for a dozen country-fresh eggs.
Twenty of them contained certificates redeemable for a
two-ounce bottle of costly French perfume. Ten of them
contained certificates redeemable for an outboard motor
and five of them—golden ones—were good for a three-
week, all-expense vacation for two at a luxury hotel in
Madrid, Paris, London, Venice or Rome. The response
was terrific and the store filled up with customers. They
reasoned that the eggs would be hidden by someone who
worked at the store and they intended to find out which
clerk it was. "It has been our experience," Mr. Freeley read
in the explanatory literature, "that there is among the
housewives in any community a large number who will
stop at nothing to ascertain the identity of the egg-hiders
and the probable position of the eggs. This has led in
some instances to an astonishing display of immorality."
It was Emile that Mr. Freeley hired to hide the eggs. Had
he checked with Narobi's he wouldn't have hired Emile at
all but he thought the boy's face clear and even virtuous.
He told Emile the details in his office. He had been given
a chart explaining where the eggs were to be hidden. They
were to be hidden between two and three on the morning
of Easter. Emile would be paid above his salary a stipend
of twenty-five dollars and in order to insure secrecy Mr.
Freeley would not speak to him again until Easter Eve.
In the meantime Emile would stamp cans.

The store closed at six on Easter Eve. The last potted
lily had been sold, but some housewives still lingered in the
museum galleries, trying to tempt from the stock boys the
secret of the eggs. At quarter after six the doors were
locked. At half-past six the lights were turned off and Mr.
Freeley was alone in the office with the eggs. He took the
chart out of the safe and studied it. A few minutes later

Emile came up the stairs. Everyone else had gone home. Mr. Freeley showed him the treasure and gave him the chart. His plan was to store the eggs in the back of Emile's car. He would be waiting on the sidewalk in front of Emile's house at two in the morning and they would begin their mission from there. Before they took the crates of eggs down from Mr. Freeley's office they made a careful examination of the waste bins and empty cartons at the back of the store to make sure that no housewife had concealed herself there. The eggs filled the luggage compartment and back seat of Emile's car. It was dusk when they began their work and dark when they had finished. They shook hands in a pleasant atmosphere of conspiracy and parted. Emile drove home cautiously as if the eggs at his back were fragile as well as valuable. The power of felicity and excitement they contained seemed palpable. There was an old garage behind the house and he put the car in here and padlocked the door. He was excited and a little oppressed by the fear that something might go wrong. The secret was not out but neither was it perfectly concealed. He knew that there were at least ten people at the store who, through a process of elimination, had come to suspect that he might be in charge of the treasure and he had had to deal with their questioning.

Mrs. Cranmer, having decided that Melissa had preyed on her son's innocence, had resumed her peaceable life with Emile. In spite of her age and the sorrows she had borne Mrs. Cranmer was still able to engage herself in friendship as passionately as a schoolgirl. She was easily slighted and easily elated by the neglect or attention of her neighbors. She had recently made a new friend in Remsen Park—the low-cost development—and talked with her on the telephone much of the time. She was talking on the telephone when Emile came in. Emile read the paper while he waited for his mother to finish her conversation. Mr. Freeley's exploitation specialists had taken the back page of the paper and the copy was inflammatory. There were pictures of the five European cities and an assurance that all you had to do was to look in your grass in the morning and you would be on your way.

They ate supper in the kitchen. When the dishes were

washed Mrs. Cranmer got back on the telephone. Now she was talking about the eggs and Emile guessed that many conversations in the village that night would be on this subject. It had not occurred to Mrs. Cranmer that her son might be chosen and he was grateful for this. After supper he watched television. At about nine o'clock he heard a dog barking. He went across the hall to his room and looked out of the window but there was no one by the garage. At half-past ten he went to bed.

Mr. Freeley felt very happy that evening. The store had begun to prosper and he felt that the trips to Madrid, Paris, London, Rome and Venice that would soon be hidden in the dewy grass were the result of his own generosity, his own abundant good nature. Kissing his wife in the kitchen he thought that she was as desirable as she had been when he married her many years ago; or if she was not that, she had at least kept abreast of the changes time and age had worked in him. He desired her ardently and happily and looked at the clock to see how long he must wait before they would be alone. There was a roast in the oven and she moved out of his embrace to baste it and then again to set the table, draw the baby's bath and pick up the toys, and as he watched her go about these necessary tasks he saw the wanness of fatigue come into her face and realized that by the time she had washed the dishes, ironed the pajamas, sung the lullabies and heard the prayers she might not have the strength to respond to his passionate caresses. This conflict in generative energies left him uncomfortable and after supper he took a walk.

The sky was dark and low but even if it rained, he thought, it would be better for his purposes than a bright moon. He walked out of his neighborhood into Parthenia and thought guiltily of how few eggs would be hidden here. Supermarkets and other changes had left the stores there mostly deserted. Filth was written on the walls and in one of the store windows, beyond the FOR RENT sign, was a display of funeral wreaths made of dry moss and false box-wood. One of these was shaped like a valentine heart and had a banner that said "Mother and Father" draped across its ventricles. This was Water Street, the demesne of the hoods. He saw three hoods standing in a doorway ahead of him and thought they looked familiar.

A week earlier Mr. Freeley had gone to the Easter Assembly at the high school to hear his daughter sing. He had come in late and stood at the back of the auditorium near the door, waiting like any other parent for the appearance of his child. His daughter, although she had no special gifts that he knew of, had been chosen to sing a solo. It was unfortunate that he had come in too late to find a seat. Standing near him at the door was a group of local hoods, whose whispering and shuffling made it difficult for him to give all his attention to the children's singing. The hoods seemed uncommitted to the performance. They kept slipping in and out the door and he thought how uncommitted they were to anything. They did not play games, they did not study, they did not skate on the ice pond or dance in the gymnasium but they menacingly circled all these activities, always in some doorway or on some threshold, in and out of the light as they were this evening.

Then the pianist began to hammer out the music for his daughter's solo and he saw the girl step shyly from the ranks of the chorus to the front of the stage. At the same time one of the hoods left his shadowy position at the door and joined a girl who was standing in front of Mr. Freeley. They blocked the view of his daughter. He moved to the left and then to the right, but the hood and his girl were always in the way and he only had a glimpse of his child. He had a good view of the hood and his maneuvers with the girl. He saw him put an arm around her shoulders. He heard him whispering into her ear. Then to the music of "I Know That My Redeemer Liveth" he saw him slip his hand into the front of her dress. Mr. Freeley seized the boy and the girl roughly by the shoulders and thrust them apart, saying so loudly that his daughter looked out at the disturbance: "Cut it out or take it out. This is no place for that kind of thing." He was shaking with rage and to keep himself from hitting the youth in the face he walked out of the auditorium and onto the schoolhouse steps.

He lit a cigarette with difficulty. He was so deeply disturbed that he wondered if what was really bothering him was not fear for his daughter. He was sure that he had been enraged as a father and a citizen at the unsuitability of what he had just been a witness to during an Easter hymn in a building that belonged, at least in spirit, to the innocent. When his cigarette had burned down he went back into the auditorium. The hoods stood aside to let him pass and he thought he had never experienced such an emanation of naked hatred as came from them toward him.

The hoods in the doorway on Water Street had the same suspenseful attitudes, showed the same choice of half-lights, and he felt a revolting strangeness toward them as if they had not come from another class or neighborhood but had come hurtling down from an evil planet. As he approached them he saw they were passing around a whisky bottle. He could not reproach them for lawlessness and depravity. Lawlessness and depravity were their aspirations. He smelled whisky as he passed the doorway and then he was struck on the back of the head and instantly lost consciousness.

Emile's alarm woke him at half-past one. While he was shaving a gust of wind slammed the door of his room and woke his mother. Waked so suddenly she sounded heavy and her voice like the voice of a much older woman. "Emile. You sick?"

"No, Mum," he said. "It's all right."

"You sick? You in trouble, dear? Those frozen crab cakes—did they make you sick?"

"No, Mum," he said. "It's nothing."

"You sick?" she asked, still heavily, and then she cleared her voice and seemed at the same moment to clear her mind. "Emile!" she exclaimed. "It's the eggs."

"I have to go now, Mum," he said. "It's nothing serious. I'll be back before breakfast."

"Oh, it's the eggs, isn't it?"

He could hear the bed creak as she sat up and put her feet on the floor, but he got by the door of her room before she reached it and went down the stairs. "I'll be back before breakfast," he called. "I'll tell you about it then." He felt for the chart in his pocket and let himself out the front door.

The stars were shining. It was much too early in the year for there to be anything blooming but a few clumps of snowdrops and the only wild flowers were the speckled skunk cabbages in the hollow but there was in the air a soft fragrance of earth as fine as roses and he stopped to fill his lungs and his head with it. The world seemed fine in the street light and the starlight and young, too, even in its shabbiness, as if the fate of the place had only just begun to be told. The earth, covered lightly with leaves, moss, garlic grass and early clover, was waiting for his treasure.

When there was no sign of Mr. Freeley at quarter after two he began to worry. It was so still that he could have heard a car in the far distance and he heard nothing. He wanted help on his mission, he did not want to do it alone, but at twenty minutes past two he decided that he would have to. He unlocked the garage doors, which, poorly hung, scraped loudly in the gravel. He looked in the back seat. His hoard was safe. When he backed the old car out onto the road the only light burning in the neighborhood was in his mother's parlor. He was too excited to imagine the mischief she might be up to and she was up to plenty. She had her new friend in Remsen Park on the telephone. "Emile's just gone out to hide the eggs," she said. "He just left. I don't know but I've got a feeling he's going to hide them in the Delos Circle neighborhood. I mean wouldn't it be just like Mr. Freeley to give everything to those rich snobs and forget his friends in Remsen Park? Wouldn't it be just like him?"

In another two hours, Emile thought, as he shifted from reverse into low, his mission would be accomplished and, this close to success, he saw how heavily the responsibility had weighed on his mind. A light was burning in a house at the corner but it was a small, narrow window, closely curtained, and he guessed that it was a bathroom. As he watched the light went out. From the top of Turner Street near the golf links he could see all over the village—see how perfect and reassuring the darkness was and how deeply the place slept, and the thought of so many men, women, children and dogs wandering through their labyrinthine dreams made him smile. He stood at the headlights of his car, reading the instructions. Eight eggs at the corner of Delwood Avenue and Alberta Street, three eggs on Alberta Street, ten eggs at the junction of Delos Circle and Chestnut Lane.

The Hazzards lived at the corner of Delwood Avenue and Alberta Street. Mrs. Hazzard was awake. She had waked from a bad dream at about two and was sitting at the open window, smoking. She was thinking about the eggs—about those that contained warrants for travel—and wondering if any would be hidden on Alberta Street. She wanted to see Europe. There was more envy than longing in her feeling. It was not so much that she wanted to see the world as that she wanted to see what other people had seen. When she read in the paper that Venice was sinking into the sea and that the leaning tower of Pisa was due to collapse, what she felt was not sadness at the disappearance of these wonders but a sharp bitterness at the image of Venice vanishing beneath the waves before she, Laura Hazzard, had seen it. She also felt that she was singularly well equipped to appreciate the pleasures of travel. It was her kind of thing. When friends and relations returned from Europe with their photographs and souvenirs she listened to their accounts of travel with the feeling that her impressions would have been more vivid, her souvenirs and photographs would have been more beautiful and that she would have fitted more gracefully into a gondola. But there were some tender sentiments mixed with her envy. Travel was linked in her mind to the magnificence and pathos of love; it would be like a revelation of the affections. She had sensed, in love, a sky much deeper than the blue sky of the Northern Hemisphere; more spacious rooms and stairways, arches, domes, all the paraphernalia of the enormous past. She was thinking of this when she saw a car come around the corner and stop. She recognized Emile and watched him begin to hide his eggs in the grass. This whole sequence of events—the bad dream that waked her, her thoughts as she sat at the open window and the sudden arrival of the young man in the starlight—seemed to her marvelous and in her excitement she called down to him from the window.

Despair swept over Emile when he heard her voice. How, short of wringing her neck, could he undo the fact that she had seen him at his secret task? "Shhh," he said, looking up at the window, but she had gone and in a minute she opened the door and ran out barefoot and in her nightgown. "Oh, Emile, you know I think I was meant to find one," she said. "I couldn't sleep and I was just sitting at the window when you came along. I have to have one of the gold ones, Emile! Give me one of the gold ones."

"It's supposed to be a secret, Mrs. Hazzard," Emile whispered. "Nobody's supposed to know. You're not supposed to look for them until morning. You have to go back into your house now. You go on back to bed."

"What do you think I am, Emile?" she asked. "You think I'm a little girl or something? You give me a golden egg and I'll go back to bed but I won't move until you do."

"You'll spoil everything, Mrs. Hazzard. I won't hide any more eggs until you go back into your house."

"You give me a golden egg, you give me one of those golden eggs or I'll help myself."

Mrs. Hazzard's voice waked old Mrs. Kramer who lived next door. Instantly alert, she installed her teeth, stepped into her slippers and went to the window. She understood the meaning of the scene at once. She went to the telephone and called her daughter, Helen Pincher, who lived three blocks away on Millwood Street. Helen woke from a deep sleep and mistook the telephone for the alarm clock. She tried to stop the ringing, shook the clock and finally turned on the light before she realized that it was the telephone. "Helen, it's Mother," the old woman said. "They're hiding the Easter eggs. Right in front of my house. I can see them out of my window. Get over here!"

The ringing of the bell had not waked Mr. Pincher but the light and the last of the conversation did. He saw his wife put down the phone and run out of the room. For the last month or so Mr. Pincher had been alarmed by his wife's conduct. She had overdrawn the checking account three times, she had run out of gasoline three times in the same week, she had forgotten to wear stockings to the Gripsers' wedding, she had lost her snake bracelet and she had ruined his good leather hunting jacket by putting it into the washing machine. Each time she had said: "I must be going out of my mind." When he heard footsteps outside and looked out of the window and saw that she was running down the front walk in her nightgown he was convinced that she really had become irrational. He got into his bathrobe but he couldn't find any slippers and so he ran barefoot out of the house after her. She had a lead of a block or more and he called loudly: "Helen, Helen, come back, dear. Come home, dear." He woke the Barnstables, the Melchers, the Fitzroys and the DeHovens.

Emile got back into his car. Mrs. Hazzard tried to open the other door and get in but it was locked. He tried to start the car but he was nervous and the motor flooded. Then into the beam of his headlights came Helen Pincher, running. Her nightgown was transparent and the curlers in her hair looked like a crown. Her mother was hanging out of the window, urging her on. "That's them, Helen, there they are!" Behind her, her husband shouted: "Come back, darling, come back, sweetheart."

Emile got the car started just as Helen reached it and she put her head in at the window. "I want the one for Paris, Emile," she said.

Emile put the car into gear and as he began slowly to let out the clutch Mr. Pincher joined them shouting: "Stop that car, you damned fool. She's sick." Now in the beam of his headlights Emile saw the approach of a dozen or more women in nightgowns. They all appeared to be wearing crowns. He continued to move the car slowly forward but some of the women stood directly in his way and he had to stop twice to avoid harming them. During one of these stops Mrs. DeHoven let the air out of one of his rear tires.

Emile felt the car settle. He knew what had happened but he went on moving slowly. The deflated tire slumped against the shoe and he could not get up much speed but he thought he might outstrip his pursuers. Alberta Street at that point went steeply downhill for perhaps half a mile. On the left was a large tract of empty land. The owner (old Mrs. Kramer) was asking ten thousand an acre and the property hadn't moved. It had gone to deep grass and scrub wood and on every wild cherry and sumac tree there was nailed the name and telephone number of some real estate agent. Emile thought that if he got to Delos Circle he might be in the clear. He speeded up going downhill, but just as his headlights reached Delos Circle he saw the housewives of Remsen Park, thirty or forty of them, most of them wearing long robes and what appeared to be massive crowns. He swung the car sharply to the left, bumped over the curb and the sidewalk into the unsold house lots and drove straight to the far boundary of the property. He was trapped but he still had some time at his disposal. He cut the motor and the lights, ran around to the back and opened the luggage compartment and began to pitch the eggs off into the deep grass. He had a good wing and by heaving the eggs far away from him he was able to divert the advancing crowd. His arm got lame before long and then he began to take the egg crates and dump their contents into the grass. He disposed of all but one before the women reached him and straightened up to see them, so like angels in their nightclothes, and hear their soft cries of longing and excitement. Then with a single egg in his pocket—a golden one—he cut back through the woods.

The pain of the blow that had stunned Mr. Freeley drew him back into consciousness. His head felt broken. He found himself lashed by wire to a post in a cellar. He shook with cold and saw that he had nothing on but his underpants. At first he thought he had lost his mind but the centralizing force of pain in his head gave a terrible vividness and reality to his circumstances. He was a big man, his body carpeted with the brindle hair of middle age. The wires that bound him cut deeply into his fleshy arms and his hands were numb. Suddenly he roared for help but there was no reply. He had been robbed and beaten and now he was trapped and helpless in some place that seemed to be underground. The outrageousness of the situation— and panic—made him feel that his brain was cracking open and when he trembled the wire cut his skin. Then he heard footsteps and voices upstairs, the voices of the hoods. They came, one by one, into the cellar. It was the same three. There was the leader, then there was one with a fat face and then a thin, pale one with long hair.

"Chicken," the leader said, looking at him.

"What do you want from me?" Mr. Freeley said. "You

have my money. Was it because of that girl at the high
school?"

"I don't know nothing about no girl at no high school,"
the leader said. "I just don't like your looks, chicken, that's
all. What's the matter, chicken? Why you shaking so? You
afraid we're going to torture you with matches and all? He
struck a match and held it close to Mr. Freeley's skin
but he didn't burn him. "Look at chicken. Chicken's afraid
of dying. That's why I don't like your looks, chicken.
Jesus, listen to chicken roar."

Mr. Freeley roared. The floor tipped first to the left,
then to the right and he lost consciousness again. Then he
felt that he was being touched. He was being cut down. He
could feel the loosening of the wires and the rush of blood
back into his arms. He would have fallen but someone
caught him and supported him. It was the pale one with the
long, oily hair. He led Mr. Freeley over to the corner where
there was an old automobile seat and he fell onto it.

"Where are the others?" he asked.

"They gone," the boy said. "They got scared when you
blacked out."

"You?"

"I'm scared all the time."

"What do you want?"

"Nothing now. It's just like he said. He don't like your
looks. You want some water?"

"Yes."

The boy got some water and held the glass to his lips.

"When can I go?"

"Go," the boy said. "Your suit's upstairs. It didn't fit
nobody. Harry took your watch. I didn't take nothing.
Good-bye, now."

He swung out of the door and Mr. Freeley heard him run
lightly up some stairs. He felt his head wound and then
he felt his arms and legs. Everything seemed to be sound
and he went feebly up the stairs. His suit was by the door
and when he got outside he saw that he was in an
abandoned roadhouse at the edge of town.

Mr. Freeley walked home. So did Emile but they took
different routes. Emile cut through some back yards to
Turner Street and started up the hill. The scene was

apocalyptic. Forsaken children could be heard crying in empty houses and most of the doors stood open in the dawn as if Gabriel's long trumpet had sounded. At the top of Turner Street he cut over onto the golf links, climbed to the highest fairway and sat down, waiting for the day. He felt tired, happy, humorous and relieved of his responsibility and of a much heavier burden. Something had happened. Something had changed. Like everyone else who reads the newspapers he had come to hold in his mind a fear that some drunken corporal might incinerate the planet and to hold in another part of his mind the most passionate longings for a peaceful life among his generations. In spite of his youth he had breathed in this concept of general infirmity. He seemed at times to listen to the planet's heartbeat as if the earth were a melancholy hypochondriac, possessed of great strength and beauty and with them an incurable presentiment of sudden and meaningless death. Now the moment of danger seemed past, and he felt joyfully that the illustrious and peaceful works of man would go on forever. He could not describe his feelings, he could not describe the dawn, he could not even describe the hooting of a train that he heard in the distance or the shape of the tree under which he sat. He could only watch and admire the vast barrel of night fill up to its last shelf and crevice with the fair light of day and all the birds singing in the trees like a band of angels whistling to their hounds.

On his way home he stopped at Melissa's and put the golden egg for Rome on her lawn.

PART THREE

CHAPTER XXVIII

❦

For someone so old, born and raised in a distant world, Honora's familiarity with the photographs of the monuments of <u>Rome</u> made at one level her entry into the city a sort of homecoming. A large, brown picture of Hadrian's Tomb had hung in her bedroom when she was a child. Waiting for sleep, suffering and recovering from illnesses, its drum-shaped form and rampant angel had taken a solid place in her reveries. In the back hall there had been a picture of the Bridge of Angels and two large photographs of the Imperial Forum had been handed backward, room to room, until they ended up in the cook's quarters. Thus, some of Rome was very familiar. But what did one do in Rome? One saw the Pope. Honora asked at the American Express Office how this could be arranged. They were very helpful, respecting her age, and sent her on to a priest at the American college. The priest was courteous and interested. An audience could be arranged. She would receive her invitation within twenty-four hours of the appointment. She was to wear dark clothes and a hat and if she wanted to have some medals blessed he could recommend a shop—he gave her an address—where there was a fine assortment of religious medals sold at a 20 percent discount.

He explained, tactfully, that while the Holy Father spoke English, he spoke the language more fluently than he understood it and that should he forget to bless her medals, she could consider them blessed by his presence. Honora was, of course, opposed to the use of medals but she had plenty of friends who would value a blessed medal and she bought a stock. Returning one evening to her *pensione*

she was handed a card from the Vatican, announcing her
audience for ten the next morning. She rose early and
dressed. She took a taxi to the Vatican, where a man in
immaculate evening dress asked for her name and her card.
He pronounced her name "Whamshang." He asked her
please to remove her gloves. His English was thickly accented and she did not understand. It took some explaining to make clear to her that one did not wear gloves in
the presence of the Holy Father. He took her up a flight
of stairs. She had to stop twice to rest her legs and get her
wind. They waited in an anteroom for half an hour. It was
after eleven when a second equerry opened some double
doors and ushered her into an enormous *salone,* where she
saw the Holy Father standing by his throne. She kissed his
ring and sat in a chair that was proffered by a second
equerry. He held, she noticed, a salver in his hands in
which there were several checks. It had not crossed her
mind that she would be expected to make a contribution to
the Church during her audience and she put a few lire onto
the salver. She was not shy but she felt herself to be in the
presence of holiness, the essence of a magnificently organized power, and she regarded the Pope with genuine
awe.

"How many children have you, Madame?" he asked.

"Oh, I don't have any children," she said, speaking
loudly.

"Where is your home?"

"I come from St. Botolphs," she said. "It's a little village. I don't suppose you've ever heard of it."

"San Bartolomeo?" The Holy Father asked with interest.

"No," she said, "Botolphs."

"San Bartolomeo di Farno," the Pope said, "di Savigli-
ano, Bartolomeo il Apostolo, Il Lepero, Bartolomeo Capi-
tanio, Bartolomeo degli Amidei."

"Botolphs," she repeated, halfheartedly. Then suddenly
she asked, "Have you ever seen the Eastern United States
in the autumn, Holy Father?" He smiled and seemed interested but he said nothing. "Oh, it's a glorious sight,"
she exclaimed. "I don't suppose there's anything else like
it in the world. It's like a harvest of gold and yellow. Of

course the leaves are worthless and I've gotten so old and lame that I have to pay someone to rake and burn them for me but my they are beautiful and they give such an impression of wealth—oh, I don't mean anything mercenary—but everywhere you look you see golden trees, gold everywhere."

"I would like to bless your family," the Pope said.

"Thank you."

She bowed her head. He spoke the blessing in Latin and when she felt sure that it was ended she loudly said *Amen*. The interview ended, an equerry took her down and she passed the Swiss Guards and returned to the colonnade.

Melissa and Honora didn't meet. Melissa lived on the Aventine with her son and a *donna di servizio* and worked on a sound stage near the Piazza del Popolo, dubbing Italian spectacles into English. She was the voice of Mary Magdalen, she was Delilah, she was the favorite of Hercules; but she had the Roman Blues. These are no more virulent than the New York Blues or the Paris Blues but they have a complexion of their own and like any other form of emotional nausea they can, when they are in force, make such commonplace sights as a dead mouse in a trap seem apocalyptic. If homesickness was involved, it was not, for Melissa, a clear string of images evoking the pathos, the sweetness and the vigor of American life. She did not long to canoe on the Delaware once more or to hear, once more, harmonica music on the dusky banks of the Susquehanna. Walking down the Corso her blues were the blues of not being able to understand the simplest remark and the chagrin of being swindled. It was the Campidolio on a rainy day, with a guide trailing her around and around the statue of Marcus Aurelius, complaining about the season and the business. It was a winter rain so cold that she felt for the host of naked gods and heroes on the rooftops without even a fig leaf to protect them from the wet. It was the damps of the Forum, the chill in the seventeenth-century stairwells and the forlorn kitchens of Rome with their butcher's marble, their fly-specked walls and their stained pictures of the Holy Virgin hung above a leaky gas ring. It was autumn in a European city with war forever in the air; it was the withering of those clumps of flowers that grow in the highest orifices of Aurelian's Wall, those clusters of hay and grass that sprout up between the very toes of the saints and angels who stand around the domes of Roman churches. It was that room on the Capitoline where the Roman portrait busts are stacked up; but instead of feeling some essence or shade of Imperial power she was reminded of that branch of her family that had gone north to Wisconsin to raise wheat. There seemed to be Aunt Barbara and Uncle Spencer and cousins Alice, Homer, Randall and James. They had the same clear features, the same thick hair, the same look of thoughtfulness, fortitude and worry. Their royal wives were helpmates—and they sat in their marble thrones as if the pies were in the oven and they were waiting for their men to return from the fields. She tried to walk through the streets looking alert and hurried—caught up in the tragedy of modern European history—as most of the people on the street seemed to be, but the sweetness of her smile made it clear that she was not a Roman. She walked in the Borghese Gardens feeling the weight of habit a woman her age or any other age carries from one country to another; habits of eating, drinking, dress, rest, anxiety, hope and, in her case, the fear of death. The light in the gardens seemed to illuminate the bulkiness of her equipment, as if the whole scene, and the distant hills, had been set up for someone who traveled with less. She walked by the moss-choked fountains and the leaves were falling among the marble heroes; heroes with aviators' caps, heroes with beards, heroes with laurels and ascots and cutaways and heroes whose marble faces time and weather had singled out capriciously for disfigurement. Troubled and uneasy, she walked and walked, taking some pleasure in that tranquillity that falls with the shade from great trees onto the shoulders of man. She watched an owl fly out of a ruin. At a turning in the path she smelled marigolds. The garden was full of lovers, very sweet with one another and candid about their pleasures, and she watched a couple kissing by a fountain. Then suddenly the man sat down on a bench and took a pebble out of his shoe. Whatever the significance of this was, Melissa realized that she wanted to get out of Rome and she took a train to the islands that night.

CHAPTER XXIX

Emile was out of work for most of the summer and in the fall his mother's brother Harry came to visit them while he attended a convention in New York. He was a pleasant, heavy man who ran a ship-provisioning business in Toledo. He could, through his influence as a provisioner, get Emile a place as an unlicensed hand on one of the ships that plied the seaway to Rotterdam or Naples and Emile agreed to the plan at once. When Uncle Harry returned to Toledo he wrote to say that Emile could sail as a deck hand on the S.S. *Janet Runckle* at the end of the week.

Emile bought his bus ticket to Toledo at a travel agency in Parthenia, said good-bye to his mother and went on into New York. The bus was scheduled to leave at nine that night but by eight o'clock there were more than a dozen passengers on the waiting platform. These were travelers and you could tell it by their finery, their shy looks and their new bags. Every people seems to have some site, some battlefield, tomb or cathedral where their national essence and purpose is most exposed, and the railroad stations, airports, bus stops and piers of his country seemed to be the scenery where his kind found their greatness. They were dressed, most of them, as if their destination were some sumptuary judgment seat. Their shoes pinched, their gloves were stiff, their headgear was topheavy, but this nicety in dress seemed to suggest that the ancient legends of travel—Theseus and the Minotaur—were still, however faintly, remembered by them. Their eyes were utterly undefended, as if an exchanged glance

between two miscreants would plunge them both into an
erotic abyss, and they kept their looks to themselves, their
bags, the paving or the unlighted sign above the platform.
At twenty minutes to nine the sign was lighted—it said
TOLEDO—and they stirred, got to their feet, pressed forward, their faces filled with light as if a curtain had just
risen on a new life, a paradise of urgency and beauty,
although it rose in fact on the Jersey marshes, the all-night
restaurants, the plains of Ohio and some troubled dreams.
The windows of the bus were tinted green and driving out
of the city all the street lights burned greenly as if the
whole world were a park.

He slept well and woke at dawn. They spent the day
crossing Ohio. The green windowglass made the landscape
baneful, as if the sun had grown cold and these were the
last hours of life on the planet, and in this strange light
people went on hitchhiking, mowing fields and selling used
cars. Late in the day they came to the outskirts of Toledo
but he might have been coming home to Parthenia. There
were hamburger stands and places where you could buy
fresh vegetables and used-car lots with strings of lights and
a dog-and-cat hospital and a woman in a bathing suit
pushing a gasoline lawn mower and a pregnant woman
hanging out her wash and the elms and the maples were the
same, he noticed, and Queen Anne's lace grew in the
fields and you couldn't tell until you got to the center of
the city whether you were in Parthenia or Toledo.

The other passengers scattered and Emile stood on a
corner with his suitcase. The air, he thought, had a grassy
smell. Perhaps this was from the surrounding farms or the
lake. The street lights burned and the store windows were
lighted but there was still a rosy light from the setting sun
and he felt that excitement he always experienced in the
ball park when, during the fourth or fifth inning of a
double-header, they would turn on the lights while the sky
was still blue. It was not cold at all but he shivered as if
at this hour and in this flat country there were some subtle
rawness in the air. He asked a policeman for directions to
the Union Hall. It was a long walk. The daylight had risen
off the buildings and up out of the sky and he walked in
the light from store fronts, restaurants and bars. The Union

Hall when he got there seemed empty, a place with green walls and an oiled floor and benches for waiting. A man behind a window took his thirty-dollar fee and said that his uncle had made the arrangements. They would board the ship that night and sail whenever the loading was completed. He sat down on one of the benches and waited for the crew to come in.

The first to come was the cook, a short man in a brown business suit, who hailed his friend behind the window and introduced himself to Emile. His skin was sallow, his nose was broken and unset. That was the first thing you noticed, that and the monkey light in his eye. It was the broken nose that dominated his face, the widespread nares that made the shrewd light in his eye seem simian, mischievous at times and at times as reflective as the eyes of any cold monkey in a Sunday afternoon zoo. "You look just like a fellow shipped out with us last year," he said. "Paff was his name. He got a scholarship in some university and left the sea. You look just like him."

Emile was happy to resemble someone who had gotten a scholarship to college. Some of the stranger's intelligence seemed to rub off on his shoulders. The rest of the crew began to straggle in and one by one they told him how much he looked like Paff. The first mate was a young man who knocked his cap to the back of his head like a ballplayer and who seemed cheerful, aggressive but not at all bellicose. The second mate was an old man with a thin mustache and a threadbare uniform who took a photograph of his daughter out of his wallet and showed it to Emile. The picture showed a girl in ballet costume, posed on the roof of a tenement. Then the cabin steward joined Emile and the cook. He was a young man with that identifiable gentility that is bred in the turf huts of Nebraska; a mode of elegance that is formed in utter despair. There were thirty-five in all. The last to come was a dark-skinned man carrying a bar bell.

Taxis took them out of the city. Emile sat in front with the driver and the cook, trying to make out Toledo. There were lights, buildings, a river in the distance, and there must have been a beach nearby because many of the people in the opposite lanes of traffic wore bathing suits. Emile 'elt with intense discomfort that he had not made his presence in Toledo a reality; that he had left the better part of himself in Parthenia. They crossed railroad tracks and went into a dark neighborhood lit by gas-cracking plants, with here and there a saloon on a corner. They stopped at a gate where a man in uniform sent them on at the sight of the cook and then they were in a wilderness until at a turn in the road they came into a broad circle of light and an uproar of engine noise where the S.S. *Janet Runckle* was being loaded in a night world independent of the fact that the sun had set on the banks of Lake Erie two or three hours ago and where, like the music of some romantic agony, the noise of cranes, winches, ore-loaders, fork lifts, donkey engines, hopper cars and boat whistles filled the air.

The passengers came aboard at midnight. The first was an old man with his wife or daughter. He climbed the long gangway directly but the woman with him seemed afraid. It was finally suggested that she take off her high-heel shoes and with a deck hand in front and one behind she was eased up the gangway. The next to come was a man with his wife and three children. One of the children was crying. The last to come was a young man carrying a guitar. At four Emile went on duty and hosed down the decks with the rest of the watch. He wore Paff's waterproofs. The captain ordered a tug for five but when the tug was delayed he put two men overside in the bosun's chair and warped the ship out into the channel with lines and winches. They blew their stack in the dawn and Emile wished on the morning star for a safe voyage.

The morning watch hosed down the decks and washed the superstructure and deckhouse with soap and water. The afternoon watch chipped paint. The work was easy and the company was cheerful but the food was terrible. It was the worst food Emile had ever eaten. There were powdered eggs for breakfast, greasy meat and potatoes for dinner and cheese and cold cuts every night. Emile was hungry all the time and his hunger took on the scope of some profound misunderstanding between the world and himself. The plate of cheese and cold cuts that he faced each evening seemed to represent, like a sacrament, stupidity and indifference. His needs, his aspirations and his time of life were all misunderstood and cheese and cold cuts exacerbated the fact. He left the galley in anger one evening and went back to the stern. Simon joined him there; Simon was the one with the bar bell. "This *Runckle,*" Simon said. "She's famous all over the world for bad chow."

"I'm hungry," Emile said.

"I'm skipping ship in Naples," Simon said. "I got four hundred dollars in travel checks. You come with me."

"I'm hungry," Emile said.

"There's this American restaurant in Naples," Simon said. "Roast beef, mashed potatoes. You can even get a club sandwich. You come with me."

"Where," Emile asked, "where will we go?"

"Ladros," Simon said. "There's this beauty contest I'm going to be in. The way I figure it is, you got just so many chances and I know one thing, I got my looks. I'm very good-looking. It's the only thing I got and I better cash in on it before it's too late. In Ladros you can pick up two, three thousand dollars in this contest."

"You're crazy," Emile said.

"Well, there's no doubt about the fact that I'm vain," Simon said. "I'm a very vain man. I never go by a mirror without looking at myself and thinking there goes a very good-looking man. Never. But you come with me. We'll go to this restaurant. Apple pie. Hamburgers."

"Blueberry pie's my favorite," Emile said. "After that lemon meringue. Then apricot."

Emile saw the Azores glumly across a plate of cheese and cold cuts. Gibraltar was meat loaf. He ate bloated spaghetti sailing down the coast of Spain and when they docked early one morning in Naples he felt, in spite of his indifference to Simon's ambitions, that he had no choice. They left the *Runckle* in the middle of the morning and went to an American restaurant where Emile put away two plates of ham and eggs and a club sandwich and felt like himself for the first time since leaving Toledo. They took an afternoon boat in a choppy sea to Ladros. Simon got seasick. The contest headquarters was in a café in the main *piazza* and although Simon's face was green the first thing

he did was to enroll and pay his entry fee. They got cots
in a dormitory near the port where twenty-five or thirty
other contestants were boarding. Simon worked conscien-
tiously on his muscle-building. He oiled and sunned himself and wore, like the others, something called a slip,
a sort of codpiece. He rented a boat and exercised in this
during the mornings. After his siesta he worked out with
the bar bells. Emile, wearing voluminous American trunks,
rowed with him in the morning and spent a pleasant time
swimming off the rocks.

It was very hot and Ladros was crowded but the sea had
a color he had never seen before and there was something
in the air, a suspension of conscience, that made the white
beaches and the dark seas of his own country seem censorious and remote. He seemed, in crossing the Bay of
Naples, to have lost his scruples. The contest was on
Saturday and on Friday Simon came down with a bad attack of food poisoning. Emile bought him some medicine
in a pharmacy but he was up most of the night and was too
weak to get out of bed in the morning. Emile felt for him
deeply and wished it were in his power to help. He had
wasted his savings and if his sole ambition was ridiculous
could he be blamed? Simon asked Emile to take his place
and in the end he agreed. It was the brute power of boredom that forced his decision. He had nothing else to do.
He got into his bathing trunks, put on Simon's numeral
and went up to the *piazza* at a little after four. The hot,
bright sunlight could still be seen at the foot of the street
but the square was in shade. There was a long wait.
Presently a boatload of English tourists came in and filled
up the tables at the edge of the square and then, in
numerical order, the procession started.

He didn't want to seem sullen, that after all would have
been unfair to Simon, but he did want to seem disengaged,
to make clear that this was not his idea, not what he
wanted. He didn't look at the faces below him but stared
at an advertisement for San Pellegrini mineral water on a
wall beyond the café. What would his mother have thought,
his uncle, the ghost of his father? Where was the dark
house in Parthenia where he had lived? When he had
crossed the *piazza* he waited around with the others and

then was led into the café by the proprietor and didn't realize until then that there were only ten and that he was one of the winners.

It was getting dark by then, deepening into the grape-colored sky that more than anything else made him feel not unpleasantly far from home. Now the *piazza* was crowded. The ten men stood at the bar drinking coffee and wine, held together by the bond of a common experience and a questionable victory and alienated by the barriers of language. Emile stood between a Frenchman and an Egyptian and the best he could do was to speak a little crude Italian and smile hopefully but fatuously to prove that he was friendly and self-possessed. As it grew darker and darker in the *piazza*, as the light of day faded and as they stood under the bare lights of the café that had been arranged sensibly and economically to light the work of the bartenders and to flatter no one, they might, but for their lack of clothing, have been a group of workmen, clerks or jurors, stopping for a drink on their way back to wherever their lives were centered, to wherever they were awaited and wanted. Emile did not understand what would happen next and he asked the proprietor in dumb show to explain. The explanation was long and it was a long time before Emile understod that they, the ten winners, would now be auctioned off to the crowd in the *piazza*. "But I'm an American," Emile said. "We don't believe in that!"

"Niente, niente," the judge said gently and explained to Emile that if he didn't want to be sold he was free to go. In his own country Emile would have gone home indignantly but he was not in his own country and inquisitiveness or something deeper held him there. He was shocked to think that unfamiliar surroundings, lights and circumstances might influence his morals. To reinforce his character he tried to recall the streets of Parthenia but they were worlds away. Could it be true that his character was partly formed from rooms, streets, chairs and tables? Was his morality influenced by landscapes and kinds of food? Had he been unable to take his personality, his sense of good and evil, across the Bay of Naples?

In the *piazza* a band began to play and from behind the café a few mortars were fired off. Then the *padrone* opened the door and called to a man named Ivan, who smiled at his companions and went out onto the terrace where there was a block on which he stood. He seemed to acquiesce gracefully at this turn of events. Emile went out onto the terrace and stood in the shelter of an acacia tree. The bidding began lightheartedly, it seemed a joke, but as the bidding increased he realized that the young man's skin was up for sale. The bidding rose quickly to a hundred and fifty thousand lire; but then it came in slowly and the stir in the crowd was erotic. Ivan seemed impassive but the beating of his heart could be seen. Was this sin, Emile wondered, and if it was, why should it seem so deeply expressive of everyone there? Here was the sale of the utmost delights of the flesh, its racking forgetfulness. Here were the caves and the fine skies of venery, the palaces and stairways, the thunder and the lightning, the great king and the drowned sailor, and from the voices of the bidders it seemed that they had never wanted anything else. The bidding stopped at two hundred and fifty thousand lire and Ivan stepped off the block and walked into the dark where someone, Emile couldn't see who, had been waiting with a car. He heard the motor start and saw the headlights shine on the ruined walls as they drove off.

An Egyptian named Ahab came next but something was wrong. He smiled too knowledgeably, seemed much too ready to be sold and to perform what was expected of him and was knocked down at fifty thousand lire in a few minutes. A man called Paolo re-established the atmosphere of sexuality and the bids, as they had been for Ivan, came in slowly and hoarsely. Then a man named Pierre climbed onto the block and there was some delay before the bidding began at all.

Something had gone wrong. The bloom was off him. He had drunk too much wine or was too tired and now he stood on the block like a stick. His slip was cut scant enough to show his pubic hair and his pose was vaguely classical—the hips canted and one hand curved against his thigh—classical and immemorial as if he had appeared repeatedly in the nightmares of men. Here was the face of love without a face, a voice, a scent, a memory, here was a rub and a tumble without the sandy grain of a personality, here was a reminder of all the foolishness, vengefulness and lewdness in love and he seemed to excite, in the depraved crowd, a stubborn love of decency. They would sooner look at the prices on the menu than at him. His look was sly and wicked, he was more openly lascivious than the others but no one seemed to care. There was some subtle change in the atmosphere of the place. Ten thousand. Twelve thousand. Then the bidding stopped. This was the worst of all for Emile to see. Ivan had sold himself to God knows whom, a face in the dark, but it seemed more shameful and more sinful that Pierre, who was willing to perform the sacred and mysterious rites for the least sacred rewards, was wanted by no one and that for all his readiness to sin he might, in the end, have to spend a quiet night in the dormitory counting sheep. Something was wrong, some promise, however obscene, was broken and Emile sweated in shame for his companion, for to lust and to be unwanted seemed to be the grossest indecency. In the end Pierre was knocked down for twenty thousand lire. The *padrone* turned to Emile to ask if he wanted to reconsider his decision and in an intoxication of pride, a determination to prove that what had happened to Pierre could not happen to him, he went forward and stood on the block looking out boldly at the lights in the *piazza* as if he had in this way managed to come face to face with the world.

The bidding was spirited enough and he was knocked down for a hundred thousand lire. He stepped off the platform and walked through the tables to where a woman was waiting. It was Melissa.

She drove him up into the hills and through the gates of a villa where he could hear the loud noise of a fountain and nightingales singing in the trees and where he discovered that he had not brought his sense of good and evil across the bay. This eruption of his senses, this severance from the burdens of his life, was so complete that he seemed to fly, to swim, to live and die independently of all the well-known facts, that he seemed violently to destroy and renew himself, demolish and rebuild his spirit on some high sensual plane that was unbound from the earth and its calendar.

There was a pool in the garden where they swam and

they ate their meals on a terrace. With her this time he never seemed to achieve consciousness; or perhaps he had discovered a new level of consciousness. There were six black dogs around the place who watched them and the servants came and went with trays of food and liquor. He had no idea of the passage of time but he guessed he had been there a week or ten days when she said one morning that she had to drive down to Ladros on an errand but that she would be back before lunch.

She hadn't returned by two and he ate his lunch alone on the terrace. When the maids had cleared the table they went upstairs to take their siesta. The whole valley was still. He lay on the grass by the pool, waiting for her to return. He felt drugged by an acuteness of sexual sensation and like the absence of a drug her delayed return left him in pain. The black dogs lay in the grass around him. Two of the dogs kept bringing sticks for him to throw. Their demands were insistent and tedious. Every few minutes they would drop a stick at his feet and if he didn't throw it at once they would howl for his attention. He heard a car in the road and thought that in another five minutes she would be with him but the car continued on to a villa farther up the cliff. He dove into the pool and swam the length of it, but as he pulled himself out of the cold water into the hot sun this contact only made his need for her seem keener. The flowers in the garden seemed aphrodisiac and even the blue of the sky like some part of love. He swam the length of the pool again and lay on the grass in a shady part of the garden where the dogs joined him and the retrievers howled for him to throw sticks.

He wondered what she was doing in Ladros. The cook bought the wine and the food and there was, he thought, nothing she needed. Her inability to resist his touch and his looks made him wonder if she could resist the touch or the look of any other man and if she was not now climbing some staircase with a stranger with hairy forearms. The degree of his pleasure in her immersion in sensuality was the exact degree of his jealousy. He couldn't credit her with any vision of constancy; and he went on throwing sticks for the dogs.

He went on throwing sticks as if some clear duty were

involved, as if their welfare and amusement were on his
conscience. But why? He had not liked them or disliked
them. His feeling was substantial enough to be traced. He
did, it appeared, feel some obligation to the dogs. There
was some mutuality here as if in the past he had been a dog,
dependent upon the caprices of a stranger in a garden, or
as if in the future he might be transformed into a dog
asking to be let in out of the rain. There were obligations
and rewards, it seemed, for the patience with which he
threw sticks. But where was she? Why was she not now
with him? He tried to imagine her on some innocent errand
but he couldn't. Then he sat up suddenly in anger and
pain and the dogs sat up to watch. Their golden eyes and
the whining of the retrievers made him angrier and he
climbed the stairs to the *salone* and poured himself a drink
but he left the door open and the dogs followed him in
and sat around him on their haunches as he stood at the
bar as if they expected him to speak with them. The house
was still; the maids would be sleeping. Then his rage at her
propinquity, her uselessness, her corruption shook him
and the gaze of the animals only seemed more questing,
as if this hour were speeding toward a climax they well
knew; as if he were traveling toward some critical instant
that involved them all; as if their dumbness and his lust,
jealousy and anger were converging. He ran up the stairs
and dressed. It was an hour's walk to the village but he
didn't expect her car to pass him because he was convinced by then that when she did return it would be with
another lover and he would have been transformed into a
dog. But when she did pass him and stopped and when he
saw that there were groceries in the back of the car, his
moral indignation collapsed. He went back with her to the
villa and returned to Rome with her at the end of the week.

CHAPTER XXX

⋅⊰ ⊱⋅

Returning to her *pensione* one morning Honora found Norman Johnson waiting for her in the lobby. "Oh, Miss Wapshot," he said, "oh, it's so good to see you. It's so good to see anybody who can talk English. I was told that all these people studied English in school but most of the ones I've seen don't speak anything but Italian. Can we sit down here." He opened his briefcase and showed her the order for her extradition, a copy of the criminal indictment passed down by the circuit court in Travertine and an order for the confiscation of all her property; but with so much documented power in his hands he seemed shamefaced and it was she who felt sorry for him. "Don't you worry," she said, touching him lightly on the knee. "Don't you worry about me. It's all my fault. It was just that I was so afraid of the poor farm. I've been afraid of the poor farm all my life. Even when I was a little girl. When Mrs. Bretaigne used to take me motoring to see the autumn foliage I used to close my eyes when we passed the poor farm, I was so afraid of it. But now I'm homesick and I want to go back. I'll go down to the bank and get my money and we'll go home in one of those flying machines."

They walked together to the American Express Office, not as a jailer and a culprit but as dear friends. He waited downstairs while she closed her account and she joined him, carrying a large bundle of twenty-thousand lire notes. "I'll get a taxi," he said. "You can't walk through the streets like that. You'll be robbed." They stepped out into the Piazza di Spagna.

It was a bright winter's day. At Fregene the catamarans would be up on rollers, the bathhouses shut, the light on the olives a sad light, the *zuppa di pesce* signs fallen or hanging from a single nail. The swallows were gone. In Rome it was hot in the sun, cold in the shade, the soft, bright light heightening the curious tidewater look of that old and crowded city as if, sometime in the past, the Tiber had risen over its banks—a flood of dark water—and stained the buildings and churches up to their pediments, leaving the limestone above still pale and still, this late in the year, overgrown at every cranny with thick tufts of grass and capers that looked so like pubic hair that they gave to the celebrated square an antic look. Americans wandered away from the office reading the news from home-sweet-home. Most of the news appeared to be humorous since most of them, from time to time, would smile. They walked, unlike the Italians, as if they accommodated their step to some remembered and explicit terrain —a tennis court, a beach, a plowed field—and seemed set apart by an air of total unpreparedness for change, for death, for the passage of time itself. There were perhaps a hundred and fifty people in the square when Honora entered it and glanced up at the sky. A Danish tourist was photographing his wife on the Spanish Steps. An American sailor was dousing his head in the fountain. There were fresh flowers on the monument to the Virgin. The air smelled of coffee and marigolds. Sixteen German tourists were drinking coffee in a café across the street. 11:18 A.M.

Honora was approached by a barefoot beggar in a torn green dress who held a baby. She gave her a lira note. She gave one to a man in a striped apron, to a little boy in a white coat carrying a tray of coffee, to a good-looking tart holding her coat closed at the throat, to a stooped woman wearing a hat shaped like a wastebasket, to three German priests in crimson, to three Jesuits in black with lavender piping, to five barefoot Franciscans, to six nuns, to three young women in the black, sleazy uniforms worn by the maids of Rome, to a clerk from one of the souvenir shops, to a hairdresser, a barber, a pimp, three clerks, their fingers stained with lavender government office ink; to one dispossessed marquesa, her ragged handbag stuffed with photographs of lost villas, lost houses, lost horses, lost dogs; to a violinist, a tuba player and a cellist on their way to the rehearsal hall on the Via Athenee; to a pickpocket, a seminarian, an antique dealer, a thief, a fool, an idler, a Sicilian looking for work, a *carabiniere* off duty, a cook, a nursemaid, an American novelist, a waiter from the Inglese, a Negro drummer, a medical-supply salesman and three florists. There was not a hint of charity in her giving. The good her money might do would never cross her mind. The impulse to scatter her money was as deep as her love of fire and she sought, selfishly, an intoxicating sensation of cleanliness, lightness and usefulness. Money was filth and this was her ablution.

By this time the roofs of the square were black with people. A clerk from the express office climbed out the window, slid down the awning and dropped to the sidewalk at Honora's feet. Bystanders stood knee deep in the water of the fountain. Then some mounted *carabinieri* came up the Via Condotti and Honora turned and climbed the stairs while the voices of thousands blessed her in the name of The Father, The Son and The Holy Ghost, world without end.

CHAPTER XXXI

Coverly's security clearance was renewed pending Cameron's return from New Delhi but Brunner had gone to England and Coverly had no way of knowing when the old man would come back. Then, through some irreversible and confused bureaucratic process Coverly was served a ten-day eviction notice by the government housing office. His feelings were mixed. Their life in Talifer seemed over, if it could ever have been said to have begun. He could easily find work as a pre-programmer somewhere else and the thought of leaving Talifer seemed to Betsey like the promise of a new life. At about this time he received a wire from St. Botolphs. COME AT ONCE. This unprecedented directness from his old cousin alarmed him and he packed and left. He arrived there late the next afternoon. The day was rainy but as they approached the sea the rain turned to snow. The fall of snow whitened the bare trees and the slums beside the tracks and gave them, so Coverly thought, a pathos and beauty that they would have at no other time in their history. All this whiteness made him lighthearted. When he got off the train Mr. Jowett was nowhere around and the station had been abandoned. He saw no one to wave to in the windows of the Viaduct House; no one in the feed store. Crossing the green he was stopped by a procession of men and women leaving the parish house of Christ Church. They were eight and they walked two by two. All the men but one, who was bareheaded, wore stocking caps. He guessed that there had been a tea, a lecture, some charitable gesture, and that these were the inmates of the poor farm. One of them, an angular man, seemed mad or foolish and was muttering: "Repent, repent, your day is at hand. Angel voices have told me how to make myself pleasing to the Lord. . . ." "Hushup, hushup, Henry Saunders," said a large Negress who walked at his side. "You just hushup until we get into the bus." A bus was parked at the curb with HUTCHINS INSTITUTE FOR THE BLIND painted on its side. Coverly watched a driver help them in and then walked on up Boat Street.

A nurse opened Honora's door. She gave Coverly a knowing smile as if she had heard a great deal about him and had already formed an unfavorable opinion. "She's been waiting for you," she whispered. "The poor thing's been waiting for you all day." There was no reason for reproach. Coverly had wired his old cousin and she knew exactly when he would arive. "I'll be in the kitchen," the nurse said and went down the hall. The house was dirty and cold. The walls, plain as he remembered them, were now covered with a paper printed in black latticing and dark red roses. He opened one of the double doors into the living room and thought at first that she was dead.

She slept in a shabby wing chair. During the months since he had seen her she had lost her corpulence. She was terribly wasted. She had been robust—hardy, as she would have said—and now she was frail. Her leonine face and the childish placement of her feet were all that was not changed. She slept on and he looked around the room which, like the hallway, seemed neglected. Here was dust, cobwebs and flowered wallpaper. The curtains were gone and he could see the light snow through the high windows. Then she woke.

"Oh, Coverly."

"Cousin Honora." He kissed her and sat on a stool by her chair.

"I'm so glad you got here, dear, I'm so glad you came."

"I'm glad to be here."

"You know what I did, Coverly? I went to Europe. I didn't pay my tax and Judge Beasely, that old fool, said they'd throw me in jail so I went to Europe."

"Did you have a good time?"

"Remember the tomato fights?" Honora asked, and he wondered if she had lost her mind.

"Yes."

"After the frost I used to let you and the others come into my tomato patch and have tomato fights. When you'd thrown all the tomatoes you used to pick up the calling cards the cows had left and throw those." That this redoubtable old woman should call a steaming pile of cow manure a calling card was a reminder of the eccentric niceties of the village. "Well, when you'd thrown all the calling cards and all the tomatoes you used to be quite a mess," Honora said, "but if anyone asked you if you'd had a good time I expect you'd say yes. That's the way I feel about my trip."

"I see," said Coverly.

"I've changed," Honora asked, "you can see that I've changed, can't you?" There was some lightness, some hopefulness, even some pleading in her voice as if he might say persuasively that she hadn't changed at all and she could then stamp out into the garden and rake a few leaves before the snow covered them.

"Yes."

"Yes, I suppose I have. I've lost a lot of weight. But I *feel* much better." This was bellicose. "However, I don't go out now because I've noticed that people don't like to see me. It makes them sad. I see it in their eyes. I am like an angel of death."

"Oh, no, Honora," Coverly said.

"Oh, yes, I am. Why shouldn't I be? I'm dying."

"Oh, no," Coverly said.

"I'm dying, Coverly, and I know it and I want to die."

"You shouldn't say that, Honora."

"And why shouldn't I?"

"Because life is a gift, a mysterious gift," he said feebly in spite of the weight the words had for him.

"Well," she exclaimed, "you must be going to church a great deal these days."

"I sometimes do," he said.

"High or low?" she asked.

"Low."

"Your family," she said, "was always high."

This was harsh, flat, that old contrariness upon which she had counted more than anything else to express herself, but now she seemed too feeble to keep it up. She followed his eyes to the ugly wallpaper and said: "I see you've noticed my roses."

"Yes."

"Well, I'm afraid they're a mistake but when I came home I called Mr. Tanner and asked him to bring me over some wallpaper with roses on it to remind me of the summer." Stooped and leaning forward in her chair, she raised her head, her eyes, and gave the roses a terribly haggard look. "I get awfully tired of looking at them," she said, "but it's too late to change."

Coverly looked up at the wall, at her mistake, and noticed that the flowers were not the true colors and shapes of roses at all. The buds were phallic and the blooms themselves looked like some carnivorous plant, some petaled fly-catcher with a gaping throat. If they had been meant to remind her of the roses that bloomed in the summer they must have failed. They seemed like a darkness, a corruption, and he wondered if she hadn't chosen them to correspond with her own sense of this time of life.

"Will you please get me some whisky, Coverly," she said. "It's in the pantry. I don't dare ask *her*." Honora nodded her head toward the back of the house where the nurse must be sitting. Then she screened her mouth with her left hand, presumably to direct her voice away from the door, but when she spoke it was in such a vituperative hiss that it must have carried down the hall. "She *drinks,*" Honora hissed, rolling her eyes wildly toward the kitchen in case Coverly should have missed the point.

Coverly was surprised to have his old cousin ask for whisky. She used to take a drink at the family parties but always with the most vocal misgivings and reservations as if a single highball might stretch her out unconscious on the floor, or still worse, lead her to dance a jig on a table. Coverly went through the dining room to the pantry. The two changes he had noticed, disrepair and an obsession with roses, were continued here. The walls were covered with dark-throated roses and the table was ringed and scored under a thick layer of dust. There was, in the lap of one of the chairs, a broken leg and arm. The place was out of hand but if she was dying, as she had said, she seemed, like a snail or nautilus, to be approaching the grave in the carapace of her own house, projecting her dimness of sight and her loss of memory in cobwebs and ashes.

"Can I do anything for you, Mr. Wapshot?" This was the nurse. She sat in a chair by the sink, empty-handed.

"I'm looking for some whisky."

"It's in the jelly closet. There isn't any ice but she doesn't like ice in her drinks."

There was plenty of whisky. There was a half-case of bourbon and at least a case of empty bottles scattered helter-skelter on the floor. This was completely mysterious. Had the nurse ordered in these cases of whisky and swigged them alone in the kitchen?

"How long has you been working for Miss Wapshot?" Coverly asked.

"Oh, I'm not working for her," the nurse said. "I just came in today to improve appearances. She thought you'd worry if you found her alone so she asked me to come in and make things look nice."

"Is she alone all the time now?"

"She is when she wants to be. Oh, there's plenty of people who'll come over and make her a cup of tea but she won't let them in. She wants to be alone. She doesn't eat anything any more. She just drinks."

Coverly looked more closely at the nurse to see if, as Honora had claimed, she was drunk and meant to shift her vices onto the old woman.

"Does the doctor know about this?" Coverly asked.

"The doctor. Ha. She won't let the doctor into the house. She's killing herself. That's what she's doing. She's trying to kill herself. She knows that the doctor wants to operate on her and she's afraid of the knife."

She spoke with perfect pitilessness as if she were the knife's advocate, its priestess, and Honora the apostate. So that was it; and what could he do? His time in the kitchen was running out. If he stayed any longer she would become suspicious. It was unthinkable that he would return and charge her with the fraudulence of the nurse and the empty whisky bottles. She would deny it all flatly and would, what's more, be deeply wounded for he would have rudely broken the rules of that antic game in which their relationship was contained.

He went back through the pantry and the dining room, reminded by its disrepair of death, as a plain fact with which she seemed to be grappling boldly. He remembered walking down from the beach at Cascada with a bagful of black clams on his back. What does the sea sound like? Lions mostly, manifest destiny, the dealing of some final card hand, the aces as big as headstones. Boom, it says. And what did all his pious introspection on metamorphosis amount to? He thought he saw on the beach the change from one form of life to another. The sea grass dies, dries, flies like a swallow on the wind and that angry-looking tourist will make a lamp base out of the piece of driftwood he carries. The line of last night's heavy sea is marked with malachite and amethyst, the beach is scored with the same lines as the sky; one seemed to stand in some fulcrum of change, here was the barrier, here as the wave fell was the line between one life and another, but would any of this keep him from squealing for mercy when his time came?

"Thank you, dear." She drank thirstily and gave him a narrow look. "Is she *drunk?*"

"I don't think so," Coverly said.

"She conceals it. I want you to promise me three things, Coverly."

"Yes."

"I want you to promise me that if I should lose consciousness you will not have me moved to the hospital. I wish to die in this house."

"I promise."

"I want you to promise that when I'm gone you won't worry about me. My life is over and I know it. I've done everything I was meant to do and a great deal I was not meant to do. Everything will be confiscated, of course, but Mr. Johnson won't do this until January. I've asked some nice people here for Christmas dinner and I want you to be here and make them welcome. Maggie will do the cooking. Promise."

"I promise."

"And then I want you to promise me, to promise me that . . . Oh, there was something else," she said, "but I can't remember what it was. Now I think I'll lie down for a little while."

"Can I help you?"

"Yes. You can help me over to the sofa and then you can read to me. I like to be read to these days. Oh, remember how I used to read to you when you were sick? I used to read you *David Copperfield* and we would both cry so that I couldn't go on. Remember how we used to cry, Coverly, you and I?"

The fullness of feeling in this recollection refreshed her voice and seemed to send it back through time until it sounded for a moment like the voice of a girl. He helped her out of the chair and led her over to the old horsehair sofa, where she lay down and let him cover her with a rug. "My book is on the table," she said. "I'm reading *The Count of Monte Cristo* again. Chapter twenty-two." When she was settled he found her book and began to read.

His recollection of her reading to him was not an image, it was a sensation. He could not recall her tears while she sat by his bed but he could recall the violent and confused emotions she left behind her when she went away. Now he read uneasily and he wondered why. She had read to him when he was a sick child; now he read to her as she lay dy-

ing. The cycle was obvious enough, but why should he feel
that she, as she lay on the sofa, utterly helpless and infirm,
had the power to weave spells that could ensnare him? He
had never had anything from her but generosity and kindness, so why should he perform this simple service uneasily? He admired the book, he loved the old woman and
no room on earth was so familiar as this, so why should he
feel that he had stepped innocently into some snare involving a fraudulent nurse, a case of whisky and an old
book? Halfway through the chapter she fell asleep and he
stopped reading. A little later the nurse came to the door
wearing a black hat and with a black coat over her uniform. "I have to go," she whispered. "I have to cook supper for my family." Coverly nodded and listened to her
footsteps pass into the back of the house and then the
closing of the door.

He went to the long and dirty window to see the snow.
There was some yellow light at the horizon, not lemony,
not confined to its color, the light of a lantern, a lanthorne,
a longthorne, the shine of light on paper, something that
reminded him of childhood and its garden parties, isolated
now by the lateness of the hour and the season.

"Coverly?" she asked, but she spoke in her sleep. He
went back to his chair. He saw how terribly emaciated she
was but he liked to think that this had not changed the
force of her spirit. She had not only lived independently,
she seemed at times to have evolved her own culture. There
was nothing palliative in her approach to death. Her rites
were bold, singular and arcane. The gloom and disrepair
of her beloved house, the fraudulent nurse, the gaping
roses—she seemed to have arranged them all around her
satisfactorily as an earlier people had confidently supplied
themselves, while dying, with enough food and wine for a
long voyage.

"Coverly!" She woke suddenly, lifting her head off the
pillow.

"Yes."

"Coverly. I just saw the gates of Heaven!"

"What were they like, Honora, what were they like?"

"Oh, I couldn't say, I couldn't describe anything like
that, they were so beautiful, but I saw them, Coverly, oh,

I saw them." She sat up radiantly and dried her tears. "Oh, they were so beautiful. There were the gates and hosts of angels with colored wings and I saw them. Wasn't that nice?"

"Yes, Honora."

"Now get me some more whisky."

He went lightheartedly through the dark rooms, as happy as if he had shared her vision, and made some drinks, consoled to think that she would not, after all, ever die. She would stop breathing and be buried in the family lot but the greenness of her image, in his memory, would not change and she would be among them always in their decisions. She would, long after she was dust, move freely through his dreams, she would punish his and his brother's wickedness with guilt, reward their good works with lightness of heart, pass judgment on their friends and lovers even while her headstone bloomed with moss and her coffin was canted and jockeyed by the winter frosts. The goodness and evil in the old woman were imperishable. He carried her drink back through the darkness and put another log on the fire. She said nothing more but he filled her glass twice.

He called Dr. Greenough at half-past six. The doctor was having his supper but he came about an hour later and pronounced her dead of starvation.

So they wouldn't all come back to a place that was changed and strange and Coverly was the only member of the family at her funeral. He had no way of finding Moses, and Betsey was busy closing up the house in Talifer. Melissa had disappeared and the last we see of her is on a bus returning from one of the suburbs to the city of Rome. It is nearly Christmas but there are not many signs of this. Either Emile or his barber has cultivated a lock of hair that hangs over his forehead, giving him a look that is arch, boyish and a little stupid. He seems a little drunk and is, of course, hungry. Melissa's hair is dyed red. One result of living with someone so much younger—and they are living together—is to have made her manner girlish. She has developed a habit of shrugging her shoulders and resettling her head, this way and that. She is not one of those expatriates who is ashamed to speak English. Her

voice is musical, genteel, and it carries up and down the
bus. "I know you're hungry, darling," she says, "I *know*
that but it's really not my fault. As I understood it they
had invited us to lunch. I *distinctly* recall that she asked us
for lunch. What I suppose happened was that after she
had invited us to lunch the Parlapianos asked *them* to
lunch and they decided to jettison us; put us off with a
drink. I noticed that the table wasn't set when we came in.
I *knew* something was wrong then. It would have been
much pleasanter if she'd telephoned and canceled the en-
gagement. That would have been rude enough but to have
us come all the way out there expecting lunch and then to
tell us that they were engaged is one of the rudest things
I've ever heard of. All we can do is to forget it, forget it,
it's just something else to be forgotten. As soon as we get
back to Rome I'll do the shopping and cook you some
lunch. . . ."

And so she does. She goes to the Supra-Marketto
Americano on the Via Delle Sagiturius. Here she disen-
gages one wagon with a light ringing of metal from a chain
of hundreds and begins to push her way through the walls
of American food. Grieving, bewildered by the blows life
has dealt her, this is some solace, this is the path she takes.
Her face is pale. A stray curl hangs against her cheek.
Tears make the light in her eyes a glassy light but the
market is crowded and she is not the first nor the last
woman in the history of the place to buy her groceries with
wet cheeks. She moves indifferently with the alien crowd
as if these were the brooks and channels of her day. No
willow grows aslant this stream of men and women and
yet is is Ophelia that she most resembles, gathering her
fantastic garland not of crowflowers, nettles and long pur-
ples, but of salt, pepper, Bab-o, Kleenex, frozen codfish
balls, lamb patties, hamburger, bread, butter, dressing, an
American comic book for her son and for herself a bunch
of carnations. She chants, like Ophelia, snatches of old
tunes. "Winstons taste *good* like a cigarette should. Mr.
Clean, Mr. *Clean*," and when her coronet or fantastic garland seems completed she pays her bill and carries her
trophies away, no less dignified a figure of grief than any
other.

CHAPTER XXXII

ঔ৳ ৳ঔ

Betsey and Binxey arrived the day before Christmas and Coverly went down to the station to meet the train. "I'm so tired," Betsey said, "I'm just so tired I could *die.*" "Was the train trip bad, sugarluve?" Coverly asked. "Bad," said Betsey, "bad. Just don't speak to me about it, that's all. I don't see why we have to come all the way down here to have Christmas anyhow. We might just as well have gone to Florida. I've never been to Florida in my whole life."

"I promised Honora that we'd have Christmas here."

"But you told me she was dead, dead and buried."

"I promised." For a moment he felt helpless before this incompatibility; felt as if his blood had been transmuted by anger or despair into something syrupy and effervescent, like Coca-Cola. It was unthinkable that he should break his promise to the old woman, it was some part of his dignity, and yet he could see clearly that it was unthinkable to Betsey that he should trouble himself. Coverly walked beside his wife with the slight crouch of a losing sexual combatant, while Betsey stood more erectly, held her head more sternly, seemed to seize on every crumb of self-esteem that he dropped. Coverly had done what he could to get the house in order. He had lighted fires, decorated a tree and put presents under it for his son and his wife. "I have to put Binxey to bed," Betsey said indignantly. "I don't guess there's any hot water for a bath, is there? Come on, Binxey, come on upstairs with Mummy. I'm just so tired I could *die.*"

After supper Coverly waited for the carol singers but they had either given up this ceremony or taken Boat Street off their route. At half-past ten the bells of Christ

Church began to ring and he put on a coat and walked out to the green. The ringing of the bells stopped as he approached the door. He was preceded by three women, all of them unknown to him. They seemed not together and they were all three past middle age. The first wore a drum-shaped hat, covered with metal disks from which the street lights flashed with the brilliance of some advertising lure. Buy Ginger-Fluff? Texadrol? Fulpruff Tires? He looked into her face for the text but there was nothing there but the text of marriage, childbirth, some delight and some dismay. The other two wore similar hats. He waited until they had entered before he went in and found that they four were the only worshipers on Christmas Eve.

He went to a pew way forward, genuflected with a loud creaking of his kneebones and said his prayers, immersed in the immemorial and Episcopal smell of ancient rains. Mr. Applegate came in without his cassock and lighted the candles. He returned to the altar a moment later, carrying the Host. "Almighty God," he intoned, "unto Whom all hearts are open, all desires known and from Whom no secrets are hid, cleanse the thoughts of our hearts with the inspiration of Thy holy spirit. . . ."

The resonance of the Mass moved into that gloomy place on Christmas Eve with the magnificence of an Elizabethan procession. Perorative clauses spread out after the main supplication or confession in breadth and glory and the muttered responses seemed embroidered in crimson and gold. On it would move, Coverly thought, through the Lamb of God, the Gloria and the Benediction until the last Amen shut like a door on this verbal pomp. But then he sensed something strange and wrong. Mr. Applegate's speech was theatrical but what was more noticeable was a pose of suavity, a bored and haughty approach to the holy words for which Cranmer had burned. As he turned to the altar to pray Coverly saw him sway and grab at the lace for support. Was he sick? Was he feeble? The woman with the lights in her hat turned to Coverly and hissed: "He's drunk again." He was. He spoke the Mass with scorn and contumely, as if his besottedness were a form of wisdom. He lurched around the altar, got the general confession mixed up with the order for morning prayer and kept saying: "Christ have mercy upon us. Let us pray," until it seemed that he was stuck. There is no point in the formalities of Holy Communion where, in the case of such a disaster, the communicants can intervene and there was nothing to do but watch him flounder through to the end. Suddenly he threw his arms wide, fell to his knees and exclaimed: "Let us pray for all those killed or cruelly wounded on thruways, expressways, freeways and turnpikes. Let us pray for all those burned to death in faulty plane-landings, mid-air collisions and mountainside crashes. Let us pray for all those wounded by rotary lawn mowers, chain saws, electric hedge clippers and other power tools. Let us pray for all alcoholics measuring out the days that the Lord hath made in ounces, pints and fifths." Here he sobbed loudly. "Let us pray for the lecherous and the impure. . . ." Led by the woman with the flashing hat, the other worshipers left before this prayer was finished and Coverly was left alone to support Mr. Applegate with his Amen. He got through the rest of it, divested himself, extinguished his candles and hurried back to his gin bottle, hidden among the vestments, and Coverly walked back to Boat Street. The telephone was ringing.

"Coverly, Coverly, this is Hank Moore over at the Viaduct House. I know it's none of my business but I thought maybe you were wondering where your brother was and he's over here. He's got the widow Wilston with him. I don't want to put my nose in nobody else's business but I just thought you might like to know where he was."

It was Christmas Eve at the Viaduct House but the scene upstairs was flagrantly pagan. This was no sacred grove and the only sound of running water came from a leaking tap but Moses the satyr leered through the smoky air at his bacchante. Mrs. Wilston's curls were disheveled, her face was red, her smile was the rapt and wanton smile of forgetfulness and she held a lovely glass of lovely bourbon in her right hand. Her jowls—the first note of pendulousness to be massively reiterated by her breasts—were very meaty. "Now you listen to me, Moses Wapshot," she said, "you just listen to me. You Wapshots always thought you were bettern everybody else but I wanna tell you, I wanna tell you, I can't remember what I wanna tell you." She laughed. She had lost the power of consecutive thought and with it all the stings and pains of living. She waked and yet she dreamed. Moses, naked as any satyr, smacked his lips and left his chair. His walk was lumbering, bellicose and a little haunted. It was on the one hand pugnacious and had on the other the lightness, the fleetness, the hint of stealth of a man who is stepping out of a liquor store after having paid for a quart of gin with an unsubstantiated check. He made his way to her, smacked her wetly in several places and gathered her up in his arms. She sighed and lolled in his embrace. He started for the bed with his jolly burden. He weaved to the right, recouped his balance and weaved to the right again. Then he was going; he was going; he was gone. Thump. The whole Viaduct House reverberated to the crash and then there was an awful stillness. He lay athwart her, his cheek against the carpet, which had a pleasant, dusty smell like the woods in autumn. Oh, where was his dog, his gun, his simple joy in life! She, still lying in a heap, was the first to speak. She spoke without anger or impatience. She smiled. "Let's have another drink," she said. Then Coverly opened the door. "Come home, Moses," he said. "Come home, brother. It's Christmas Eve."

Christmas Day in the morning, when Coverly woke and romanced Betsey, was dazzling. The frost on the window-glass, shaped like shrapnel, distilled and amplified the light. Maggie came early and opened the furnace drafts and presently hot air and coal gas began to pour out of the registers. Binxey emptied his stocking and unwrapped the presents that Coverly had bought for him and they all had breakfast in the warm kitchen off a wooden table that was as slick and porous as hand soap. The kitchen was not a dark room but the power of light on the new snow outside made it seem cavernous.

Moses woke in a crushing paroxysm of anxiety, the keenest melancholy. The brilliance of light, the birth of Christ, all seemed to him like some fatuous shell game invented to dupe a fool like his brother while he saw straight through into the nothingness of things. The damage he had done to his nerves and his memory was less painful than a sense he suffered of approaching disaster, some pitiless fatality that would break him without making itself known. His hands had begun to shake and in another fifteen minutes he would begin to sweat. This was the agony of death, with the difference that he knew the way to life everlasting. It was in the bottles of bourbon Honora had left in the jelly closet. He thought of bourbon while he shaved and dressed but when he went down to the kitchen and found them sitting at the table there he saw them not as the members of his family but as cruel obstacles, standing between himself and the alpine landscapes in a bottle of sour mash. The coffee and orange juice that Maggie gave him seemed innocuous and nauseating. How could he get them out of the room? If he had only thought to buy some presents and left them under the tree, he might have been alone for a minute. "Jelly," he exclaimed. "I want some jelly for my toast." He went into the closet and shut the door.

Going through the dining room after breakfast Coverly saw that Maggie had set the table for twelve guests and he wondered who they would be. Honora had always had a large table at Christmas. After Thanksgiving she would begin—in public places—trains, buses and waiting rooms— to look around for those faces that bore the inexpungeable mark of loneliness and invite them to her house for Christmas dinner. Intuition and practice had made her discerning and she could single out her prey unerringly and yet, knowing as she did how the passion of loneliness runs through the lives of all men, she was oftener rebuffed than accepted by strangers who, she saw, as they turned away from her, would sooner spend their holiday in a bare room than admit to her or even to themselves that they lacked a host of friends and relations and a groaning board. Wayward pride had been her adversary, and a formidable one, but the wish to fill up her table seemed, like her love of fires and her disinterest in money, aboriginal, and she had once gone up to the railroad station waiting room on Christmas morning and corraled the strays who were warming themselves there at the coal stove.

Coverly cleared the walks after breakfast. The loud ringing of his shovel on the paving had a singular and a foolish charm, as if this rude music, this simple task, evoked the spirit of Leander in a happier role than he had seemed damned to play out in the wreckage of the old house on River Street. The blinding light on the snow seemed to ring again and again around the boundaries of the village like the vibrations of a rubbed water glass, but even that early in the day the brilliance of the light could be seen to shift, to be the lights of one of the shortest days of the year.

The Bretaignes and the Dummers came in at eleven. Maggie gave them sherry and raspberry shrub. There was such a hard and mischievous light in Moses' eye by this time that they did not stay for long. Some time after noon Coverly was standing at a window when he saw the yellow bus he had seen on the night he returned. There was the same driver, the same passengers and the legend HUTCHINS INSTITUTE FOR THE BLIND. The bus stopped in front of the house and Coverly ran down the stairs, leaving the hall door open. "Wapshot?" the driver asked. "Yes," said Coverly. "Well, here's the company for your Christmas dinner," said the driver. "They told me to pick them up at three." "Won't you come in?" asked Coverly. "Oh, no, thanks, no," the driver said. "I got stomach trouble and all I want is a bowl of soup. I'll get something in the village. Turkey and all that. It makes me sick. You'll have to show them up the steps though. I'll give you a hand."

Coverly opened the door and said to the Negress he had seen on the green: "Merry Christmas. I'm Coverly Wapshot. We're very happy to have you here." "Merry Christmas, Merry Christmas," she said while from a portable radio she carried a chorus of hundreds sang "Adeste Fideles." "There are seven steps," Coverly said, "and then one more into the house." The woman took his arm with the trust of custom and helplessness and lifted her face to the brilliance of the sky. "I can see a little light," she said. "Just a little. It must be bright out there." "Yes, it is," said Coverly. "Five, six, seven." "Joyeux Noël," said Moses, bowing from the waist. "May I take your wraps?" "No, thank you, no, thank you," the woman said. "I took a chill in the auto and I'll keep them on until I warm up." Moses led her into the parlor while the driver brought up the angular prophet, who was saying: "Have mercy upon us, have mercy upon us, most merciful Father; grant us Thy peace." "Hushup, hushup, Henry Saunders," said the Negress. "You spoil everybody's party." Her radio sang "Silent Night."

There were eight in all. The men wore stocking caps that seemed to have been pulled down over their ears with impatience and severity by the hands of some attendant who was anxious to get off and enjoy his own Christmas dinner. When Coverly and Betsey had got them all seated in the parlor Coverly looked around for the wisdom of Honora's choice and thought that these eight blind guests would know most about the raw material of human kindness. Waiting for unseen strangers to help them through the traffic, judging the gentle from the self-righteous by a touch, suffering the indifference of those who so fear conspicuousness that they would not help the helpless, counting on kindness at every turn, they seemed to bring with them a landscape whose darkness exceeded in intensity the brilliance of that day. A blow had been leveled at their sight but this seemed not to be an infirmity but a heightened insight, as if aboriginal man had been blind and this was some part of an ancient, human condition; and they brought with them into the parlor the mysteries of the night. They seemed to be advocates for those in pain; for the taste of misery as fulsome as rapture, for the losers, the goners, the flops, for those who dream in terms of missed things—planes, trains, boats and opportunities— who see on waking the empty tamarc, the empty waiting room, the water in the empty slip, rank as Love's Tunnel when the ship is sailed; for all those who fear death. They sat there quietly, patiently, shyly, until Maggie came to the door and said: "Dinner is served and if you don't come and get it now everything will be cold." One by one they led the blind down the brightness of the hall into the dining room.

So that is all and now it is time to go. It is autumn here in St. Botolphs where I have been living and how swiftly the season comes on! At dawn I hear the sound of geese, this thrilling cranky noise, hoarse as the whistling of the old B & M freights. I put the dinghy into the shed and take up the tennis court tapes. The light has lost its summery components and is penetrating and clear; the sky seems to have receded without any loss of brilliance. Traffic at the airports is heavy and my nomadic people have got into their slacks and haircurlers and are on the move once more. The sense of life as a migration seems to have reached even into this provincial backwater. Mrs. Bretaigne has hung a blue-plastic swimming pool out on her clothesline to dry. A lady in Travertine has found a corpse in her mint bed. In the burial ground where Honora and Leander lie, there is a carpet of green, drawn like a smile over the tumultuous conversion to dust. I pack my bags and go for a last swim in the river. I love this water and its shores; love it absurdly as if I could marry the view and take it home to bed with me. The whistle on the table-silver factory blows at four and the herring gulls in the blue sky sound like demented laying hens.

This late in the year the Williamses still drive down to Travertine for a swim in that dark and nutritious sea and after supper Mrs. Williams goes to the telephone and says to the operator: "Good evening, Althea. Will you please ring Mr. Wagner's ice-cream store." Mr. Wagner recommends his coffee and delivers a quart a few minutes later on a bicycle that rings and rattles so in the autumn dusk that it seems to be strung with bells. They play a little whist, kiss one another good night and go to sleep to dream. Mr. Williams, racked by the earth-shaking, back-breaking, binding, grinding need for love, dreams that he holds in his arms the Chinese waitress who works in the Pergola Restaurant in Travertine. Mrs. Williams, sleepless, sends up to heaven a string of winsome prayers like little clouds of colored smoke. Mrs. Bretaigne dreams that she is in a strange village at three in the morning ringing the doorbell of a frame house. She is looking, it seems, for her laundry, but the stranger who opens the door cries suddenly: "Oh, I thought it was Francis, I thought Francis had come home!" Mr. Bretaigne dreams that he is fishing for trout in a stream whose stones are arranged as coherently as those in any ruin and have as profound a sense of the past as the streets and basilicas of some ancient place. Mrs.

Dummer dreams that she sails down one of the explicit waterways of sleep, while Mr. Dummer, at her side, climbs the Matterhorn. Jack Brattle dreams of a lawn without quack grass, a driveway without weeds, a garden without aphids, cutworm or black spot and an orchard without tent caterpillars. His mother, in the next room, dreams that she is being crowned by the governor of Massachusetts and the state traffic commissioner for the unprecedented scrupulousness with which she has observed the speed limits, traffic lights and stop signs. She wears long white robes and thousands applaud her virtue. The crown is surprisingly heavy.

Some time after midnight there is a thunderstorm and the last I see of the village is in the light of these explosions, knowing how harshly time will bear down on this ingenuous place. Lightning plays around the steeple of Christ Church, that symbol of our engulfing struggle with good and evil, and I repeat those words that were found in Leander's wallet after he drowned: "Let us consider that the soul of a man is immortal, able to endure every sort of good and every sort of evil." A cavernous structure of sound, a sort of abyss in the stillness of the provincial night, opens along the whole length of heaven and the wooden roof under which I stand amplifies the noise of rain. I will never come back, and if I do there will be nothing left, there will be nothing left but the headstones to record what has happened; there will really be nothing at all.

— how can we use
          a novel (Q)

— writing techniques
          of 1950s

— Settys
— social change
— of
— intellectuals
— kind of problems?

tensabt $